Praise for The Country Club Murders

"A sparkling comedy of errors tucked inside a clever mystery. I loved it!"

— Susan M. Boyer,
USA Today Bestselling Author of *Lowcountry Book Club*

"Readers who enjoy the novels of Susan Isaacs will love this series that blends a strong mystery with the demands of living in an exclusive society."

— *Kings River Life Magazine*

"From the first page to the last, Julie's mysteries grab the reader and don't let up."

— Sally Berneathy,
USA Today Bestselling Author of *The Ex Who Saw a Ghost*

"This book is fun! F-U-N Fun!...A delightful pleasure to read. I didn't want to put it down...Highly recommend."

— *Mysteries, etc.*

"Set in Kansas City, Missouri, in 1974, this cozy mystery effectively recreates the era through the details of down-to-earth Ellison's everyday life."

— *Booklist*

"Mulhern's lively, witty sequel to *The Deep End* finds Kansas City, Mo., socialite Ellison Russell reluctantly attending a high school football game...Cozy fans will eagerly await Ellison's further adventures."

— *Publishers Weekly*

"There's no way a lover of suspense could turn this book down because it's that much fun."

Suspense Magazine

D1707731

"Cleverly written with sharp wit and all the twists and turns of the best '70s primetime drama, Mulhern nails the fierce fraught mother-daughter relationship, fearlessly tackles what hides behind the Country Club façade, and serves up justice in bombshell fashion. A truly satisfying slightly twisted cozy."

– Gretchen Archer,
USA Today Bestselling Author of *Double Knot*

"Part mystery, part women's fiction, part poetry, Mulhern's debut, *The Deep End*, will draw you in with the first sentence and entrance you until the last. An engaging whodunit that kept me guessing until the end!"

– Tracy Weber,
Author of the Downward Dog Mysteries

"An impossible-to-put-down Harvey Wallbanger of a mystery. With a smart, funny protagonist who's learning to own her power as a woman, *Send in the Clowns* is one boss read."

– Ellen Byron,
Agatha Award-Nominated Author of *Plantation Shudders*

"The plot is well-structured and the characters drawn with a deft hand. Setting the story in the mid-1970s is an inspired touch...A fine start to this mystery series, one that is highly recommended."

– *Mysterious Reviews*

"What a fun read! Murder in the days before cell phones, the internet, DNA and AFIS."

– *Books for Avid Readers*

"If you liked *Gilmore Girls*, you'll love *Watching the Detectives*. It has the same sarcastic humor and wit, with a loving, but dysfunctional multi-generational family of strong women. You'll have all the feels following the adventures of life, love, and murder with the Russell women."

– *A Cozy Experience*

BACK STABBERS

The Country Club Murders
by Julie Mulhern

Novels

THE DEEP END (#1)
GUARANTEED TO BLEED (#2)
CLOUDS IN MY COFFEE (#3)
SEND IN THE CLOWNS (#4)
WATCHING THE DETECTIVES (#5)
COLD AS ICE (#6)
SHADOW DANCING (#7)
BACK STABBERS (#8)

Short Stories

DIAMOND GIRL
A Country Club Murder Short

BACK STABBERS

THE COUNTRY CLUB MURDERS

JULIE MULHERN

HENERY PRESS

Copyright

BACK STABBERS
The Country Club Murders
Part of the Henery Press Mystery Collection

First Edition | October 2018

Henery Press
www.henerypress.com

Trade Paperback ISBN-13: 978-1-63511-455-3
Digital epub ISBN-13: 978-1-63511-456-0
Kindle ISBN-13: 978-1-63511-457-8
Hardcover ISBN-13: 978-1-63511-458-4

Printed in the United States of America

For Matt, Meredith and Katie

ACKNOWLEDGMENTS

Thank you to Steve Kirk and Edie Peterson, your eagle eyes are deeply appreciated. Thank you to my editors at Henery Press, you are wonderful. And, thank you to Gretchen Archer for turning on the flashlight when I'm wandering in the dark.

ONE

March, 1975
Kansas City, Missouri

The woman in the chair opposite me was hacking up a lung.

If the sick woman died, Mother would have a conniption fit.

Not because the poor woman was dead. No, Mother would be upset I'd been present at her passing. Mother took a dim view of death. She took a dimmer view of my unfortunate habit of stumbling over bodies.

I glanced at my watch. My broker, Winthrop Marshall, had kept me waiting for nearly thirty minutes.

The woman's eyes streamed. Her nose ran like a faucet. Overwhelmed by her cold, she didn't cover her mouth when she coughed.

Cough, cough.

I sympathized. I did. But the woman should have stayed home. In bed. With chicken soup, a bottle of 7UP, a box of Kleenex, and a gross of cold pills.

I abandoned the leather club chair (where I sat) and the most recent copy of Barron's (where I'd found nothing of interest—the magazine had no fashion stories and probably didn't even block the woman's germs) and approached the receptionist's desk.

"I'd like to wait someplace else." I said.

The receptionist, an exceedingly pretty woman with very white teeth, donned a I-know-you've-been-waiting-with-the-plague-but-there's-nothing-I-can-do smile. "I'm sorry. We don't have another waiting area but—" her smile grew brighter "—Mr. Marshall should arrive momentarily."

Winthrop wasn't even here? That meant his office was empty.

Cough, cough. COUGH!

"Either I wait in Winthrop's office, or I'm leaving."

The receptionist eyed the germ (masquerading as a woman) who was busily infecting the brokerage's elegant waiting room. A wrinkle marred her pretty brow. "I can check with his assistant."

"Please do." I stood at the front desk (as far from the sick woman as possible) and waited.

I did not tap my fingers against the high polish of the receptionist's desk as Mother would have. I did not dig in my purse for a travel pack of tissues as my housekeeper, Aggie DeLucci, would have (then she'd have given them to the sick woman). I did not roll my eyes as Grace, my daughter, would have. I simply fixed a polite but firm smile on my face.

The receptionist pushed a button on what looked like a very complicated switchboard. "Debbie, Mrs. Russell would like to wait in Mr. Marshall's office." She glanced (more of a glare) at the coughing woman and lowered her voice to a whisper. "There's a sick woman up front."

Cough, cough.

She listened, glanced at me, and manufactured a small smile of her own. "She insists. If she can't wait in his office, she'll reschedule."

She listened again. "Debbie will be right out."

Winthrop Marshall's assistant appeared a moment later. Debbie, another exceedingly pretty young woman, had bouncy blonde hair, bright blue eyes, and vivid red lipstick. She wore a dress so short that I hoped, for her sake, she never dropped anything—bending over would give anyone watching a view of everything God gave her.

In her shoes, working for Winthrop as she did, I would have worn a nun's habit. As it was, I wore pants and a turtleneck sweater in the most serious shade of gray I could find.

In my experience (acquired since my husband died), a single woman dealing with her stockbroker, insurance agent, or estate lawyer seemed to be asking for attention of a too-personal variety. Showing up at their offices was apparently some kind of invitation. And Winthrop was the worst of the lot. The odious man had offered to see me through my grief by scratching any itch I might have.

I had no itch. Especially not around Winthrop who'd lost most of his hair and carried an extra fifty pounds around his middle. Also, he had thick lips. Bleh. A small shudder shook my shoulders just thinking about those lips.

One of these days—soon—I'd make finding a new broker a priority.

I'd have done it before, but, for all his faults, Winthrop was good at his job. The portfolio flourished in both bull and bear markets. I could put up with a leer or two and a few sleazy come-ons for a fifteen-percent return.

"I'm sorry Mr. Marshall is late, Mrs. Russell," Debbie offered me a smile so apologetic it bordered on worried. "It's not like him. He must be stuck in traffic."

It was half past nine. Any rush hour traffic had long since dispersed.

She pulled out a key, unlocked the door to Winthrop's office, and asked, "Would you care for coffee?"

Did the wind blow in Kansas?

"I'd love some, thank you."

"How do you take it?"

"With cream."

She reached inside the door, flipped a light switch, and said, "I'll be back in just a moment. Please make yourself comfortable."

"Thank you." I walked into Winthrop's tastefully decorated corner office alone.

Except, I wasn't alone.

Winthrop sat behind the desk, leaning back in his chair as if he were looking for stock prices on the ceiling. He'd rolled up his sleeves to his elbows and he'd loosened his tie. Winthrop Marshall was the very picture of a man hard at work, one who'd taken a quick break to consider some new angle. But Winthrop wasn't working. Or considering.

"Winthrop?" I needn't have bothered. His skin was gray and there was a rusty blossom on his white shirt. He'd been dead for a while.

Still, I walked toward him. "Winthrop?"

I stepped behind the desk and froze.

There are things once seen that cannot be unseen.

My hands flew to my eyes, covering them.

My hands were too late.

The image of bald, overweight, thick-lipped Winthrop Marshall dead in his desk chair with his boxers and pants pulled down to his skinny ankles was seared into my brain for all time.

I backed away and the heel of my shoe caught on the carpet. I fell, putting me at eye-level with Winthrop's—oh dear Lord—I scooted (crab-walked) away.

"Mrs. Russell?" Debbie stood in the door. She held a mug emblazoned with the brokerage logo.

Thank, God. I needed a coffee.

Her gaze found me and my spot on the carpet then traveled to Winthrop.

She dropped the mug.

Dammit.

My coffee stained the rug.

Debbie grabbed the door frame. "Wha-wha-what happened? Did you kill him?"

Me? Kill Winthrop? I dragged myself off the floor. "Heavens, no. He's been dead for hours." Probably.

"Dea-dea-dead?" Why was she yammering about death after asking me if I'd killed him?

"Dead as a doornail." Not the most empathetic response, but I had just been confronted with Winthrop's flaccid—I couldn't go there. Plus, she'd asked if I committed murder *and* dropped my coffee. "We need to lock this room and call the police."

"The po-po-police?"

"I know a homicide detective. Take me to a phone and I'll call him."

Debbie (looking decidedly green) staggered to a desk just outside Winthrop's office. Its surface held a phone, typewriter, steno pad, ashtray, cup of steaming coffee, and photograph.

I picked up the receiver but was flummoxed by a plethora of buttons.

With a red-tipped finger, Debbie jabbed at the phone and a button turned the same shade as Debbie's skin—sickly green.

I dialed.

While the phone rang, I stared at the photograph of Debbie and a handsome young man. "Boyfriend or husband?"

She shook her head, apparently too distraught to answer.

I shifted my gaze to her left hand where a small diamond and a gold band glittered on her ring finger. Husband.

"Jones." Anarchy's voice calmed my just-been-at-eye-level-with-a-dead-man's—oh dear Lord—nerves.

"It's Ellison."

A few seconds passed. "I thought you had a meeting with your stockbroker." He sounded grim. In addition to being a homicide detective, Anarchy was the man in my life. Telling him Winthrop Marshall had promised to increase my returns to twenty percent if I let him scratch my itch had been a mistake.

Anarchy had kept his lips tightly sealed but I'd gleaned his thoughts from the expression in his coffee brown eyes. *Fire Winthrop and get a new broker.*

Good advice but a moot point now.

I cleared my throat. "Winthrop's been murdered."

"Not funny."

"No," I agreed. "It's not funny. He's been dead for a while. Hours."

"You're not kidding?"

As if I'd ever cry wolf about a body. I didn't kid about corpses.

"I'm not."

"Tell me where you are. I'll be there as soon as I can."

I rattled off the address.

"On my way." He hung up and I was left listening to a dial tone.

"May I please have some coffee?" I asked Debbie.

She nodded but didn't move.

"Perhaps you can tell me where it is? I'll get it myself."

"The kitchen." She wore a deer-in-the-headlights expression.

I gently pushed her into her chair. "Just point me in the right direction."

She pointed.

If I walked down the hallway—windowed offices on the left and desks like Debbie's on the right—I'd find the coffeepot.

I walked.

A few of the women sitting at the desks gave me curious looks. One asked, "May I help you?"

"Just looking for coffee."

"Three desks down and to the right."

"Thank you. No, don't get up. I'll find it."

I found the kitchen, took a mug from the cabinet, and poured. A refrigerator stood at one end of the counter. I opened its door, located cream, and poured that too. Then I wrapped my hands around the mug and sighed.

Soon, the sheer awfulness of finding a body would hit me. When that happened, I might need more than coffee. But, for now, coffee was all I wanted.

I leaned against the counter, sipped, and sighed again.

Soon, Anarchy would arrive.

Soon, I'd have to tell Mother I'd found our stockbroker dead.

But for a few blissful minutes, I could pretend I'd never seen Winthrop Marshall dead with his pants around his ankles.

"Marcy!" The voice was so loud—so angry—I straightened and prepared for flight.

A murmur followed. I assumed it was Marcy's reply.

An attractive young woman burst into the kitchen. Like Debbie, her skin looked a bit green (maybe it was the lighting). Unlike Debbie, she didn't look as if a strong wind might blow her over. In fact, she looked as angry as the voice had sounded.

"Who are you?" she demanded.

"One of Mr. Marshall's clients."

"Where's Debbie? What are you doing in here?"

"Debbie's had a bit of a shock. She's sitting down."

The woman sniffed. "You shouldn't be in here."

It wasn't as if I had access to confidential files. "I needed a cup of coffee."

She sniffed again. "What shock?"

No. I was not going there. "I'll let her tell you about it."

A third sniff. She brushed past me, grabbed a mug from the cabinet, filled it with coffee, and muttered something I couldn't make out.

"Pardon me?"

"I wasn't talking to you."

Well, wasn't she just a ray of sunshine? One would think she'd use better manners when speaking to the firm's clients.

"I apologize. That was rude." Had she read my mind or my face? Probably my face.

I sipped. "Are you all right?"

She considered. "Yes—" she added a sugar cube to the coffee and speared it with a spoon "—No. There's an examiner coming."

As if that explained anything. "An examiner?"

Her mouth set in a grim line and she nodded. "From the Securities Exchange Commission. I was here late last night and still have a mountain of reports to prepare. Whenever I hit a groove, Mr. Wallace asks me to fetch coffee."

Frank Wallace was one of Winthrop's partners.

"Marcy!" Frank had a voice that carried.

"Excuse me." Marcy and Frank's coffee hurried through the door.

I drained half my mug, refilled it, then followed her.

Oomph!

My second visit with the carpets at Bisby, Marshall & Wallace was better than the first (no half-naked dead men at eye-level).

"Watch where you're going," said the man who'd knocked me down. "You got coffee on my pants."

I looked up at Buzz Bisby.

His pale blue eyes widened. "Ellison. Oh my God. Ellison. I apologize. Are you all right?" He extended a hand and helped me off the floor. "I am terribly sorry."

Now was the part when I was expected to absolve him.

But, I was covered in hot coffee and he'd been beastly when he thought I worked for him. "You should watch where you're going, Buzz."

"I should. I should. You're absolutely right." He smoothed his striped tie then glanced at the door to the kitchen. "What were you doing in there?"

"Getting coffee." Coffee which now stained my pants and sweater.

"Why didn't Debbie get it for you?"

"She needed to sit."

"Why? What's wrong?" Buzz's eyes narrowed. "Is she pregnant?"

How would I know? I stepped closer to Buzz and whispered, "Winthrop's dead in his office."

"Winthrop?" he squeaked. "Dead?"

Several of the women at desks outside of offices glanced our way.

I nodded and lowered my voice. "The police are on their way."

Buzz's skin acquired a soft celadon hue. It wasn't the lights. He hadn't looked green until now. "The police?"

I glanced at my watch. "They should be here any minute."

Buzz rubbed his chest and his eyes rolled back in his head. "I don't feel so good."

Buzz keeled over, claiming my spot on the carpet.

Mother was going to be furious enough over one dead

stockbroker. Her head would spin in full circles if I told her about two. "Help!"

TWO

A bevy of attractive young women surrounded me. Well, their legs were attractive. They all wore short skirts and from my spot on the floor next to Buzz, their skirts and legs were all I could see without craning my neck.

Not a single one of them offered any advice.

I gauged Buzz's color (not good), his breathing (shallow), and his eyes (glazed).

"Doesn't he have some pills?" one of the young women ventured.

Spittle ran from the corner of Buzz's mouth and he worked his mouth as if he was trying to speak—to tell me something vitally important.

I reached into his suit coat and felt around. In the inside pocket, my fingers found a pillbox. "These?" I held up the little box.

Buzz managed a desperate nod.

"Stick it under his tongue," said Marcy, who'd abandoned her examiner's report for the crisis. "That's what my dad does when he has an episode."

I stuck the pill under Buzz's tongue and said a silent prayer. *Please don't let him die.* Not only did I like Buzz and his wife, Bea, but two bodies in one day was pushing it—even for me.

With the pill under his tongue, Buzz relaxed slightly. Was his color better? Was he breathing easier?

"What the hell is going on out here?"

The women startled and parted, allowing me a view of Frank

Wallace, and Frank a view of me and Buzz.

"Dear, God." Frank eyed Buzz with real concern. "Has anyone called an ambulance?"

"Not yet," Marcy admitted.

"What are you waiting for?" Frank boomed. "Judgment day?" Marcy scurried to the nearest phone.

Frank hurried across the space that separated us and crouched across from me. "Buzz—" his voice was gentler "—you doing okay?"

Buzz was on the carpet with spittle running down his chin.

"He has pills." Frank shifted his gaze from Buzz to the pillbox in my hand. "Did you give him one?"

"Yes."

Frank nodded his thanks. "Hear that Buzz? The pill will kick in and you'll be right as rain." He took Buzz's hand in his. "Hang in there. Help will be here soon."

Frank seemed to be a good friend. Too bad he was a horrible boss.

"I thought he was shot."

Every head swiveled. Even Buzz's.

Detective Peters, Anarchy's partner, scowled down at me, Buzz, and Frank. "You said he was shot and that he'd been dead for a while. That guy's not even cold."

I looked up into the confused faces of the young women. I looked across Buzz's body at Frank Wallace. I swallowed. "This is not the gentleman I called about."

"Well, where is he?" Detective Peters gifted me a you'd-better-not-be-wasting-my-precious-time look.

"In his office."

Frank Wallace, the only partner at Bisby, Marshall & Wallace capable of speech, spoke. "What in the Sam Hill is going on?"

I looked at Detective Peters.

Detective Peters looked back and smirked. No way was he getting me out of the hole he'd dug for me.

With his rumpled overcoat, permanently disagreeable expression, and tendency to blame me for the world's ills, Detective

Peters was not my favorite person to look at—especially not when he was smirking at my discomfort. I shifted my gaze to Frank. "It's a matter for the police."

Frank's cheeks flushed and he puffed his chest. "What happened?" He glowered. At me. "I want an explanation. Now."

No one replied.

They couldn't. They didn't know.

Debbie, Buzz, and I were the only ones who knew Winthrop was dead in his office.

Debbie couldn't answer Frank—she wasn't in the group surrounding me. Buzz couldn't answer Frank—Buzz couldn't speak. I could have answered Frank but I abhorred bullies—I kept my lips sealed just to spite him.

When it became obvious I wasn't going to serve up the information he'd demanded, Frank shared his scowl with the rest of the women.

Silence reigned.

With a disgusted grunt, Frank cast a final scowl my way, stood, and strode down the hall toward Winthrop's office.

I shifted my gaze back to Detective Peters. "He's about to contaminate your crime scene."

Detective Peters' expression let me know he held me personally responsible—for all of this. The dead man, the hopefully-not-dying-man on the floor, and the man who was about to find Winthrop and befoul his crime scene. Peters swiveled and followed Frank.

Where was Anarchy?

"Get out of my way." Frank's voice boomed from down the hall.

Whoever replied wasn't nearly as loud. We couldn't hear a response.

"This is my firm. Move." Frank had an impressive set of lungs inside that puffed chest.

Again, the reply was inaudible.

The young women had all shifted their attention from the man on the floor to whatever was happening in front of Winthrop's office. Their legs blocked my view.

"He's gorgeous."

Well, now I knew who'd stopped Frank. I returned my attention to poor Buzz. "Do you want some water?"

He nodded and his lips moved as if he had something important to say.

"Would one of you get Mr. Bisby a glass of water, please?"

With apparent reluctance, one of the young women turned away from the scene unfolding in front of Winthrop's office and hurried into the kitchen.

She returned with a Dixie cup of water.

"Thank you." I propped Buzz up against my knees and held the cup to his lips.

He drank slowly. Tiny sips.

"He's coming this way." The young woman who spoke fluffed her hair.

Backs straightened, shoulders shifted backward, and skirts were smoothed.

Anarchy Jones had that effect on women. Without trying.

The women were an attractive lot. All of them. Young and pretty, with legs for miles, and substantial chests (although how much of that was related to their thrown-back shoulders I didn't know).

"Ellison—" Anarchy stopped at the edge of the circle without seeming to notice anyone but me "—are you all right?"

"I'm fine but Buzz needs an ambulance."

His brows drew together. "Buzz?"

"Mr. Bisby." One young woman (blonde hair, brown eyes, a skirt so short it was probably illegal in some states) pointed at the man draped across my lap.

Anarchy was a detective. He'd already figured that out. He just couldn't believe there was a man with a name as odd as his own. One of these days I'd have to introduce him to Forest Woods.

"His given name is Balthasar," I explained.

"Wasn't Balthasar one of the wise men?" A young woman in a very mini-dress asked.

Balthasar, the bringer of gold, was not a bad name for a stockbroker—but Buzz had been Buzz his whole life. It was probably too late to use his given name.

"No." A blonde with back-combed hair shook her head vigorously. "The wise men were Shadrach, Meshach, and Abednego."

Had she never been to Sunday school? I had. Every Sunday until I was old enough to sit through service without so much as a fidget. I knew my Bible stories. "King Nebuchadnezzer had Shadrach, Meshach, and Abednego thrown into a fiery pit when they wouldn't bow to him. An angel came to the three men and they walked out of the pit unharmed. Balthasar, Caspar, and Melchior were the wise men."

"Are you sure?" asked the back-combed blonde.

"Positive."

Poor Buzz, who at that moment had zero interest in Bible stories, groaned.

Anarchy looked over his shoulder. "The EMTs are on their way."

A few seconds later two men pushed the crowd of young women away.

They strapped a cuff to Buzz's arm and took his vitals.

A third man appeared with a gurney and they transferred Buzz from my lap.

"Ellison." Buzz's voice was rusty. "Don't leave me."

"I won't. I promise." I glanced at the circle of young women. "Would one of you please call Mrs. Bisby. Ask her to meet us at the hospital."

"Right away," said a brunette.

"I'll need to take your statement," said Anarchy.

He could do that later. "You know where to find me."

I rode in the ambulance. I held Buzz's hand. When we arrived, I exchanged pleasantries with the admitting nurse. We saw each other regularly.

I picked the most comfortable chair in the waiting room and settled in.

Ten minutes later Bea flew through the door and rushed to the admitting desk. "I'm Bea Bisby, my husband is here."

"One moment, Mrs. Bisby."

Poor Bea looked beside herself.

I hurried across the waiting room. "Bea."

She saw me and her face crumpled. "Ellison." My name was a sob. "How is he?" Apparently the brunette had given Bea the full story. How else would she know I'd come in with Buzz?

"The men in the ambulance seemed calm." I dredged up an encouraging smile. "I'm sure he'll be all right."

"We're ready for you, Mrs. Bisby," said the admitting nurse.

Bea gave me a quick, distracted hug. "Thank you for getting him here."

"Of course. Keep me updated?"

"I will." She disappeared through the swinging doors that led to the treatment area.

There wasn't much point in waiting so I took a cab back to Bisby, Marshall & Wallace. I thought about going inside, imagined Detective Peters' outraged glare, and climbed into my own car.

I drove home slowly. Pondering.

Who had killed Winthrop Marshall? And why? And why had news of Winthrop's murder nearly killed Buzz?

I pulled into the drive, parked the car, and wandered inside— all the way to the kitchen where Mr. Coffee, loyal to his core, waited for me.

"How was your meeting with your broker?" Aggie, also loyal to her core, looked up from the silver candlestick she was polishing. She knew about Winthrop's come-ons and his thick lips—I'd told her. "Did he hit on you again?"

"No." I rubbed the back of my neck and tilted my face toward the ceiling. "I found him dead."

The blackened cloth in Aggie's hand fell to the floor and her mouth dropped open. "You're kidding,"

My fingers sought the tightest vertebrae and pressed. "I'm not. I wish I were."

She settled the candlestick onto the counter and pointed at a stool. "Sit. I'll get you a cup of coffee."

I sat and Aggie brought me a cup of ambrosia.

"What happened?" she asked after I'd taken a few restorative sips.

"He'd been shot." I stared into my coffee cup for a few seconds. "Probably sometime last night."

"Didn't his wife miss him?" Aggie and her late husband Al had enjoyed a marriage based on love, trust, and mutual respect. If Al Delucci had failed to come home, Aggie would have found him.

I suspected Ruth Marshall did not care that much about Winthrop.

"I don't know." I shook my head. "Maybe he told her he was working late. Maybe they had separate bedrooms." If I were Ruth, I'd have insisted on separate bedrooms. I'd have insisted on separate houses. "When I got there, his office was locked. His assistant opened the door and I found him dead behind his desk. Shot in the chest." I did not tell her about the pants, or the ankles, or my eye-level views. Instead, I shuddered.

She looked on me with sympathy in her eyes. "You knew him well?"

That eye-level view. "Well enough."

"When I finish the silver, I'll make a Bundt cake." Bundt cake, a sign of caring and comfort for me to take to Ruth Marshall and her family.

I thought about the pants and boxer shorts pooled around Winthrop's pale, skinny ankles. "This death might call for a ham."

THREE

Anarchy arrived at my house shortly after lunch. Shadows lurked under his eyes but his smile was as warm as the summer sun.

I basked in the sunshine for a few seconds. "Have you eaten? The quiche is still warm."

"Sounds good." His voice was tired—as if Frank Wallace and the bevy of young women had already worn him thin.

He took my hand and we walked to the kitchen with Max, my dastardly dog, trotting at our heels.

Aggie nodded a welcome, her gaze catching on our linked hands.

"Anarchy hasn't had lunch yet." I let go of Anarchy's fingers and pulled a plate from the cupboard.

Aggie took the plate from me and had Anarchy's lunch—quiche Lorraine, greens dressed in her secret vinaigrette, and crusty bread—ready in no time.

I positioned a placemat on the kitchen island and added a napkin and silverware. "Iced tea, coffee, or water?"

"Iced tea, please." Anarchy settled onto a stool and picked up the fork.

Max settled on his haunches and stood watch next to Anarchy's stool. He'd be happy to pick up any dropped bites.

"Mrs. Russell tells me she found another body." Aggie didn't sound judgmental or aggravated as Mother would have. Aggie sounded almost blasé. Blasé was worse than aggravated.

Aggravated suggested that finding bodies should stop.

Immediately.   Ellison-find-a-new-hobby-or-I'll-disinherit-you. Ellison-you-won't-have-a-friend-left-in-this-town. Ellison-people-are-talking-about-you-over-the-bridge-table.

Blasé suggested I was a woman who found bodies as a matter of course.

I was many things.

Mother.

Artist.

Even widow.

All were preferable to being a woman who found bodies—as a matter of course.

Anarchy took a second bite of quiche. "How's Bisby?"

"Admitted to the hospital. I'm pretty sure he's in stable condition but I haven't heard from Bea yet."

"Bea?" His brows rose.

"Yes."

"Bea and Buzz Bisby?" Anarchy's eyes sparkled.

"Yes." My lips twitched (in response to the sparkle, not because I thought the Bisbys' names were odd). "What did you find out at the brokerage? Who killed Winthrop?"

"No idea. According to his colleagues, he was well-liked and seldom worked late. His secretary swears he'd already left when she went home at five."

"What did the other women say about him?"

"The other women?"

"The secretaries, the receptionist, the copy girl."

"They said he was a good boss."

I rolled my eyes.

The fork paused on its way to Anarchy's mouth. "You heard something else?"

"If he hit on me, I can guarantee you, he hit on those young women."

"I don't see how that follows."

I gaped at him. Was he kidding? "The women in that office are young and pretty with legs for miles. We're not talking about a man of high moral fiber."

"Hitting on you shows a certain discernment."

Anarchy really thought that? I smiled at him like a moon-struck calf.

"The man had good taste."

I strongly suspected Winthrop had very broad tastes. He didn't hunt with a rifle but with a shotgun. If the pellet spray was wide enough, he was bound to hit something. Some misguided woman would fall for his lines. "Be that as it may, he asked about scratching my itch within three months of Henry's death. Thank God I was in a position to say no. The young women in his office might not have had that luxury."

Anarchy chewed his quiche, considering. "We'll ask more questions. What do you know about Debbie?"

Poor Debbie. "Finding Winthrop was quite a shock for her."

"She was so upset she could hardly talk to me. Had she been working for him long?"

"I know she's been there since Henry died. Before that?" I shrugged. "Henry dealt with all things financial."

A cat coughing up a hairball—that's the noise Aggie made.

Max abandoned his steady focus on Anarchy's plate, tilted his head, and gazed at her with a quizzical look on his doggy face.

I pretended I hadn't heard Aggie's audible opinion of my late-husband. "Can't the office manager tell you how long Debbie's been there?"

"The office manager was out sick today. She's not answering her phone. Peters is checking on her."

I wouldn't care to be that office manager. Detective Peters was tough to take when one felt on top of the world. If I had to deal with him when I was sick, I'd pull the covers over my head and hide till next Tuesday. After the morning I'd had, I might do that anyway.

"Ellison!" Mother's aggrieved call carried from the front hall.

Why, why, why had I ever given her a key to my house? And why was she yelling?

There could only be one answer.

I glanced at Aggie then at Mr. Coffee's near empty pot. "I'll need more coffee."

Feeling like Daniel on his way into the lion's den (without the Lord's protection), I pushed through the kitchen door.

Mother stood in the foyer wearing a Chanel suit that couldn't decide if it was beige or ecru. The suit was new. It had to be. Normally she would save such a light color for later in the spring. She was rushing the season. Something she never did unless a new suit or dress was simply begging to be worn. In addition to the suit, she wore an expression that couldn't decide if it was sour or outraged. "Another one, Ellison? Really?"

She was lucky (I was lucky) Buzz hadn't died too. Otherwise the number would be two.

"What happened?" she demanded.

I studied the braided piping on her jacket—there was a subtle gold thread that completely made the ensemble. "I had an appointment with Winthrop and when I got there he was dead."

"Why didn't someone else find him? Why you?"

Why me? How many times had I asked myself exactly that?

"It's a long story. One I was about to tell Anarchy. Would you care to join us?"

"He's here?"

She'd recognized his car in the drive. I'd bet the cost of her new suit on it.

"Yes." My tone was butter-wouldn't-melt-in-my-mouth cool.

She sniffed and glanced at her watch as if I were keeping her from something important. "How long is this story?"

My mind veered toward an image of Winthrop's naked lap. "Not that long."

A second sniff. "I'll take the condensed version."

"There was a sick woman coughing all over the reception area. I asked to wait in Winthrop's office. When his secretary opened the door, I found Winthrop dead."

"That's it?" She patted the perfect helmet of her hair. "In a nutshell."

"Not a long story."

Not when I left out the pants around his ankles, and Debbie's reaction, and Buzz.

Mother drew a deep breath. She followed the breath with a deep sigh. "Why do these things happen to you?"

We were back to *why you.* "I wish I knew."

Her nod was positively regal. "Perhaps you should figure it out, then you could avoid making the mistake in the future."

My disappointing propensity for finding bodies was an evergreen topic. Mother never tired of pointing out the error of my deplorable ways (at least she wasn't blasé). It was time for a change of subject. "You look very nice. Where are you off to?"

"The hospital foundation's board meeting." She looked down at the black tips of her ecru shoes. "How did you get Major Jenkins to make that enormous gift to the Chinese event?"

I was chairing a gala opening for the Chinese exhibition that would arrive in Kansas City in April. In addition to deciding everything from menu to décor (I had a wonderful ambiance committee), I had to make sure the event was profitable for the museum (I was on my own). That meant asking for money. Lots of money. Major Jenkins had pledged a six-figure gift. The museum was waiting for the stock transfer. "He's on the museum board and his granddaughter is on the event committee. Why?"

"The capital campaign for the hospital. He turned us down flat."

Major Jenkins cared about art not hospital wings. I shrugged.

Mother sniffed. "It's not as if he'd miss the money."

"You don't give money to everyone who asks." If she did, she'd wouldn't be able to afford Chanel suits.

The sour expression returned. "Supporting the hospital is a civic duty."

I sealed my lips. Anything I might say would further sour her expression.

"You gave. And you care about art not hospitals."

"True. But you asked and I care about you. If you want Mr.

Jenkins to give, have someone he cares about ask him."

Brnng, brnng.

Mother pursed her lips and glanced at her watch. "I've got to run. Please try not to find any more bodies."

I had never, ever, *tried* to find a body. "I promise."

Brnng, brnng.

She closed her hand around the door handle. "I mean it, Ellison."

"I know you do."

Brnng, brn—

"I'll let you take your call." She paused and leveled a death glare at me. "Remember, you promised."

"Mrs. Russell—" Aggie spoke from down the hallway "—I'm sorry to interrupt but Mrs. Bisby is on the phone. She says it's important."

Mother's right brow rose slightly and she released the door handle. Her expression spoke volumes. Was I somehow involved in a second murder?

"Buzz is in the hospital. I asked Bea to call me with any news."

Thunder settled on her brow. "Hospital?"

"He had a heart incident."

She narrowed her eyes. "No one tried to kill him?"

"Absolutely not."

"You're sure?"

"Positive."

Mother sniffed and opened the front door. "Remember your promise." Without another word, she strode like a lion into late March's lamb-like sunshine.

I shut the door behind her, resting my forehead against its solid expanse.

"Should I tell Mrs. Bisby you'll call her back?"

I lifted my head. "No. I'll take the call in the study."

My late husband's office had defied my attempts at redecoration. Dark paneling. Ugly carpet. Heavy drapes. One of these days, I'd have them all changed.

I picked up the receiver. "Bea, is Buzz all right?"

"He'll be fine. They're keeping him for a day or two to monitor his heart."

"Thank heavens."

"Ellison—" there was an Ellison's-not-going-to-like-this quality to her voice "—may I ask a huge favor?"

I swallowed sudden dread. "Of course."

"There's a man with whom Buzz and Winthrop and Frank do business, Chauncey Nelson. He's in town from New York for meetings and he brought his wife. I promised to entertain her tomorrow."

Given that half the people who were supposed to attend the meeting were unavailable, one would think Chauncey Nelson (Chauncey? Really?) would return to New York.

"Frank has decided to proceed with the meeting and I just can't entertain Hester Nelson. I need to be at the hospital. Would you please take her shopping or to a museum?"

"Of course." The words slipped, unconsidered, past my lips.

"Thank you." Never in the history of *thank yous* had a woman sounded so grateful.

"My pleasure."

"I was to pick her up at The Alameda at ten tomorrow morning."

"I'll do it."

"I've never met her but—"

That dread I'd swallowed crept back up my throat.

"I don't think she's too thrilled to be here."

Then why had she come?

"Buzz told me she's one of those Easterners who thinks we keep cattle in our backyards."

I knew the type. When I went to the gallery in New York that carried my work, I endured countless questions. Did we ride horses as a matter of course? Did we eat anything but beef and corn? Were seven-story skyscrapers as high as we could go? And always, how did I survive in a cultural wasteland?

It was no use talking about Kansas City's art museums, or art institute, or the vast number of working artists employed by Hallmark. It was no use talking about Charlie Parker or jazz. If I pointed out that John Kander, who wrote the music for *Cabaret*, was from Kansas City, they'd smile indulgently and point out the operative word was *from*.

I'd grit my teeth and smile back. "You really must come visit."

An invitation that never failed to earn me a second indulgent smile.

Tomorrow was my chance to show an Easterner that Kansas City was more than stockyards, barbeque, and a song from *Oklahoma!*

"I'll take her to The Nelson," I promised. "And Swanson's. She needs to see the Plaza."

"You're sure?"

"Of course, I'm sure. It's a day of art and shopping, what could go wrong?"

FOUR

Anarchy listened to everything I had to tell him about Winthrop, scratched Max behind the ears, and devoured the last bite of the quiche Aggie had prepared. Then he nodded at her, "Thank you, Aggie. That was delicious."

She responded with a lukewarm smile. "You're welcome."

One of these days, Aggie might bring herself to like Anarchy. Or not.

Anarchy checked his pager, stood, and dropped a kiss on my cheek. "May I use the phone before I go?"

"Of course." Aggie and I shifted our gazes to the kitchen phone with its stretched-to-Timbuktu cord. "Do you need privacy?"

Anarchy's lips flirted with a smile. "Please."

I led him to the study, which didn't look so awful when he was in it. "Help yourself."

Max, who'd followed us, whined softly and rubbed his head against my leg.

"Do you want to go for a run?" I asked.

His stubby tail wagged.

"I'll leave you to your call." Hopefully I didn't sound too wistful.

Anarchy had already switched to cop-mode. His expression was serious and he had the receiver in hand.

"Can you let yourself out?" I definitely sounded too wistful.

"Yeah." He glanced at his pager, stuck his finger in the dial, then looked up at me with eyes so warm they could melt a glacier.

"Thanks, Ellison. For everything. Dinner tonight?"

"That would be nice." That would be more than nice.

"I'll pick you up at seven."

"See you then." The part of me that still couldn't believe a man like Anarchy was interested in an almost middle-aged widow did cartwheels. The rest of me simply smiled. I led Max from the study, went upstairs, and changed into running clothes.

Anarchy's voice was just audible through the closed study door when I clipped Max's leash on his collar and slipped outside.

Max and I ran to Loose Park. Each lap around its edges measured a mile. "How many laps today? Four?"

Max just grinned and pulled against the leash. *Faster.*

After the first lap, Max's pace slowed.

My breath came in regular huffs. Three pounds of my heels against the path—exhale. Three pounds of my heels—inhale. Max trotted next to me, his jaw hinged open in a happy grin.

We headed up one of the park's hills (third time) and I concentrated on keeping my pace steady.

Max pulled on his leash. Hard.

"I'm done racing. Slow down."

He pulled again. Harder.

A pair of sassy squirrels were shaking their bushy tails in his direction.

I tightened my grip on the leash.

In a lightning fast maneuver, Max cut in front of me.

I tripped over him and fell. Hard enough that an inventory of parts was required. Ankles—okay. Knees—might be bruised. Hips—okay. Hands—scraped. Leash—gone.

I stood. Slowly. "Dammit, Max."

The outraged squirrels chittered at him from the branches of a Bradford pear tree. He stood beneath them, his smile bigger than ever (the prospect of munching on squirrels filled him with joy).

I limped into the little copse of trees and reclaimed his leash just as a maroon Lincoln Continental pulled into the small parking lot next to the path.

A man in a suit got out of the Lincoln, shoved something into the trash barrel, then climbed back in his car and drove away.

Odd. Very odd.

"Curiosity killed the cat," I told Max.

He grinned at me. He was all for killing cats.

"Maybe he was getting rid of a bag from a takeout lunch."

Max still grinned. Leftovers were one of his favorite food groups.

"It wouldn't hurt to look."

Max's grin widened. He never said no to rooting in the trash.

I limped over to the barrel and peered over the rim—half hoping for a crumpled McDonald's bag.

There, at the bottom of the barrel, was a manila envelope.

I glanced over my shoulder then peered again into the barrel. What was it? A ransom payment? Love letters?

The squirrels stopped their chittering and stared at me. A robin leveled a most serious gaze my way. The other birds (there were many) silenced their tweeting. It was as if I was Snow White, the envelope was a poisoned apple, and the park animals were telling me not to bite.

Well.

I bent over and reached for the envelope—quickly—the inside of the barrel smelled appalling.

My fingers grabbed the edge and I stood.

Then I peeked inside.

Someone had torn up papers—halved them, quartered them, then halved them again. I pulled a fragment out of the envelope. "Confid—, Win—, and Spec—"

"What do you think?" I asked Max.

He yawned. Pieces of paper were far less interesting than squirrels or hamburger wrappers or running.

I thought it was pretty interesting. Someone had left their office in the middle of the day, driven to a near-empty park, and pitched the envelope into a barrel that would be filled with the leavings of the under-seven, after-school crowd within the hour. It was a mystery without a body. My favorite kind of mystery.

I folded the envelope and slipped it into the waistband of my sweats. All those little pieces of paper pressed against the small of my back.

Max tugged at the leash. We still had another lap and he wasn't delaying another minute so I could ponder boring (not a bite of food) trash.

I followed him back onto the path and my banged knee sent me a warning shot. *No more running. Not today.* "We're walking," I told Max. "And you have only yourself to blame."

Hmmph.

We walked the last lap and headed for home.

The corner of the envelope (poisoned apple) poked at me. Max pulled on me. My knee complained to me. I'd never been so happy to see my front door.

I stepped inside and unhooked Max's leash.

He trotted off to the kitchen for a slurp of water and a nap.

Aggie appeared in the kitchen door. "Oh good, you're home. Nan Roddingham called. She'd like you to call her as soon as possible."

Nan Roddingham? Really? "Did she say what she wanted?"

"No."

Nan Roddingham was eight years older than I. She collected master bridge¹ points like most women collected Herend figurines. Rumor had it she'd actually read *War and Peace*. At the pool. She played decent tennis, better golf, and kept horses at Saddle & Sirloin. We were friendly but not friends. If she was calling, she wanted something—a painting for an auction or a warm body for a committee.

"I'll shower first."

I climbed the stairs to the second floor then took another set of steps to the third. Once a ballroom, I'd converted the top floor of the house into a studio. The enormous room smelled of paint and turpentine and was comfortably cluttered with mason jars filled with paintbrushes, stacked canvases, a club chair too shabby for the downstairs, piles of sketchbooks, books on art, two easels, and a drafting table of impressive size.

I pulled the envelope, now slightly damp with sweat, from my waistband and dropped it on the table. There was plenty of room to piece the papers together.

The slightly bedraggled envelope looked suspect.

Whatever was inside was none of my business.

Plus, there was that whole curiosity and cat thing.

I didn't care.

The envelope held a simple mystery. And when I'd solved it, I could pitch the whole thing in the trash. Until then, the scraps of papers would stay.

I turned on my heel, hurried down the stairs, and grabbed a quick shower. I took my time blow-drying my hair—dinner at seven.

Then I headed to the kitchen, grabbed a cup of coffee, and wagged my finger at Max. "My knee is swollen and I blame you."

He yawned.

At least Mr. Coffee looked sympathetic.

Mug of nirvana in hand, I strolled into the family room, located the country club directory, found Nan's number, and dialed.

"Hello," she answered.

"Nan? Ellison Russell returning your call."

"Ellllison—" Nan's way of drawing out the first syllables of words made her sound as if she was from the east coast. She wasn't. She was born less than ten blocks from where she now lived. "Thaaaank you for returning my call."

"My pleasure. What can I do for you?"

"I caaaalled to talk to about the Sunset Hills Boooook Club."

"Wow." Wow was an understatement.

There were umpteen-million book clubs around. Even Libba belonged to one. But Sunset Hills was different. First off, everyone actually read the book. Secondly, while a nut covered cheese ball might be served during the book discussion, wine was reserved till after. Most book clubs (certainly Libba's) were just an excuse to drink. Finally, Sunset Hills limited its membership. No one under the age of thirty-five could join and once a member had reached fifty-five, she moved up to the seniors group (where wine was served early and often).

Sunset Hills was the book club many women aspired to join, but given its limited membership, few succeeded. Conventional wisdom said, if you weren't a legacy, you might as well drink Liebraumilch and read Erica Jong elsewhere.

I wasn't a legacy (book clubs weren't Mother's thing) so I repeated, "Wow."

"We think you'd make a woooonderful addition. Would you please consider joining?"

Watership Down sat on my bedside table as it had for months. It was tough to get through a book when bodies turned up on a far too regular basis. "Do you think we might meet for coffee and go over expectations?"

It didn't matter what the expectations were, she had me. We both knew it. I couldn't turn them down. If I joined, Grace would be a legacy. And, if there was the slightest chance of Mother finding out about this invitation and that I'd declined it, my life wouldn't be worth living.

"I'd be deeeelighted. Can you meet in the morning?"

"Early. I have an appointment at ten."

"Perrrfect. La Bonne Bouchée? Say eight thirty?"

"I'll be there. And, Nan, thank you for your call. Of course, I'm flattered."

"We'd be luuuucky to have you as a member."

I hung up the phone and stared at nothing. The Sunset Hills Book Club? Really? Maybe the members were willing to overlook a few bodies to have an artist, who presumably was an intellectual (boy, were they wrong) as a member. That couldn't be it—I knew too many of the current members and they knew I'd rather read Richard Adams than Marcel Proust.

I picked up the phone and dialed.

"Walford residence."

"Penelope, this is Ellison calling. May I please speak to Mother?"

"One moment, Mrs. Russell."

Penelope put down the phone, but the sound of her retreating footsteps tapped loud and clear through the receiver.

Mother had her quirks but she was always on my side.

Always.

And she would know if there was something off about this invitation.

"Ellison, what's wrong?" Worry pitched Mother's voice higher than was usual. She might as well have asked *did you find another body?*

"Nothing's wrong."

"Then why are you calling?"

"I need your advice."

She marked the occasion with a moment of silence. "About what?"

"The Sunset Hills Book Club."

"They asked you?" The amount of surprise in her voice was a bit insulting.

"They did."

"Of course you're accepting."

That decision was made, or I wouldn't have mentioned it to her. "I'm just surprised."

"I'm not," said the woman who regularly told me no one would want to know me if I continued to find bodies. "You're smart. You're accomplished. You read." She paused. "I wouldn't mention finding Winthrop's body to anyone."

"No."

"Who called you?"

"Nan Roddingham."

Mother made an I-don't-like-the-way-she-talks-it's-affected noise. "Just tell them you can't join until after the gala. The last thing you need right now is a thousand-page book that needs to be read in two weeks."

Amen to that. "You think they'll let me defer for a month?"

"Of course. Every single one of those women understands the pressures of volunteer work." There was not a hint of irony in Mother's voice.

"If you hear anything—"

"I'll let you know. I'm proud of you, Ellison."

Always nice to hear. It would have been nicer hearing those words on Mother's lips at an art opening or about how well Grace was turning out but I'd take my compliments as I could get them. "Thanks, Mother. I've got to run—a million things to do."

"I'm sure you do. The gala is only weeks away."

If she wanted to believe gala chores were the reason I was ending our call, I wasn't about to correct her or tell her I had a date with Anarchy.

FIVE

I stood in my closet and glared at my clothes. I had racks of them. Racks. And not a stitch to wear. I glanced at my watch. The situation was dire. I needed help.

I hurried into my bedroom and from there into the hallway. "Grace!"

No answer.

Hardly surprising given the volume of the music pouring out of my daughter's room. It was a good thing Mother never listened to popular music. If she ever heard the lyrics coming from Grace's room—well, it didn't bear thinking about.

"Grace!" I stood in the doorway to her room

My daughter was sprawled across her bed with her nose in a book. Oblivious.

"Grace!"

She looked up, then reached over to the radio and turned down the volume on "Lady Marmalade."

"Too loud."

"Sorry." She wasn't. The decibels would go back up as soon as I left her.

We could have waged a war over loud music. Instead, we'd come to an agreement. The dial would go down—way down—after dinner and I didn't complain when the house shook before the evening meal.

"What's up?" she asked.

"I can't decide what to wear."

Her grin widened and she waggled her eyebrows. "You have a date?"

I nodded.

"With Anarchy?"

"Yes." Who else?

She dropped her book on the bed and swung her feet to the floor. "Okay, I know just the thing."

I followed her to my closet.

"This." She held up a pair of silk pants and a gauzy blouse.

"Too revealing."

She rolled her eyes. "They're pants."

"I meant the top."

She glanced at her watch. "What time is he picking you up?"

"Seven."

"Then you don't have time to argue." She pressed her selection into my arms. "Just wear it."

"Fine." It wasn't as if I'd be going to the country club. I could be a little daring.

"You need more blush. You look too pale."

"Anything else?" Why had I invited such a bossy teenager into my closet?

"Let your hair down."

My hair was up in a perfect French twist—my signature style. "Why?"

"Just do it. It looks pretty around your shoulders."

Who was I to argue with teenage wisdom?

When Anarchy rang the bell at seven, I wore the outfit Grace had selected, my cheeks were pink, and my hair floated around my shoulders.

"Wow." Anarchy's eyes widened. "You look great."

Somewhere, out of sight but within hearing distance, Grace was smirking—maybe even mouthing *I told you so.*

I pulled my new Guy Laroche safari jacket from the closet. "How chilly is it?"

"You might need that later."

I folded the coat over my arm. "Where are we going?"

"Nabil's."

"Lovely." Sort of. We'd see people I knew. Normally Anarchy took me to steak houses or a fried chicken place under a bridge. Normally we existed in our own bubble. No bubble tonight. "It's one of my favorites."

"Grace told me."

Grace was just full of helpful advice.

Together, we walked to his car. Anarchy opened the door. I got in.

He settled behind the wheel. "How was your run?"

"Max cut in front of me and I fell."

"Dogs will do that."

"Especially when they spot lazy-looking squirrels." Now was my chance to tell him about the envelope, but I couldn't. My reasons for retrieving that envelope from the bottom of the trash barrel weren't clear to me; explaining them to Anarchy was impossible.

"You're not hurt?"

"My knee is a bit stiff but I'm fine."

We drove the short distance to the Country Club Plaza listening to Supertramp's "Dreamer" on the radio.

Anarchy turned left onto Nichols Road. "I have to tell you—" he jerked his chin toward a six foot tall rabbit wearing a jaunty jacket "—I think those bunnies are creepy."

Each spring, nine rabbits took up residence on the Plaza. They had names. They wore cute clothes. The female bunnies carried baskets filled with eggs. The male bunnies wore jaunty bow ties. Mothers and fathers took pictures of their children next to the bunnies. Kids had their favorites (Grace was always partial to Nicholas and his polka dot coat). And at night, the bunnies' eyes glowed red. They looked like demon bunnies.

"They're friendly during the day," I argued.

"Ellison—" Anarchy pointed at the rabbit "—that thing looks like it was sent here to collect souls."

"I grew up with them. I think they're charming."

Anarchy muttered something I didn't quite catch, circled the block, and parked in front of Halls. "Do you mind walking?"

"Not at all."

We strolled down the sidewalk, pausing to peer in windows. "What about your afternoon?" I asked. "What did you do?"

"I went to the hospital and talked to your friend, Buzz."

"How is he? Bea was supposed to call me." I should have called her.

"They're keeping him for a few days."

Anarchy opened Nabil's door for me and I stepped inside.

The maître d', Henri, spotted me and his face fell. "Mrs. Russell, we are booked tonight." He glanced down at his ledger and shook his head as if he saw nothing but bad news. "If you'd care to wait at the bar, I'll see if we can squeeze you in."

"We have a reservation," said Anarchy. "For Jones."

Henri ran his finger down the list of names, his face cleared, and he picked up two menus. "Wonderful. This way please."

He led us to a table for two. "If I'd known you were coming, Mrs. Russell, I would have reserved your usual table."

"This is perfect, Henri." I draped my jacket over the chair and sat.

Henri waited until Anarchy was seated then presented us with menus. "Greg will be your server."

Anarchy watched Henri hurry back to his post. "They know you well."

"It's one of my favorites."

My favorites. Anarchy's favorites. Perhaps it was time we found our favorite. "If you could eat any kind of meal, what would it be?"

"A steak. What about you?"

"French bistro."

George appeared tableside. "Would you care to order a drink?"

"A Stoli martini, please. Dirty."

Anarchy's brows rose. "A beer. Whatever you've got on tap."

"Very good, sir." George nodded and disappeared.

Anarchy looked at the menu. "What do you normally order?"

"Always the same thing. The chicken breast in lemon-caper sauce. But I hear the steak is quite good."

"Ellison." Prudence Davies stood next to our table. Some demon (a demon bunny?) had forgotten to guard the gates of hell and Prudence had escaped. There could be no other explanation for her presence. "How sweet that you brought your detective out to dinner."

I loathed Prudence. The woman resembled Mr. Ed. But that major hiccup in the looks department hadn't stopped her from having an affair with my late husband or half the married men of my acquaintance.

"You look nice, Prudence? Orthodontia?" I'd met horses with smaller teeth than hers.

"So amusing. Hunter's here. Did you notice? With Gaye Hardy."

If Mother had her way, I'd be the fourth and final Mrs. Hunter Tafft. On paper, Hunter and I were perfect for each other. Same clubs, same friends, same backgrounds. Plus, he was a successful attorney who'd helped me out of more than one jam. Add to that handsome features, silver hair, and an impeccable wardrobe. He drank vodka martinis. Dirty ones.

But perfect on paper didn't translate. Not when a beer-drinking detective who wore too much plaid could make me forget my middle name with just a smile.

Mother was destined for disappointment.

"I hadn't noticed them. I'll have to say hello before we leave."

Prudence blinked. Hunter having a date hadn't wounded me. "I heard you found Winthrop's body this morning."

"Hmm." I had no response.

"And I hear his pants were around his ankles."

The tip of Anarchy's shoe knocked softly against my shin.

I got the hint. "Where did you hear that?"

"Ruth. She figures that slut of a secretary got tired of giving it up."

"Debbie? She's a sweet girl. I doubt she was fooling around with Winthrop."

Prudence snorted.

"Have you even met her?"

"As a matter of fact, I have. Winthrop managed my portfolio." She glared at me as if I was responsible for Winthrop's death and a possible decline in her returns.

"You seriously think that pretty young woman with the handsome husband was fooling around with Winthrop Marshall?" Distaste curdled my tone.

"I do." Of course she did. Prudence would have ignored Winthrop's wedding band, spare tire, and thick lips in a heartbeat if he offered to scratch her itch. I credited Debbie with better taste.

"Hmm." I raised my shoulders and let them fall.

"Stay away from the other partners."

"Pardon me?"

"That's the highest-yielding brokerage in town. Its clients can't afford another death."

Greg angled around Prudence and put the martini down in front of me. Thank God. With Prudence at the table, I needed it.

Then he set down Anarchy's beer.

Prudence's gaze caught on the mug and her lip curled. "Beer, detective?"

Anarchy looked up at her—a slow, chilly look. "Yes."

"You know—" Prudence looked down her long nose "—gentlemen stand when a lady comes to the table."

I took a big sip of vodka.

"Thanks for the tip," Anarchy replied. "If any ladies come by, I'll get up."

Prudence's lips pulled away from her teeth.

I lifted my martini glass and tilted it slightly toward Anarchy's stein. "To us."

Prudence huffed.

I stared across the table into Anarchy's coffee-brown eyes. If we ignored her, maybe she'd go away.

I took another sip of icy vodka.

Anarchy sipped his beer.

Our gazes held.

Prudence huffed again, then she walked away.

"I thought she'd never leave." Anarchy's voice was a velvet whisper, meant just for me.

"We got off easy. Normally someone has to lure her away with fresh meat."

Anarchy's lips stretched into a grin and my heart somersaulted. Oh dear Lord.

"I shouldn't have been so rude."

"To Prudence? You weren't rude enough."

"She's jealous."

"Of me?" I stared into my martini and considered. "Maybe. But Prudence has always wanted what other people have." She'd wanted Henry.

And she could have had him. If I'd known all the things my late husband was up to, I'd have gift-wrapped and delivered him.

The man who'd pledged to be faithful to me till-death-do-us-part preferred Prudence (and countless other women) and had left me with an issue or two (or twenty).

"Ellison."

I looked up from my drink. Hunter and Gaye stood next to our table.

Anarchy rose from his chair.

Hunter bent and brushed a kiss across my cheek. "Ellison, you know Gaye."

"Of course, it's nice to see you."

"You as well." Gaye's pursed lips suggested she wasn't exactly thrilled with this tableside visit.

"And Gaye, this is Anarchy Jones." Hunter shoved his hands in his pockets. "Anarchy, my friend, Gaye Hardy."

"A pleasure to meet you, Gaye."

Gaye merely nodded.

"I hear you caught the Winthrop case," said Hunter.

Anarchy nodded. "Word gets around fast."

"You have no idea," I muttered.

Gaye rested her hand on Hunter's arm. "If we're going to make that movie, we should go."

Hunter raised his arm and glanced at his watch, shaking off her hand. "You're right. Ellison, lovely to see you. Jones—" Hunter extended his hand.

The two men shook.

Anarchy watched them walk away with the oddest expression on his face. When they disappeared from view, he resumed his seat. "Are you sure?"

"Sure about what?"

"Sure about us. All you have to do is crook your little finger and he'd drop that woman in a heartbeat."

The man had lost his mind. "What are you talking about?"

"Tafft. He still has feelings for you."

A light bulb went on. Brighter than a hundred watts. I might wonder what Anarchy saw in an almost middle-aged widow, but he wondered what I saw in him.

I reached across the table and took his hand—warm and strong and slightly damp from the beer stein. "I'm sure."

Anarchy's eyes warmed to freshly percolated and he smiled.

Greg appeared at the edge of my vision. "May I—"

"We'll both have the chicken in lemon-caper sauce." Anarchy's gaze never left my face.

We stared. We grinned. Neither of us willing to be the one who looked away.

We might have stayed liked that all night, but Greg asked, "Soup or salad?"

I shifted my gaze to the waiter. "Salad."

Then I took a third sip of martini. I needed that one too. Something big had just happened. Something without a name.

And because I wasn't ready to name it, I asked, "Do you think Prudence was right? Was Debbie sleeping with Winthrop?"

Anarchy took the sudden change in conversation in stride. "I don't know. He was definitely sleeping with someone."

Which explained the pants and the ankles and the—I closed my eyes. Nope. No good. The memory was burned on the back of my eyelids too. "Who?"

"Someone in the office. I'm hoping you can help me find her."

SIX

I walked into La Bonne Bouchée a few minutes early. The wind followed me inside and I wrapped my wool coat (Bill Blass and fabulous) more tightly around me. Last night, the air had held the promise of spring. This morning, the temperature was better suited to January. Typical Kansas City weather.

I claimed a window table and shed my winter gear.

A waiter appeared as soon as I sat. "Just one today?"

"A friend will be joining me."

"May I get you something while you wait?"

"A café au lait."

If Mr. Coffee had a fault, it was that he couldn't steam milk. Not that I'd ever tell him such a thing. I wouldn't hurt his feelings for all the steamed milk in the world.

At precisely eight thirty, Nan pushed past the crowd surrounding the pastry case. She dug in her purse and pulled out a pair of glasses. With the glasses on her nose, she spotted me, smiled, and returned the glasses to her bag.

I wouldn't have guessed her for the vain sort.

I stood.

We hugged.

I sat.

She shrugged out of her mink jacket. "Beeeeastly weather."

Beastly. One didn't meet too many Midwesterners who used that word. None who pronounced it the way Nan did. Maybe she was a bit vain.

"Perfectly awful." I glanced around the small seating area. "The waiter should be back any minute. I went ahead and ordered a coffee."

"I'm glad you didn't wait." Nan sat down, put her purse (a Coach feedbag) on the table, and dug inside. After a moment's search, she pulled out an envelope with my name on it. "There!" She pushed the envelope across the table slowly, carefully—as if it were a Fabergé egg. "That has all the information you need."

The envelope rested directly in front of me.

"Nan, I'm incredibly honored to be asked but, with the gala next month, I can't add a single thing to my plate till May."

"Not a problem." Nan jammed her gloves into her purse and hung the strap over the back of her chair. "We know how busy you are."

"So May is all right?"

"Perrrfectly fine. Now—" she pushed up the sleeves of her cashmere sweater and rested her forearms on the little table "—what's in the envelope outlines everything but, in a nutshell, the club is limited to twenty active members. We meet ten times a year on the second Tuesday of the month. No meetings in August or December."

Summer vacations and Christmas. Got it.

"We expect our members to attend and we expect them to read the selection."

The waiter arrived and put my decadent coffee on top of the envelope.

Nan paled.

"May I get you something, ma'am?"

"Coffee. Black." Her gaze was fixed on my hands lifting the coffee and moving the envelope to a safer spot. "You might want to put that in your purse. I'll answer any questions you have now, but you might want to refer to the contents later."

Such fuss over an envelope. I slipped the information into my handbag, took a sip of coffee, and suppressed a satisfied sigh (barely).

"Each member is allowed to pick a book once every two years."

"What kind of books?" I didn't want to reread my college English syllabus.

"They're usually current. This month we read *Centennial*."

Exactly the kind of thousand-page book I dreaded.

"Next month we're reading *Postern of Fate* by Agatha Christie." She speared me with a look. "I imagine that would be right up your alley."

Because I found bodies? "When would I host?"

"July. I know it's just around the corner, but every membership is numbered and you're getting one of the sevens."

At least I'd have May and June to see how things were done.

"The meetings are from six thirty to nine. Thirty minutes to socialize, an hour to discuss the book, then dessert. Evvvveryone is expected to contribute to the discussion."

The waiter put a cup of black coffee down in front of Nan. "Anything to eat today?"

"No, thank you." We spoke at the same time.

She sipped her coffee and a beatific expression settled onto her face. "Nectar of the gods."

I couldn't argue.

"I heard you had some exxxcitement at Bisby, Marshall & Wallace."

Excitement. Why did people assume finding a body was exciting? Finding a body was dreadful.

Nan patted her perfectly coiffed hair. "I know it's not nice to speak ill of the dead, but he was an odious man."

I couldn't argue that.

"He absolutely preyed on the young women in that office. Frankly, I'm surprised he made it as long as he did. I would have thought some outraged husband would have killed him long ago."

"Oh?" I murmured. Who would have thought Nan would be such a font of information? I leaned forward. "Did he have a favorite girl? Was he seeing anyone?"

"That I don't know. I just know he forced himself on the girls who worked for him because my nephew, Tim, worked there for a few months. He couldn't stomach what was happening."

And I'd heard her nephew, Tim Vanderlay (Nan's sister's boy), was fired.

"He was working late one night when a girl burst out of Winthrop Marshall's office. Torn dress. Mussed hair. Tear-stained cheeks." She leaned forward. "Well, of course, Tim demanded to know what had happened. She said it was all a misunderstanding."

"Poor girl."

Nan snorted. "The next day the girl acted as if nothing had happened. She acted as if she didn't know what Tim was talking about. So—" Nan took a restorative sip of coffee "—Tim confronted Marshall."

"How did that turn out?"

"Marshall told him to mind his own damn business. Three weeks later, Tim was out of a job." Nan seemed blissfully unaware that she'd supplied her nephew with a motive for murder.

"How awful."

"Last I heard, the girl was still working there." Nan shook her head as if Tim's troubles were the girl's fault.

"What was her name?"

"I don't know." Another sip of coffee. "But I can find out."

I pulled up in front of The Alameda a few minutes before ten, left my car keys with the doorman, and dashed inside.

Brrr. I should have believed the weather girl, Cheryll Jones, when she said there was a chance of snow.

A woman wearing a navy suit and a pinched expression stood near the front desk. If the lines on her face were any indication, she was ten or fifteen years older than I . Her long, thin face might have been pretty if she smiled. She didn't. She tapped her toes. She glanced at her watch. She idly stroked the mink coat folded over her arm.

I approached her. "Excuse me, are you Hester?"

She looked me up and down and bit her lip, as if weighing her answer. "Yes."

I thrust my hand toward her. "I'm Ellison Russell, Bea Bisby's friend. She's so sorry she can't make it today."

"Half the reason we came here was to meet her husband."

Wasn't she charming? "Well, heart attacks are seldom convenient."

Hester's already stiff spine straightened even more. Then she softened. "That came out wrong. I hope Mr. Bisby makes a speedy recovery."

"We all do. Is this your first trip to Kansas City?"

"Yes."

"What would you like to do today? We have a wonderful art museum—"

"Mrs. Bisby mentioned you were an artist." Her lips said *artist.* Her tone said *leper.*

"I am. We also have wonderful shopping just across the street."

"I need some gloves. I didn't realize how cold it was here."

"Shopping it is. My car's right outside." I waved toward the hotel's circle drive. "Where are you from, Hester?"

"New York."

"Originally?"

"Darien."

"I have some friends who live in Darien."

"I doubt I know them."

Well, la-ti-da.

"I haven't lived there in years."

We stepped outside into the cold. "That's my car." I pointed to the Mercedes Mother and Daddy gave me for Christmas. The sedan needed to be traded—I just hadn't gotten around to it yet.

A valet brought the car to us and we climbed in.

I gripped the wheel. "Let's start at Swanson's."

"I defer to you."

It took all of two minutes to drive from The Alameda to

Swanson's. I even found a parking spot next to the door.

Winter might have returned, but in my favorite store, spring was in full bloom.

There was a bouquet of fresh colors, a dizzying array of floral prints, and a perfume girl spritzing anyone who got too close with Creed's Fleurissimo. I shrugged off my coat and breathed easier.

Esme, my saleswoman, appeared at my side. "Good morning, Mrs. Russell, may I take your coats while you shop?"

"Thank you, this is Mrs. Nelson who's visiting from New York."

"Pleased to see you, ma'am."

Hester didn't bother answering.

With an apologetic smile, I handed over winter and dove into spring. "Esme, that dress over there—" I pointed to a black and white polka dot coat dress.

"Givenchy," she replied. "Linen lined with silk."

"Do you have it in my size?"

"I already have it put back for you."

Hester sniffed. "Where are the gloves?"

"That case over there, Mrs. Nelson. I'm afraid our selection is a bit picked over."

Hester sniffed again then walked away.

"Please forgive Mrs. Nelson. She's a bit overwhelmed." What she was, was rude. "This is her first trip to Kansas City and things aren't going as planned."

"What?" Esme tilted her head.

"What?" I repeated.

"She's been in here on at least three occasions. She's tried on half the store."

"She has?"

Esme nodded. "She never buys."

Why had Hester lied? My gaze traveled to the display case for gloves. Hester wasn't there. I searched the sales floor and my gaze caught (and held) on a swath of Chinese red. "Esme, what's that?"

"New Halston. I went back and forth on pulling it for you."

"I'd better see it."

I'd already bought three dresses to wear to the gala. What was one more? Especially when it was exactly the right shade of red.

Esme held up the long Ultrasuede wrap dress with a halter neckline. "It's gorgeous but—"

"It's not dressy enough."

"Exactly."

I fingered the fabric. "Where else could I wear it?"

"When are you going to wear Chinese red?" she asked.

That's what I loved about Esme. Most saleswomen would have rattled off an array of dinner parties and fêtes to make a sale and a commission. Not Esme. She knew red wasn't my color.

I sighed and looked around. "Where did Hester go?"

"She's tried on the same Yves St. Laurent pants set every time she's been in here."

"Maybe today she'll buy it."

Esme's tight smile said she wasn't holding her breath.

"I ought to find her. I'm supposed to be entertaining her." We walked toward the fitting rooms. "You're sure she's been here before?"

"Positive."

One of Esme's gifts was a perfect memory. She remembered she'd already sold me three silk blouses in ecru and, strictly speaking, I didn't need a fourth. She remembered Libba purchased a gold jumpsuit last October and talked her out of a second one. She remembered shoe sizes, shades of lipstick, dress sizes, and children's names. Her eye for detail was astonishing. If Esme said Hester had visited Swanson's three times, I believed her.

The fitting rooms were large and luxurious, filled with flattering three-way mirrors, delicate chairs, and china cups just waiting to be filled with coffee.

The attendant was ready in case a customer wanted a different size, or a different pair of shoes, or the alterations lady.

"Is there anyone in here, Sally?" Esme looked down the length of the short hallway lined with closed doors.

"The lady who can't decide on the Yves St. Laurent pant set," Sally whispered.

"Hester?" I called. "It's Ellison. Did you find something?"

Hester emerged from a dressing room wearing the Yves St. Laurent. The ensemble was fun and flirty and happy. Everything Hester wasn't. She stared at herself in the mirror at the end of the hall and smoothed the fabric over her hips. "Chauncey will have a conniption, but I love it. I'll take it."

Esme did not try and dissuade her.

I opened my mouth—some women shouldn't wear loud prints, or ruffles, or fuchsia. Hester was one of them. The woman was built for simple navy shifts, cable-knit sweaters, and those Nantucket basket purses that cost an arm and a leg.

Then again, who was I to argue Hester's fashion choices.

I closed my mouth and kept it closed.

"Can you ship this to New York for me?"

"Of course, Mrs. Nelson."

We completed our purchases (I bought the Givenchy) and I asked, "More shopping?"

Hester nodded her sharp chin in assent.

We went to Halls and Woolf Brothers and Harzfeld's. Hester bought gloves (which she wore out of Woolf's). I bought a Gucci silk scarf covered with flowers and edged in a soft pink.

At noon, I asked, "Are you hungry?"

"I am."

"What would you like?"

"A cup of soup?" Having warm hands seemed to have warmed Hester's disposition.

"I know just the place." We walked around the corner to Plaza III. "They have marvelous steak soup."

We sat. We settled. We ordered drinks.

Hester looked out the window at the cars passing on Ward Parkway. "This is a lovely area. Do you live nearby?"

"I do and I grew up not far from here."

"The pace is slower. The people are friendlier—thank you for stepping in for Mrs. Bisby." She took a sip of wine. "It's so distressing when men are ill."

"Buzz will be in the hospital for a few days but he'll be fine." I too took a sip of wine. "I suspect his cardiologist will make him lose a few pounds." And start exercising. And quit smoking. And cut the martinis down to one a day. I was glad I didn't have to live with him.

"I don't know what I'd do if Chauncey had a heart attack."

"What does your husband do? For a living?"

"He's an investment banker."

I nodded as if I understood what that meant. "My husband was a banker."

"Was?"

"He died last summer."

"Ohhh." The sound of sympathy. "I'm so sorry."

"He was a wonderful father." I'd not speak ill of Henry to a stranger. We needed a new topic. "You've never been to Kansas City before?"

"Never. I already told you that."

"I only ask because Esme thought you looked familiar."

Hester paled (which was quite a feat given the already milky shade of her skin). "I must have a twin. I've never been here before."

People have told me I'm a bad liar in pitying tones (if you asked me, being a good liar wasn't exactly a character reference). Hester was a terrible liar.

The question was why? Why lie about visiting Kansas City?

SEVEN

I pulled into the driveway just after four.

Aggie bustled out onto the front stoop and crossed her arms against the cold. Her expression was grave and the yellow of her kaftan no longer looked like a daffodil—it looked like a caution sign.

What was Mother rampaging about now? How many times had she called?

With a sigh, I tossed my keys in my purse and stepped onto the drive.

"Your father called." Aggie clasped her hands. "He wants you to call him back. He says it's urgent."

The world tilted and I stumbled on the smooth pavement. "Did something happen to Mother?"

"He didn't say—just that you're to call him the minute you get home."

"Call him where?"

"At his office."

If something had happened to Mother, Daddy would be with her—not at the office. The world returned to its axis.

I hurried inside to the phone and dialed my father's private line. "Daddy." I spoke as soon as someone picked up the receiver. "What's wrong?"

"Mrs. Russell, this is Brenda. If you'll hold please, I'll find your father.

"Of course, Brenda. Thank you." Brenda had worked for Daddy for years. Mother called her his work-wife.

I shrugged off my coat and hung it over the back of a chair. I tapped my foot against the ugly carpeting. I drummed my fingers on my late husband's desk. Whatever was wrong, Daddy was taking his time picking up the phone.

I glanced at my watch.

"Ellison." Daddy's voice boomed through the phone line.

"What's wrong?"

"Nothing's wrong."

"Aggie said you needed to speak with me urgently."

"Oh. That."

I waited for more.

And waited.

"What? What's happened?"

"Your sister is coming for a visit. Can she stay with you? Please?"

"Has she left her husband again?" My sister, Marjorie, and her husband had their ups and downs.

"Not that sister."

It's a good thing I was already sitting on the edge of the desk because my knees stopped working. And my spine. And my jaw. That was me—jelly-legged and slack-jawed. "What?"

"Your half-sister is coming and I'm asking if she can stay with you. Please."

Had Daddy taken leave of his senses? "Does Mother know about this?"

"Not exactly."

Oh.

Dear.

Lord.

"Daddy, do you have a death wish?"

"Don't be flip, Ellison."

"I'm not. It's a serious question." Mother had kept Daddy's first daughter a secret for more than forty years. She would not welcome Karma's introduction to Kansas City society.

"Aside from her mother, you and Marjorie are the only family

Karma has."

"Daddy, this is a really bad idea." It was an epically terrible, bring-about-the-apocalypse bad idea. Rivers would run backward. The locusts would descend. Mother's face would melt.

"Ellie, please."

"I have a gala coming up. The timing is terrible."

"The timing will never be good."

"But it's especially bad now."

"This means a great deal to me."

Either I disappointed Daddy or enraged Mother. "Why here? I'll go to San Francisco. Pick a date."

"She's coming here."

"Does she understand how this will affect your family—your marriage?"

"She's also my family and part of my life, Ellison. She wants to meet you."

"Fine. I'll hop on a plane. Tomorrow." The gala was planned. I didn't actually *need* to be here.

"She's already on a plane."

Lord love a duck.

"It's your house or mine."

Mother's head would explode. Kaboom!

Woof! Woof, woof, woof, woof.

I glanced out the window. What fresh hell was Max into?

Woof! Woof, woof, woof.

"Daddy—" Mother would be angry for a month of Sundays.

"She's arriving in two hours."

WOOF!

"Daddy, I've got to run."

"Give me an answer. Your house or mine?"

I'd lived through Mother and Daddy on the outs and I didn't want to go through that again. Ever. As unpleasant as life would be, having Mother mad at me was better than having her mad at Daddy.

"Fine. She can stay here. But you have to explain to Mother." I hung up before he convinced me to claim this whole ill-conceived, doomed-to-failure visit as my idea.

Woof!

I ran to the backyard, hoping against hope that Max hadn't treed my neighbor's cat. Again.

The neighborhood cats had traded notes and avoided our property. Except for Margaret's cat—and I was pretty sure her cat visited my backyard expressly to make trouble.

Max had treed a cat but it wasn't my next-door-neighbor Margaret's familiar feline (thank God for small favors).

The cat stuck in my tree was a scrawny ginger who looked extremely unhappy Max had interrupted his trip through our backyard.

"Where did you come from?"

The cat didn't answer me. Not so much as a meow. Instead it tracked my movements with enormous yellow eyes.

Woof!

"Oh, be quiet, you."

Woof!

The cat climbed to a higher branch.

I grabbed Max's collar and pulled him away from the tree. He pulled against me. "Stop that. It's cold out here." And I'd run outside without a coat.

Woof!

"Max, what are you doing?" Grace stood at the backdoor.

"He's treed a cat."

"McCallester!" Grace ran to the tree and shook her finger at Max. "He's a friend."

"You know this cat?"

"He's ours."

My stomach took the elevator to my ankles and all strength left my fingers (not just left but packed its bags and took off for Palm Springs). Max slipped from my grasp.

He lunged at the tree.

"Mom," Grace scolded. "Hold onto him!"

"Our cat?"

She managed an expression both sheepish and pleading. "I rescued him."

"From where?"

"The shelter. His time was up."

"You have to take him back."

"I can't. They'll kill him."

"Max will kill him."

She crossed her arms and shook her head. "Max might kill him. They definitely will." Her eyes filled with tears. "Please, Mom. I couldn't stand by and let him die."

The tears nearly did me in. Grace had been through so much in the past year—her father's murder, attempts on my life and hers, crazy relatives, homicide investigations, and heartache.

"I'll take care of him. You won't even know he's here." She wiped her eyes then pressed her hands together as if she was praying. It was as if she could sense my weakening resolve.

Woof! Max's resolve remained steadfast. His gaze remained glued to McCallester.

McCallester stared unblinkingly back.

"What about Max?"

"He'll adjust."

I did not share her youthful optimism.

Neither did Max. He looked over his shoulder and grinned as if Grace had said something ridiculously funny. Or at least ridiculous.

"He will," she insisted.

McCallester and I remained unconvinced. The cat climbed higher. I merely shook my head.

"Please?" A single tear ran down her cheek.

I took a deep already-regretting-my-decision breath. "McCallester can stay until you find him a home." What else could I do? Send the cat to his death? Break Grace's heart?

"Thank you!" She threw her arms around me and squeezed. "I'll find him the best home! I promise."

"While you're promising, how about you promise not to bring

home any more animals."

"Promise." Her smiled warmed the chilly temperature by a good ten degrees.

Woof! Max hadn't given up on ending McCallester's life.

"I'll put Max in the study." I reclaimed my hold on his collar. "You rescue the cat."

Three out of the four of us were on board with my plan. Max was the hold-out. I dragged him two feet toward the house. He dragged me one foot toward the tree. Progress was slow.

Aggie opened the back door. "What's going on?"

"Grace adopted a cat." And because that wasn't enough bad news, I added, "And my illegitimate half-sister will be staying with us—starting tonight."

The one-two punch had Aggie clutching the door frame for support. "A cat?"

I nodded.

"Oh dear Lord."

Given the circumstances, Aggie was allowed to steal my line.

Brnng, brnng.

Aggie shifted her gaze to the phone. "Should I answer that?"

"Why wouldn't you?" I tugged Max another two feet closer to the door.

"Bad news comes in threes."

Aggie had a point.

Brnng, brnng.

I glared at the dog. "Not answering won't make the bad news go away."

"Ignorance is bliss," she countered.

"We're past the ignorance stage."

Aggie inclined her head, ceding my point.

Brnng, brnng.

"You're sure?" she asked.

"Let's get it over with."

She shrugged (*it's your funeral*) and let the door fall closed.

I bent my knees and moved Max three feet closer to the house.

He looked over his shoulder at Grace, who was cooing at the tree, tugged, and erased our progress.

"Max!"

Aggie appeared in the doorway. "You'd better take this."

That didn't sound good.

"C'mon, Max." I tugged and managed another few feet.

Aggie stepped out into the cold with a leash which she clipped onto Max's collar. "Go take your call. I'll get him inside."

"Who's on the phone?"

"The Detective."

Not bad news, unless (like Aggie) Hunter Tafft was your preference. I hurried inside and lifted the receiver to my ear. "Hello," I purred.

"Mrs. Russell, this is Detective Peters—" not the detective I was hoping for, not one I would ever dream of purring at "—you need to come down to the station."

"Why?"

"We've arrested Debbie Briscoe and her husband."

"Who?"

"Winthrop Marshall's secretary."

"You can't think that sweet girl killed Winthrop. Does Anarchy know about this?"

"I'm the Senior Detective." Icicles traveled through the phone line and froze my fingers. "You need to come to the station. Now."

"I have an out-of-town guest arriving in two hours."

"Should I send a squad car to pick you up?"

So my across-the-street neighbor, Marian Dixon, could tell everyone she knew I'd been hauled to the station?

"I don't know how I can help you, Detective."

"Neither do I—not until I take your statement."

"I told Anarchy everything."

"And now you'll tell me."

Aggie burst through the back door with a rebellious Max in tow. She shook her finger at him. "Bad dog."

The bad dog merely looked over his shoulder at the backyard

and the intruding cat.

I covered the receiver's mouthpiece with my palm. "Detective Peters insists I go down to the station."

"I told you bad things come in threes."

"You were right. Can you get the house ready? The blue guest room and something for dinner?"

"Of course."

"What are we going to do with the cat?"

Max's ears perked. He knew what to do with the cat.

"Can Grace keep it in her room?" asked Aggie.

"I don't think we have much choice."

"Mrs. Russell! Mrs. Russell!" Detective Peters' voice was loud enough I could hear him clearly even though the receiver was miles from my ear.

I removed my palm. "Sorry, Detective. I did tell you I had a guest coming."

"I'm sending the squad car."

"Don't bother. I'm on my way."

He grunted at me. "I'll expect you within the hour."

"Goodbye, Detective." I hung up.

Max scratched at the back door.

"Not in a million years, bucko."

"We may need a few supplies," said Aggie. "For the cat."

"Supplies?"

"Cat food. Kitty litter. A litter box. Catnip."

"I draw the line at catnip. Do we need anything else?"

"No. I went to the store earlier today because we were running low on coffee—"

I shot Mr. Coffee a comforting glance—we would never, ever run out of coffee. He had my solemn vow.

"I bought a ham to fix for Ruth Marshall and a few staples. As long as your sister isn't on a special diet, we should be fine."

"She's from San Francisco." A special diet was a distinct possibility.

We pondered brown rice cakes, alfalfa sprouts, and carob.

Aggie rubbed her chin. "Maybe you should pick up some granola, just in case."

"Fine." I retrieved my coat and hopped into the Mercedes. Maybe now was the time to trade it in—Mother was going to be hair-on-fire furious anyway. She and Daddy had given me the car for Christmas because she disapproved of my Triumph. *Ellison, a grown woman needs a car that seats more than two people.* That Mother was right didn't thrill me. That someone I loathed had broken into the car and had sex in the passenger seat filled me with revulsion. The car had to go.

Soon.

I drove to the police station, parked, and went inside. "I'm here to see Detective Peters."

"Your name?"

"Ellison Russell."

The sergeant behind the desk actually looked up. Studied me. Smirked. "Have a seat. I'll let him know you're here."

Detective Peters kept me waiting forever. I-don't-care-about-the-consequences-if-he's-not-available-I-have-shopping-to-do forever. It smelled of stale-smoke-fear-and-hopelessness-in-here forever.

When he finally led me back to an interview room, he didn't even offer me coffee. I knew better than to accept police station coffee—but still.

We sat.

"You found Marshall?"

"I did." I explained the circumstances.

"What did Mrs. Briscoe say when she saw the body?"

"She dropped my coffee."

"Did she say anything?"

"She asked me if I'd killed him."

A flame of interest lit in Detective Peters beady eyes. "Did you?"

"Of course not."

"Then why did she ask?"

"Because I found him."

"What else did she say?"

"Not much. The poor woman was traumatized."

"But you weren't?"

"I've found bodies before." The other bodies had been fully clothed. Winthrop's state of undress (and not the actual body) had been the traumatic part for me.

Peters favored me with a suspicious stare.

"What else?"

"Nothing. Debbie could barely speak." She'd been a green-hued wreck. "Are you sure she did it? She didn't strike me as a killer."

"That's right." His lip curled. "You're a detective now."

I clenched my hands in my lap and bit my tongue.

"It was either her or her husband."

"How can you be so sure?"

"Debbie Briscoe was having an affair with Winthrop Marshall. Either the affair went bad or the husband found out."

"You're not looking at other suspects?"

Detective Peters combined the beady-eyed stare and lip curl for an expression that said I had the IQ of a particularly dim-witted post. "You're free to go."

That was it? Detective Peters had brought me down here for nothing.

I stood, much as I wanted to help poor Debbie, much as I wanted to point out that Detective Peters had wasted my time, I had cat supplies and granola to buy. I gathered my handbag and coat and exited the interview room.

"What are you doing here?"

I looked up at Anarchy. "Your partner invited me down for questioning."

Anarchy's lips thinned. "Did he ask nicely?"

"He offered to send a squad car for me."

A muscle ticked at the corner of Anarchy's lips. "What did you tell him?"

"Exactly what I told you." Maybe a little less. I looked around the squad room. Every single cop was watching us. "Would you please walk me to my car?"

When we were outside, I asked, "You are looking at former employees, aren't you?"

"Of course. Why? What do you know?"

We walked toward me car. "I'm not going to betray a confidence, but Winthrop preyed on the women at his firm. If I were you, I'd look at former employees who were unhappy with him."

"You're not going to tell me who gave you this tip?"

"Absolutely not." I opened the Mercedes' door and held my breath. My not being completely forthcoming had been an issue in the past.

Anarchy shifted his gaze to the station house and nodded. Once. "I guess I have to respect that." Then he leaned forward and brushed a kiss across my lips. "If you get anymore anonymous tips, you'll tell me?"

"I promise."

EIGHT

I dashed through the grocery store, rushing straight to the pet aisle. If they didn't have cat supplies, we were in trouble. They did. I threw both dry and wet food into my cart, along with kitty litter, and a litter box.

Then I looked for granola. My choices were limited. There was something called C.W. Post. I picked up the box and read the ingredients—brown sugar, wheat, oats, rice, honey, almonds, coconut, and raisins. Raisins! I shuddered and returned the box to the shelf and grabbed some Grape-nuts. Despite the *grape* in its name, that cereal was blessedly raisin free.

I glanced at my watch. If I hurried, I might make it home before Karma arrived.

"Ellison?"

I turned and swallowed a sigh. "Good evening, Celine."

"How are you, dear? Frank told me everything. So awful." Celine was married to Frank Wallace. The Wallace of Bisby, Marshall & Wallace. "First Winthrop and then poor Buzz." She shook her head. "A terrible day."

"True but the silver lining is that Buzz will be okay."

"I can't stop thinking about Winthrop." Celine waved her hand at her cart. "I'm making a Bundt cake for Ruth." She eyed the contents of my cart and pursed her lips as if wondering where my Bundt cake ingredients were hiding.

"Aggie's cooking a ham."

"I see." Her voice was tight because ham trumped Bundt. "Did you get a cat?"

"More of a houseguest. Grace brought it home, but it's not staying."

"Young Frank brought a dog home once. It stayed for fifteen years."

"My dog doesn't much care for cats. If you hear of anyone who'd like a cat—"

"Of course." Half of Celine's mouth curved into a smile—a she'll-have-that-cat-through-nine-lives smile. "I know it's soon, but who would you like to manage your accounts? Frank's returns are equal to Winthrop's."

"It is soon."

"Someone needs to manage your portfolio."

That someone would be Buzz.

"I'll keep that in mind." I inched my cart toward the checkout. "Good luck with your cake."

"Good luck with your new cat."

"It's not staying."

Celine simply waved and pushed her cart down the cereal aisle.

I paid for my groceries and drove home in record time.

Daddy's car was already parked in my drive.

I turned off the ignition and sat. What did one say to a secret half-sister? I had no idea.

The front door opened and light spilled onto the stoop. Grace stood framed in the doorway.

I grabbed the brown paper bags' handles and got out of the car.

Grace stepped outside, closing the door behind her. "Something you forgot to tell me?"

Oh dear Lord.

"Surprise." I handed her the bag filled with cat supplies. "I am sorry. I meant to tell you."

"She looks exactly like Aunt Marjorie."

"Really?"

"You won't believe it."

Together we walked toward the house.

"Where are they?"

"Living room."

I steeled my spine and entered my home.

"It'll be fine," whispered Grace. It was almost as if she could sense how conflicted I was. What if I didn't like Karma? What if she didn't like me? How did I feel about a sister who arrived fully formed? Like Athena but with Harrington Walford as her father.

I handed Grace the bag with the Grape-nuts. "Wish me luck."

I stepped into the living room.

Daddy was sitting in a wingback chair in front of the fire. He was nursing a scotch.

Karma sat across from him. Her scotch was on empty.

I blinked. Twice.

Grace hadn't been kidding. At first glance, Karma and Marjorie could be twins.

"I'm sorry to keep you waiting. I found a body yesterday and the police had some questions that couldn't wait."

Daddy stood. "Aggie told us."

I went to his side, kissed his cheek, smiled at my sister, and thrust out my hand. "Hi, I'm Ellison."

Her grip was cool. "Karma. Thank you for welcoming me into your home."

"My pleasure."

I'd expected a California version of Aunt Sis—a hippy-dippy woman wearing Boho chic. Karma was nothing like that. And while Karma looked like Marjorie, her clothes were all wrong. Karma wore a conservative dress, low-heeled pumps, a pearl pin on her collar, and understated makeup.

Daddy took Karma's empty glass and walked over to the bar cart. "What can I get you, Ellie?"

"I think I'd like a glass of wine. When Grace comes back, I'll send her to the kitchen for it. Please—" I waved my hand at Karma's chair "—sit." I sat on the settee (I had to—my knees were jelly).

"How was your flight?"

"Uneventful."

"The best kind."

Karma smiled and she used Daddy's smile.

I blinked.

She accepted the scotch Daddy held out to her. "Thank you." She smiled up at him. "Dad tells me you're an artist."

Dad? "I am. What do you do?"

"I work for a brokerage."

"Karma's being modest. She runs the place." Daddy puffed his chest and beamed at my new sister then settled back into his chair.

"Wow. That must be challenging."

"I love investments."

"I meant dealing with the men."

"Oh." She glanced at Daddy. "That. If the portfolios are performing, no one cares I'm a woman."

What happened in bear markets?

Grace appeared in the doorway.

"Honey, would you please ask Aggie to pour me a glass of wine?"

"Sure." She turned on her heel.

I stopped her with a question. "Where's Max?"

Grace looked over her shoulder. "Sitting outside my room."

"Where's McCallester?"

"In my room." She disappeared into the hall.

"Grace came home with a cat today and our Weimaraner isn't a fan."

"She said you were letting her keep it," said Daddy.

"Until she finds it a good home." The clarification was important.

My father chuckled into his drink then looked at his watch. "Speaking of home, I need to go. You girls have a good time." He put his drink down on the table next to his chair and stood. "Karma, I'll pick you up at nine tomorrow morning. I've arranged for a tour of the Board of Trade."

At least ten of Mother's friends' husbands worked at the Board of Trade. When (not if) she heard Daddy had taken Karma there, she'd have apoplexy.

"Or I can take you to The Nelson-Atkins. It's our local art museum."

"I read about it. The Chinese exhibit is heading there next."

Daddy grinned at me. "Ellison is planning the opening night gala."

"That sounds like quite a task. I'd love to see the museum." Karma turned to Daddy. "You don't mind about the Board of Trade, do you?"

"Not at all. You've seen one exchange, you've seen 'em all."

I'd never seen an exchange, nor had my father ever offered to take me.

Grace reappeared with a glass of wine and a pink message slip written in Aggie's neat script. "Who's Hester Nelson?"

"She's in town from New York. I took her shopping because Bea couldn't."

Karma tilted her head. "Hester Nelson?"

"Yes. Do you know her? Her husband, Chauncey, is an investment banker."

My sister's brows drew together. "Do you do business with him?"

"No."

Karma's face cleared.

"Why do you ask?"

"He's slightly shady."

"Slightly? Shady?"

She winced. "I've said too much. Just don't invest with him."

Aggie popped into the living room. "Dinner is served."

"I'll take my leave," said Daddy.

"You don't want to stay for dinner?" Hopefully I didn't sound too desperate.

"Your mother is expecting me." Men on their way to the guillotine sounded happier.

We all walked into the foyer where Daddy put on his coat then kissed every woman related to him.

When he left, we stood—suddenly awkward.

Aggie saved us. "Come on now, dinner's getting cold."

Dinner was a grilled chicken breast, sautéed green beans, and roasted potatoes.

We talked about movies and books and television programs.

"What do you think of President Ford?" asked Karma.

"He wears too much plaid." He wasn't alone in that. Anarchy's penchant for cross-hatched color was one of his few faults. "Plaid is fine for the golf course and kilts but other than that—" I shook my head.

"I meant his politics."

"I don't discuss politics."

"Not even with family?"

"Especially not with family."

"Sounds like me and my mother."

"What was she like?" I was curious about the woman Daddy almost married.

Karma's expression softened. "She was a feminist. Strong and opinionated and stubborn."

Frankly, she sounded a lot like Mother. Except for the feminist part.

"What did she do?" I asked.

"She was an environmental lawyer."

"She must have been a very strong woman."

"She was." Karma's voice was wry. And sad.

We smiled at each other. Perhaps having a second sister wouldn't be so bad.

Ding dong.

"I'll get it," Aggie called.

"Busy place," observed Karma.

Grace rolled her eyes. "You have no idea."

A moment later, Anarchy stepped into the dining room and the memory of our last kiss brushed across my memory. My cheeks flushed.

"Marjorie, I didn't realize you—" Anarchy's voice died as he stared at the woman sitting at my table.

"Anarchy this is—"

"Karma." He finished for me.

"You know each other?"

"A long time ago."

Now Karma's cheeks flushed.

Oh. My. "Have you eaten?"

"Yes." He shook his head. "I mean no."

"Aggie, will you please set another place?"

"Of course." She cast a suspicious glance Anarchy's way then disappeared into the kitchen.

"How do you know each other?" Keeping my voice even and mildly curious counted as a win.

"From school." They spoke at the same time. Their cheeks flushed similar shades of red.

"Which school?" asked Grace.

"Stanford." Karma reached for her water goblet. "It was years and years ago."

College sweethearts?

Anarchy chose the seat across from my sister. "What brings you to Kansas City?"

"I wanted to meet Ellison."

"You're Harrington's other daughter?" Realization dawned in his tone.

"Guilty."

"I should have guessed." He stared at her. "You look just like Marjorie."

"Maybe I should go to Ohio next."

I choked on my wine. Choked on a vision of Marjorie's reaction to Karma.

"Are you okay, Mom?"

I held up my hand. "Fine."

"What are you doing in Kansas City?" Karma asked.

"I'm a homicide detective."

"You did it." She smiled—the kind of smile usually reserved for precocious children or Nobel laureates.

He nodded. "I did."

The smile didn't budge. "Is your father speaking to you?"

"Barely. And what do you do?"

"I run a brokerage firm."

"Didn't your mother want you to be a lawyer?"

"She never got over it."

They laughed. A laugh I couldn't share.

Grace shot me a sympathetic look.

I fisted my hands under the table.

Aggie bustled in with a placemat, silverware, and a napkin. She took the room's temperature and plonked everything down in front of Anarchy. "I'll be back with your plate." Her tone suggested his food might be sprinkled with arsenic.

"Did Ellison tell you her stockbroker was murdered?"

We were going to chat about one of his cases? Seriously?

"No." Karma's gaze traveled between Anarchy and me as if she was trying to divine our relationship. "She just mentioned she'd found a body. What happened?"

"I showed up for an appointment with my broker and found him dead."

"How awful for you."

"She does it all the time." Grace's tone equated my finding bodies with running yellow lights. Bad, possibly dangerous, but not the end of the world.

Karma opened her mouth then paused as if waiting for the punch line.

There wasn't one.

I did find bodies all the time. More often than I ran yellow lights.

The silence stretched.

"What happened with Debbie and her husband?" I asked Anarchy.

"Peters cut them loose."

"He let them go? He seemed so sure one of them was guilty."

Aggie served Anarchy his plate, putting it on the table with enough force to make the chicken jump.

If Anarchy was concerned with her ire, he hid it well. He picked up his fork and speared a potato wedge. "Their alibis checked out."

"She seemed like a sweet girl." Except for when she asked me if I'd committed murder. That wasn't sweet.

"I'm looking into former employees."

Thank heavens.

"I stopped by to ask if your friend Bea would tell you if Winthrop was seeing someone in the office?"

"She might. If she knew."

"I called the hospital. They're keeping her husband for a few more days."

"I'll stop by with a Swedish ivy. Then Bea and I can grab a cup of coffee and a slice of pie." Since I started finding bodies, the hospital coffee shop had become one of my regular haunts.

"Thank you." He smiled at me and his coffee-colored-eyes twinkled.

The hands still fisted in my lap relaxed. A bit.

"I'll go tomorrow afternoon. I'm taking Karma to The Nelson-Atkins in the morning."

"Hopefully we won't find any bodies." Was that Karma's idea of a joke?

To me it sounded like tempting fate.

NINE

"Tell me about the museum," said Karma.

Karma and I stood at the north entrance.

"It was built in the 1930s under the auspices of two major gifts. One from Mary McAfee Atkins. The other from William Rockhill Nelson. The timing was auspicious."

"Oh?"

"The curators had cash during The Depression. They bought art when no one else was. Especially Chinese art."

We stepped inside, checked our coats, and walked to Kirkwood Hall where the ceiling rising forty feet above us was held up by twelve massive black and white marble columns.

Karma tilted her head and looked up at the ceiling. "This is fabulous."

"You sound surprised."

"I guess I am. People who live on the coasts tend to think they've cornered the market on culture."

"You thought we were nothing but barbeque and jazz?"

She grimaced. "I didn't know about the jazz."

"Count Basie? Charlie Parker? When Henry and I were first married, we went to jazz clubs all the time. I haven't been in ages."

"I'd love to go."

"I'll take you to Milton's." What had I just done? I swallowed. "The Asian gallery is upstairs. Shall we start there?"

I led her into one of the gallery rooms.

"Wow." She stopped in front of an elaborate Chinese bed. "Can you imagine sleeping in that thing?"

"No. You?"

She grinned. "Not in a million years."

We viewed landscapes considered to be masterpieces. Karma lingered in front of one of my favorites, "Fisherman's Evening Song".

"I saved the best for last." I led her across the hall.

Nan Roddingham, who wore a docent nametag, stood in my favorite gallery reviewing her notes.

"Ellllison. How nice to see you!" Her gaze shifted. "Marjorie, I didn't realize you were in town."

Oh, hell.

"Nan, this is Karma."

Nan extended her hand. "You look just like Elllllison's sister, Marrrrjorie."

Now was my chance to claim my sister. If I did, Mother's head would explode. If I didn't, Daddy might never forgive me. "This is my—"

Karma interrupted me. "I understand Marjorie's quite lovely. Thank you."

"You're welcome. Norrrrmally. I'd tell you about the art, but I suspect Ellison knows more than I do."

I shook my head. "You've had the training, Nan."

"And you're the arrrrtist."

The Asian gallery held pieces that were nearly a thousand years old. I was a contemporary painter.

"I muuuust fly. I'm supposed to meet a group of school children for a tour in a few minutes." Nan nodded her chin at Karma. "Nice to meet you." She turned her gaze in my direction. "Elllllison, I'll see you at the gala—and book club."

"Nice seeing you, Nan."

Karma and I turned to one of the Nelson's most amazing pieces—a reconstructed Buddhist temple. Inside, Guanyin of the Southern Sea sat and contemplated the people who wandered past him. Behind him was a mural that never failed to rob me of breath.

"That's amazing."

"Isn't it?"

We walked toward the entrance.

"You don't need to tell anyone I'm your sister." Karma's voice was soft. "I wanted to meet you, not upend your life."

I didn't know how to answer.

"I've always known about you. Always wanted to meet you and Marjorie. Not to force my way into your lives but to—" she glanced around the gallery as if the words she wanted might be hanging on the walls "—to know you. To know my sisters."

"I'm glad you're here."

We smiled at each other and walked into the temple.

Guanyin of the Southern Sea looked down at us and at a woman on the floor.

Something was wrong.

I stepped toward her but Karma stopped me with a hand on my arm. "It's a child's pose. She's meditating."

In my experience, women didn't practice yoga poses in short skirts.

"Let me check on her."

Karma released me and I walked toward the woman, the heels of my flats too loud on the parquet floor.

"Are you all right?" I asked quietly.

The woman didn't respond.

I glanced at Karma who wore a mildly concerned expression.

I knew what came next. I touched the woman's arm.

She wasn't cold.

Maybe I'd been wrong. Maybe I hadn't found another corpse. "Are you all right?" I spoke louder this time.

Nothing.

"Her neck."

"What?" I glanced at Karma.

My half-sister had gone pale. "Her neck's at a funny angle."

I looked more closely at the woman on the floor. Her face pressed against the floor at an angle at odds with human ability.

"Oh dear Lord."

"What?" demanded Karma.

"She's dead."

Karma stared at me for a few seconds. Her cheeks lost their color, her eyes rolled back in her head, and her knees gave way. She hit the parquet before I could get to her.

Guanyin of the Southern Sea looked on with a Zen expression.

I was not feeling remotely Zen. "Help!" I bellowed. Had Karma hurt her head? The floor wasn't exactly soft. I knelt next to her.

A doughy guard with apple red cheeks appeared in the entrance to the temple. "What? What's wrong?"

Two things.

"My sister needs an ambulance."

The guard's gaze shifted between the two women on the floor. "Which one's your sister."

"This one." I brushed the hair away from Karma's face.

"Then who is that?"

"No idea. Can you call for help? Please?" We could play twenty questions after someone with some medical knowledge arrived

The guard unclipped a walkie-talkie from his belt and pressed a button. "We need medical assistance in the Asian gallery. Call an ambulance."

"You might want to close the gallery."

"Why?"

I pointed at the other woman. "This is a crime scene. Tell them to call the police and ask for Detective Jones."

The guard was trained to ask people not to touch the art. Murder was outside his job duties. Now he turned pale.

"Please don't faint."

He leaned over, braced his forearms against his legs, and took a deep breath.

I held mine.

Endless seconds passed and he straightened.

"There's a school tour coming. Can you cordon off the entrance?"

The thought of children seeing the two women on the floor galvanized him and he pulled stanchions and a velvet rope across the entry to the main hall.

"What happened?" He scrubbed his ruddy face with open palms.

"My friend fainted when she realized that woman was dead."

"But where did the first woman come from?"

I rested on my heels. "No idea. She was on the floor when we walked in here."

The guard rubbed the back of his neck. "She wasn't here at ten thirty."

I glanced at my watch. A quarter after eleven. "You've just established the window for when this happened."

He bent at the waist again.

On the floor next to me, Karma stirred.

"Don't move. An ambulance is coming."

"What happened?" Karma's voice was hardly a whisper.

"You fainted."

"I what?"

"You fainted."

"I did not."

"How do you explain being on the floor?"

Her face scrunched in thought. "I fainted?"

"Yep."

"Help me up."

"Nothing doing. Stay where you are."

"I'm fine."

"You hit your head."

"Is that why there are two of you?"

"Probably."

"The guard—" I turned to the guard. "What's your name?"

His skin was a shade of celadon not often seen and his eyes were red-rimmed. "Murphy."

"Murphy called for an ambulance. You're going to the hospital so they can check you for a concussion."

"What about—" her gaze shifted to the body.

"The police are also on their way."

"Anarchy?" The way she said his name twisted something inside me. There was a history there. One I wasn't sure I wanted to know.

"Yes. And probably his partner, Detective Peters."

She nodded then winced. "I feel sick."

"Concussion." Been there. Done that.

Voices reached us from the hall outside the gallery.

"In here," Murphy called.

Two men wearing uniforms and pushing a gurney moved the velvet rope out of the way. They hurried toward the temple, but their steps slowed when they saw two women on the floor.

"Here," I said. "My sister needs help."

One of the men came toward us. The other approached the woman with the broken neck.

"I wouldn't touch—"

Too late. He moved the body.

The woman's face was no longer covered by the fall of her hair.

My stomach lurched.

I knew that face. From where?

It was at that moment that Detective Peters tromped into the temple. He saw me, stopped in his tracks, and curled his lip. "I should have guessed you'd be here."

The paramedic wrapped a huge donut-y thing around Karma's neck.

It gave me a reason to ignore Peters.

The paramedic who'd touched the body spoke up. "I touched the body. I wanted to make sure there wasn't a pulse."

Peters nodded once—a sharp jerk of his chin. "Did you touch it?" He was talking to me.

"Yes." Where was Anarchy?

"What happened?"

"We came in here, saw her, realized she was dead, and Karma fainted."

"Karma?"

I lifted my chin slightly. "Yes."

The paramedics transferred Karma from the floor to the gurney.

"That how you remember things?" Peters asked Karma.

"Yes, but I don't remember fainting."

Peters grunted.

The medics raised the gurney.

I gathered Karma's and my handbags and stood.

"Where do you think you're going?"

"I'm going with Karma. They're taking her to the hospital."

"You're staying here. I have questions."

"Questions?"

"Questions."

"Here are my answers. Karma and I entered this gallery at ten minutes after eleven. We spoke to Nan Roddingham. When Nan left, we came in here and found Marcy." I'd remembered her and I wished I hadn't.

"Marcy?"

"Yes. Marcy." I took a deep breath. "She was Frank Wallace's secretary."

"The broker?"

"Yes."

"What's her last name?"

"I haven't the slightest idea." I pointed to Murphy. "Murphy says she wasn't in here at ten thirty. So, I figure you've got a forty-minute window when someone might have killed her."

"What time did you speak with this Nan Roddingham?"

"At around five after eleven. She's here now. She volunteers as a docent."

Peters turned to one of the uniformed officers who'd come in with him. "Find her."

"She's giving a tour to some school children," I offered.

Peters took a few seconds to scowl at me then growled at the uniform. "Go."

"If that answers all your questions, I'm going to the hospital."

"You're not going anywhere until this Roddingham woman corroborates your story."

I weighed arguing.

"I'll be fine," said Karma. "I just hit my head. That poor woman is dead."

I scowled at Peters then turned to Karma and softened my expression. "I'll be there soon as I can."

"Will you let Dad know? Please?"

That would be a fun conversation—*Daddy, I took Karma to The Nelson-Atkins. We found a body and Karma is in the hospital.* I nodded. "Of course. I'll call him as soon as I can get to a phone."

The medics wheeled Karma away, which left me with Murphy, a uniformed officer, and Detective Peters.

"What were you doing here?" Detective Peters demanded.

"Looking at art."

He snorted.

"It's what people do in art museums."

"What's she doing here?" He pointed toward Marcy.

"I don't know. I need to sit down."

We stepped into the outer gallery, leaving the body alone on the floor. Murphy found me a folding chair and I sank onto the metal seat.

The second uniformed officer returned with Nan.

Detective Peters gave me a look that said I'd better not utter a single word, then asked, "Mrs. Roddingham?"

"Yes. What's going on?"

"Did you talk with Mrs. Russell today?"

"Yes. What—"

"At what time?"

"Shortly afffter eleven. Why?"

"And you talked to her in this room?"

"Yes," said Nan.

"Did you see anyone else this morning?"

"Yes."

"Who?" Peters demanded.

"Frank Wallace. I saw him walk in there." She pointed toward Guanyin of the Southern Sea. "I think he was meeting his—" Nan looked pained "—his girlfriend."

"Can you describe her?"

"Young. Pretty. She was wearing a red sweater and a black skirt."

Exactly what the corpse wore.

"Do you have a strong constitution, Mrs. Roddingham?"

"I do."

"Please come with me." Peters led her into the temple and I trailed after them. "Is that the woman Mr. Wallace was meeting?"

"Yes. Oh, dear. I need to sit down." Nan sat. On the floor. Hard enough to rock Guanyin of the Southern Sea on his perch.

Of the three partners at Bisby, Marshall & Wallace, one was hospitalized, one was murdered, and one was a murder suspect. I could kiss those phenomenal returns goodbye.

I cleared my throat. "If there's nothing further, Detective?"

Peters rubbed his chin and scrunched his face as if he were fabricating a reason to keep me. "You can go."

I hurried to the exit before he changed his mind.

"Ooomph."

I looked up at the man who'd almost knocked me down. He regarded me with worried brown eyes. "Are you all right?"

"Yes."

"And, Karma? Is she all right?"

"They took her to the hospital." I pretended not to notice the way Anarchy's skin blanched. "I'm on my way there now."

"What happened?"

"We found a body and Karma fainted."

"But she's okay?" Had he ever sounded so concerned before?

I nodded. With effort. "I imagine so. She hit her head."

Anarchy's gaze shifted to the gallery where Peters was grilling Nan. "Will you keep me posted? Please?"

"Yeah. Sure."

Anarchy nodded his thanks then hurried into the gallery.
I stood and watched him for a moment.
He didn't notice when I left.

TEN

I stopped by the museum director's office and asked to use the phone. Laurence's secretary ceded her desk with a polite smile. "So nice to see you, Mrs. Russell."

"Nice to see you too, Luanne. I'll only be a minute." Hopefully.

I dialed Daddy's direct number.

"Harrington Walford's office." Brenda's voice—always professional and slightly remote—was as familiar as a favorite blanket, a comfort when bodies turned up.

"Brenda, this is Ellison calling. I need to speak with my father, please."

"He's in a meeting, Mrs. Russell."

"This is an emergency."

"Oh." She paused—a long pause. "I see. Please hold."

Laurence stuck his head out of his office, spotted me and tilted his chin. "Ellison, how lovely to see you."

Had no one told him about the corpse in one of his premier galleries?

"Ellison?" Daddy sounded worried. "What happened?"

"Karma fainted. She's been taken to the hospital."

"Fainted?"

"Yes."

"Why?" The suspicion in Daddy's voice was reminiscent of Mother.

I glanced at Laurence. I straightened my shoulders. I tightened my grip on the receiver. "We found a body."

"What?" A wall of sound blasted through the receiver and from Laurence. Who knew two men could pitch their voices so high and so loud.

"I'm afraid so. I'm in Laurence's office right now, but I'll leave for the hospital shortly."

"How could you drag Karma into this?" Not only did Daddy sound like Mother, now he was using her *Ellison-how-could-you* line.

"Daddy, Laurence is waiting to speak with me. I'll see you at the hospital." I hung up before my father could say any more hurtful things.

"You found a body? In my gallery?" Laurence looked less pleased than Daddy sounded.

"In the Asian gallery. Right in front of Guanyin of the Southern Sea. The police are there now."

"Why wasn't I informed immediately?"

That was between him and his staff.

"Laurence, I've got to run. My—my friend was taken to the hospital."

He didn't care. He was already striding toward the door.

I descended the stairs, reclaimed Karma's and my coats, drove to the hospital, and hurried to the information desk. "My friend was just brought in. Would you please tell me if she's been admitted?"

The volunteer looked at me over the rims of her glasses and pursed her lips. "Name?"

"Ellison Russell."

She bent her head and ran her finger down the list.

"I'm Ellison Russell. My friend is Karma."

"Is that the first name or the last name?" Now the woman sounded grumpy.

"First."

"What's her last name, please?"

I didn't know.

I had a sister and I didn't know her last name.

"Could you please search by first name?"

The purse on the volunteer's lips became more pronounced. "You don't know your friend's last name?"

"It's complicated."

"Ellison!"

I turned. Daddy was hurrying across the lobby. When he stopped at the desk, his breath came in short pants.

The volunteer looked down her nose a little further. "Does he know Karma's last name?"

"Michaels. Karma Michaels."

"Room 246."

"Thank you," I said over my shoulder. We were already hurrying toward the elevator.

Daddy's hand closed around my upper arm. "What happened?"

I gave him the abbreviated version while we waited for the glacially slow elevator.

"Why does this happen to you? Over and over and over again."

We stepped into the elevator.

I jabbed the button for the second floor. "I don't know. If I did, I'd do something to change it."

He shook his head. "You're sure she's not badly hurt?"

The doors slid closed and we inched our way upward.

"She hit her head. My guess is she's got a mild concussion and a goose egg."

"And you didn't see anything. No killer. No clues. No one is going to show up at your house with a gun, right?"

"Right." It was the easiest answer and more positive than *I hope not.*

We walked down the hall to room 246, paused outside the door, and knocked.

"Come in."

We stepped inside. The blinds had been pulled and the room was dim. Karma lay in the hospital bed looking pale and beautiful.

Daddy hurried to her side, took her hand in his, and kissed her cheek. "How are you?"

"I've got a killer headache and they want to keep an eye on me for twenty-four hours, but I'm fine."

"Thank goodness." I hung Karma's coat over the back of a chair. "What can I bring you from home?"

"A brush, a toothbrush, my makeup, clean underwear."

"Consider it done."

"I'm so sorry this happened to you." Daddy brushed a strand of hair away from Karma's face.

"It's my fault. I never figured myself for a fainter."

"Such a shock," said Daddy.

"The first one's the worst."

My father and my half-sister looked at me as if I'd sprouted a second head.

"After finding my third body, the shock became less—" I searched for a word "—shocking."

Apparently the second head was firmly attached—they continued staring. Daddy's mouth opened and closed. A perfect O. Like a goldfish.

"Listen." I ran my damp palms down the sides of my coat. "I'm going to peek in and see how Buzz is doing. It will give you two some time to visit."

I backed toward the door, ready for objections.

None came.

I took the stairs to the third floor and knocked on the door of Buzz's room.

"Come in." Bea's voice was flat.

I stepped inside.

Unlike Karma's room, the blinds were pulled wide and Bea and Buzz were practically drowning in light. All that light wasn't Bea's friend. The poor woman looked positively haggard—like she should be the one in the hospital bed instead of Buzz.

"How are you?" I asked. "Both of you?"

"On the mend," said Buzz.

"Glad to hear it."

"They've got me on this horrible diet. I don't suppose you'd sneak me a cheeseburger?"

"How can you even joke about that?" Poor Bea. She sounded as gray as she looked—like a steamroller had run her down.

"Bea, have you eaten?" I asked.

"She has not," replied Buzz.

"Why don't we go grab a bite in the coffee shop?"

"Excellent plan." Buzz glanced around the plant-filled room. "This place gets old after an hour and Bea has been here for two days."

"But—" Bea shook her head.

"No buts, Bea. Go. Eat a sandwich. Relax for a little while. I'll be fine."

Bea glanced at the door then at her husband. "But—"

"We'll have pie for dessert," I promised.

She didn't move.

"A la mode." I upped the ante.

"Fine." She scowled as if Buzz and I were causing her great inconvenience.

The scowl slipped off her face as soon as we stepped into the hallway.

We reached the elevator and she'd pushed the down arrow. "I'm so glad you stopped by. I've been dying for pie."

"You could have fooled me."

"The important thing is that I fooled Buzz."

I raised my brows.

"The only way he'll follow doctors' orders is if I look tragic."

"He had a heart attack. You'd think he'd take his health seriously."

"You'd think." She stepped onto the elevator as the doors opened. "But he doesn't. He is actually insisting that the firm send over some files for his review."

"What do his doctors say?"

"They want to monitor him for a few more days. They say if he makes lifestyle changes, he should be fine."

"Lifestyle changes?"

We stepped out into the lobby and walked toward the coffee shop.

"No salt. More fiber. More exercise."

She had my sympathies. "That doesn't sound so bad."

Bea rolled her eyes and chose a table.

I sat across from her.

A bee-hived waitress ambled over with two water glasses overflowing with crushed ice. "What'll it be?"

"Coffee," I replied. "And a ham and Swiss on rye."

Bea ordered the same and we stared across the table at each other.

I cleared my throat. "Something happened this morning."

"Oh?" Bea poked at the crushed ice in her glass with a straw then covered her mouth with her hand. "What you must think of me."

"What?"

"I should have thanked you when you walked in. How did things go with Hester?"

"Fine. I took her shopping. About this morning—"

"I really am grateful."

"Anything I can do. Listen, about this morning—"

"You ladies need cream?" The waitress placed two mugs on the table

"Yes, please." As often as I ate there, you'd think they'd remember.

She ambled off.

"About this morning." I swallowed. "I took a friend from out of town to The Nelson and we found—"

"Here's your cream." The waitress deposited a little dessert dish filled with those plastic creamer-holding containers on the table.

"Thank you." I opened a container and dumped cream into my mug.

Bea doctored her coffee as well. Three creamers and a sugar.

"This morning—"

She looked up from stirring.

"We found a body."

"Oh, Ellison. Another one?" She reached across the table and patted my hand.

"It was Marcy."

"Marcy?"

"Frank Marshall's secretary."

The air around Bea seemed to still. "What was she doing at The Nelson?"

"No idea."

"She should have been at work."

An excellent point. "Be that as it may, Nan Roddingham was there and she spotted Marcy with Frank."

"Marcy and Frank?" Bea shook her head. "I don't think so."

"What about Winthrop? Did he carry on with any of the staff?"

"I hate to speak ill of the dead—"

Something good was coming.

The waitress put sandwiches in front of us. "You need a warm-up on your coffee?"

"Please." I spoke through gritted teeth.

She ambled over to the burners, picked up one of the glass coffeepots, then ambled back.

When she finally ambled to another table, I gave Bea an encouraging smile. "You were saying?"

"Oh. Right. Winthrop."

"Yes?"

"He chased every girl in that office. Caught most of them too."

"Does any girl stand out?"

"Not really." She stared down at her sandwich. "Are the police going to arrest Frank?"

"They're definitely going to talk to him."

She dropped her head to her hands. "There will be no keeping Buzz in bed if he finds out about this."

"Can you unplug his phone?"

"Maybe. But he needs something to keep him busy. He's going

crazy up there."

"Would you like me to pick up the files he wants?"

"Would you?" She brightened.

"Of course." Running by the brokerage office was a small thing to do.

"I'll call his secretary. Her name is Bonnie. When you get there just ask for her."

I bit in to my sandwich. Bea might not know who Winthrop had been preying upon but I bet Bonnie did.

And what of poor Marcy? Had Frank really killed her?

There might be answers at the office.

"I'll head over there after we've finished lunch."

"You're a good friend, Ellison. Thank you."

When we'd devoured our pie (coconut cream for both of us—and we both scraped our plates), I gave Bea a quick hug. "I'll swing by the brokerage offices now and be back soon."

"Don't drive fast. They hire those girls because they're pretty not because they're efficient. It may take Bonnie a little while to pull all the information Buzz wants."

"Not a problem." It would give me time to check on Karma and Daddy.

I watched Bea disappear into the elevator, then I climbed the stairs to the second floor.

Daddy looked over his shoulder when I entered Karma's room and laid his index finger against his lips. "She's sleeping."

And he was watching her sleep?

I jerked my head toward the hallway.

Daddy nodded and followed me out, blinking in the brightly lit hallway.

"I stopped by and saw Bea and Buzz. They've asked me to run an errand for them."

"Did you tell them about the girl at The Nelson?"

"I told Bea. She doesn't want Buzz to know about it yet."

He snorted.

"Everyone keeps secrets, Daddy." The woman sleeping on the

other side of the door was a case in point. "After I pick up the file for the Bisbys, I'll swing by home and get the things Karma wants, then I'll be back."

"Be careful at that brokerage, Ellie. Something odd is going on there. And, finding bodies may not be all that shocking to you, but it shocks the hell out of me. Every. Single. Time. I want you safe."

"Thank you, Daddy." I rose up on my tiptoes and kissed his cheek.

He caught me in a short, fierce hug. "I love you, honey."

"Love you too."

"Daddy?"

"What?"

"What did you tell Mother? About Karma?"

He grimaced and rubbed the spot between his brows. "Let's just say you're lucky you didn't find my body."

ELEVEN

When I arrived at Bisby, Marshall & Wallace, the receptionist's desk sat empty. I waited long enough for a trip to the powder room plus a minute or two extra then gave up. I walked back to the office area unannounced.

A crime scene tape still stretched across the door to Winthrop's office. In front of the door, Debbie's desk sat as empty as the receptionist's.

"Excuse me," I said to a pretty (of course) young woman who was actually at her desk. "Would you please tell me where I can find Bonnie?"

She lifted her gaze from the document in front of her and stared at me with red-rimmed eyes. Her mouth dropped open. "You're the woman who found Mr. Marshall."

"I am."

She wiped her nose with a wadded-up tissue. If she hadn't been crying, she would have been exceptionally pretty. "What do you want with Bonnie?"

Pretty she might be, but she was terrible at customer service.

"Mr. Bisby would like some files. Bonnie collected them for him."

Now her gaze narrowed. "Mr. Bisby is in the hospital. Why would he want files?"

"He's bored near to death."

She shook her head as if she couldn't understand working when she wasn't at the office. "I guess it's none of my business."

She was right about that. "Where is Bonnie?"

"Her desk is right outside Mr. Bisby's office."

I would have been better off just wandering around. "I don't know where Mr. Bisby's office is."

"Far corner." Her tone was that of a teenager—a mix of attitude, boredom, and you're-so-uncool.

"Thank you."

I made my way to the far corner and found yet another empty desk.

"Where is everybody?"

"Half the girls called in sick."

I jumped. I wasn't accustomed to my rhetorical questions being answered. A pretty (no surprise) young woman stood not far behind me with a stack of file folders in her arms.

"Are you Bonnie?"

"I am. You must be Mrs. Russell. It's a pleasure to meet you."

"Things seem a bit—" I searched for a word "—quiet around here."

"They are. With Mr. Bisby in the hospital, Mr. Marshall dead, and Mr. Wallace out of the office, it's very quiet." She smiled brightly. "I've got almost all the files collected. It should only take me another few minutes. Would you like to wait in Mr. Bisby's office?"

"That would be lovely. Thank you."

Bonnie put the folders down on her desk and opened the door to Buzz's office.

Like Winthrop's office, Buzz's was elegantly appointed. Impressive desk. Leather wingback chairs. Art on the walls.

I stopped and stared. Buzz had one of my paintings hanging on his wall. A landscape—a golf-course-scape.

His desk was crowded with silver picture frames. Photos of Bea and their two sons smiled up at me. A credenza against the far wall held more photos. Vacation photos of the four of them—skiing, at the beach, in a canoe.

I sat down in one of the wingback chairs and waited.

A few minutes later, Bonnie stepped into the office. "I think I've got everything ready. I'm sorry you had to make the trip. I would have been happy to deliver the files."

"That's kind of you. When Bea—Mrs. Bisby—decided to call for them, asking you to bring them didn't occur to her." There was no way Bea would have let someone from the office come to the hospital. The potential for Buzz learning about Frank's troubles was too high.

She smiled. "I'm sure Mrs. Bisby appreciates your helping out."

At least one of the pretty young women understood customer service. "How long have you been with the firm?"

"Five years in June."

"And you've worked for Mr. Bisby the whole time?"

"Not at first."

I glanced at the closed door to Buzz's office. "I have heard a few things about the way women are treated here."

The smile ran away from her face.

"Have you noticed that certain partners or brokers prey on the women who work here?"

"No. Never." Bonnie crossed her arms and her lips thinned to a barely-there line.

"What about at other firms?"

She stared at me for at least a minute. "Maybe."

"Maybe?"

She shifted her gaze to the wide expanse of Buzz's windows. "Maybe. Maybe a broker—a broker at another firm—tells a girl she looks pretty in a certain dress, or with her hair down, or in a new sweater. Maybe she says *thank you*." Her hands gripped her upper arms. "Maybe he takes her to lunch as a reward for doing extra work. Maybe he orders a martini and says he can't drink alone."

Whatever Bonnie saw outside Buzz's window existed only in her head. "Maybe the next day he pats her bottom. What can she say? She's accepted his compliments. She's been out with him. And, he's her boss."

I knew where this was going and my heart squeezed. If it could happen to Bonnie or Debbie or Marcy, it could happen to Grace. Daughters and sisters and wives devalued by men who had daughters and sisters and wives they cherished.

"Maybe he asks her to work late. Maybe he presses her against an office wall and puts his hands on her most intimate places. Maybe he bends her over a desk and—" her voice broke.

"Buzz? Did Buzz do that to you?"

"Never." She looked me straight in the eye. "Never. Mr. Bisby has always treated me with respect."

We'd given up on the fiction of another brokerage. "Wallace and Marshall?"

She looked away. "Look around this office. We're all young. We're all pretty. For them, coming to work is like going to an all-you-can-eat buffet."

"And no one says anything?"

"If they do, they're out." She shook her head. "It's not all that easy to find a job right now. Especially not when you were fired from your last one."

"Debbie and Marcy were involved with Winthrop and Frank?"

"Debbie was not. Not since she got married. Marcy, I'm not so sure about. She did a lot of closed door dictation with Mr. Wallace."

I shuddered.

"Maybe things will get better now that Winthrop is gone."

"It's not just them. It's in the water. All the brokers do it."

"What can we do to change things?"

"We?" She shifted her gaze to me. "There are no consequences for the men. There have to be consequences."

There had been consequences for Winthrop. "If Mr. Marshall was leaving Debbie alone, who did he prey on?"

"Joanie. She sits not far from his office."

"Blonde bob, pointed chin, big blue eyes?"

"That's her. How did you know?"

"I asked her how to find you."

"And she told you?"

"Not exactly."

"She has issues."

If Winthrop Marshall chased me around a desk, I'd have issues too.

We stood, both at a loss for what to say next.

Bonnie cleared her throat and looked at her watch.

"I should get going."

Bonnie filled a banker's box with the files Buzz had requested.

I took it from her. "Thank you for your help."

"I can carry that to the elevator for you," she offered.

"I can manage." I wanted a word with Joanie on my way out.

"You're sure?"

"Positive." I settled the box on my hip and walked away.

"Mrs. Russell."

I stopped.

"Please don't repeat what I told you."

"If no one is willing to talk about what happens here, nothing will change."

Bonnie stared at me. She was pretty and young and pale and undecided.

I waited.

After an eternity (thirty seconds), she squared her shoulders. "Tell who you need to tell."

"Thank you, Bonnie.

On my way out, I walked by Joanie's desk, but the cover was on her typewriter. "Did Joanie leave?" I asked a passing woman.

"She didn't feel good. She took the afternoon off."

"What's Joanie's last name?"

The woman's brow wrinkled and she tilted her head. "Wilson. Why?"

"She looked familiar," I lied. "I thought I might have met her before."

"She got married not all that long ago. Her maiden name was Phillips."

"Not the Joanie I know. Thank you."

I carried the box to the elevator, threw it in the back of the car, drove home, collected the things Karma wanted, and returned to the hospital.

I parked and reached into the backseat. During the drive, the box had tipped over and there were file folders and papers everywhere. *Dammit.* I gathered everything together as best I could. But papers ended up in the wrong files. I didn't know where they were supposed to go and there were just too many of them.

With the documents jammed into files and the files returned to the box, I carried everything inside and took the elevator to the third floor.

Buzz's door stood open.

I stuck my head in his room. "Hello." I sounded cheerier than I felt.

"Come in."

Buzz was alone.

"Where's Bea?"

"She went home to take a shower and rest. The doctors insisted." His gaze caught on the banker's box. "My files?"

"Fair warning. The box tipped in the backseat and they may be a bit mixed up."

He waved his hand (the one without the IV). The mix-up didn't matter.

I put the box down on the end of the bed and closed my eyes.

When I opened them, I looked straight at Buzz. "Did you know that Winthrop and Frank preyed on the women in your office?"

He stared back at me and his free hand bunched the blanket on his bed. "That's none of your business."

He was probably right, but I was making it my business. "Did you know?"

His gaze shifted to the window. "It's the way things are, Ellison. I protect who I can."

"You protect Bonnie. One woman in an office of how many?"

"If they don't like working there, they can always quit."

Well. I stared at him for a moment. "Do you think it's right?

What Frank and Winthrop have been doing?"

"Of course not."

"But you won't do anything to stop it?"

"They're my partners." His voice rose and the monitor next to his bed beeped faster.

"Those young women are your employees."

"Like I said, this is none of your business."

"I found Winthrop's body. With his pants around his ankles. Surely it's crossed your mind that his office antics got him killed."

"You should go."

"Buzz, you're a partner. If you don't stand up for those women, who will?"

His face was closed and stony but the monitor had gone crazy. *Beep-beep-beep-beep.* "Thank you for the files, Ellison."

"Would you feel differently if you had daughters? If Bea had to work?"

"Everything okay in here?" A nurse stepped into Buzz's room and gazed at his monitor.

"Mrs. Russell dropped something off for me. She was just leaving."

I stared at the stranger in the bed—a stranger I'd known for years. I'd always considered him a good man. "Goodbye, Buzz."

I stopped outside Buzz's door, rested my back against the wall, and studied the ceiling. If a man like Buzz wouldn't lift a finger or raise his voice, how would things change?

One thing was certain, I was moving my accounts. I wouldn't keep them in a place where women were exploited.

I took a deep breath, pushed off the wall, and made my way to Karma's room.

I knocked softly then opened the door. "It's me." My voice was quiet in case she was asleep.

She wasn't.

It's tough to sleep with an angry snow queen in your room.

"Hello, Ellison." Mother's voice was icy.

This wouldn't end well. "Hello." I turned to Karma. "I brought the things you asked for."

"Thank you." Her voice was weak.

Weakness was not the way to handle Frances Walford.

"I'm surprised to see you here," I said to Mother.

"Someone called and told me that Marjorie had been admitted to the hospital under an assumed name."

"Obviously they were mistaken."

"Obviously." Sarcasm dripped thick as simple syrup.

"Just when were you and your father going to tell me about your guest?"

I glanced at Karma. She looked as pale as her sheets. "Mother, perhaps we can discuss this another time?"

"Now is the perfect time. We're all here. Together."

With a sigh, I settled into the second chair.

"Were you going to tell me you found another body?"

"I was. I've been busy."

"Busy?" More sarcasm.

"I saw Karma settled, had lunch with Bea who's not doing well—" and she might never speak to me again "—went to Bisby, Marshall & Wallace and picked up some files for Buzz, stopped by the house for Karma's things, and came back here. Busy."

Mother snorted. I hadn't seen her this coldly angry since she discovered Marjorie's husband, the Rubber King of Ohio, manufactured condoms not tires. Obviously, Daddy had not told her Karma was in town.

"Where's Daddy?"

Mother shook her head. "I have no idea."

"He had to go back to his office," said Karma. "He had a meeting he couldn't reschedule."

Karma should have kept her mouth shut.

She knew where Daddy was when Mother didn't.

I held my breath and waited for the apocalypse.

Mother collected her coat and handbag and gloves. "You need your rest, Miss Michaels. Ellison and I will leave you now." She stood and death-glared me until I stood, then she swanned out the door.

"I'd better go with her. Are you all right?"

"I thought my mother was a dragon." Karma shook her head and winced. "Good luck."

"I'll talk to you later."

Mother waited for me in the hall. "How could he?"

This was between Mother and Daddy. I wanted no part of it. I shook my head.

She raised her chin another inch. "How could you?"

"He said it was my house or yours."

She staggered.

"There are a lot of women he's trying to keep happy."

"I'm. His. Wife." Her chin wavered. "How could he do this to me?"

Oh dear Lord. Mother only cried at weddings.

"He loves you more than anything, but she is his daughter. I suspect he feels guilty that Karma got the crumbs of his affection as a child. When she said she was coming, he couldn't tell her no."

"And he couldn't warn me? I'll be a laughingstock."

"You will not. Daddy met someone before he met you. It didn't work out, but they had a daughter. It's simple math. Karma is two years older than Marjorie."

"No one will care about a forty-year-old timeline. All they'll care about is that Harrington Walford has an illegitimate daughter."

"Own it."

Mother narrowed her eyes. Infinitely better than a wavering chin. "Pardon me?"

"Own the story. Welcome Karma. Tell everyone about Daddy's little indiscretion and that Karma is such a lovely woman we couldn't keep her a secret anymore."

Mother glanced around the deserted hall. A full minute passed. "I'll consider it." She turned on her heel and left me.

I stumbled to the waiting room, put my head in my hands, and reviewed my day—dead body, half-sister in the hospital, potentially friendship-ending argument with Bea's husband, Mother and Daddy at odds, and—I glanced at my watch—it wasn't even four o'clock.

TWELVE

The hospital waiting room was a good spot for thinking. Bland. No distractions—nothing but a six-month-old copy of *Life*, a dog-eared copy of *Reader's Digest*, and a vending machine. I sat and I thought—and thought—until the scent of worry, accumulated over decades, overcame the hospital's usual odor of mercurochrome and iodine. I stood.

Slowly, I walked back to Karma's room.

I wouldn't apologize for Mother. She was protecting what she saw as hers—her standing in society, her role as the center of Daddy's life, her daughters. That said, Karma had received quite an introduction to Frances Walford.

I pushed open Karma's door and froze.

Anarchy sat next to Karma's bed. They were both smiling. At each other. Her hand was in his.

Anarchy slipped free of her hold and stood. Abruptly. "I brought Karma flowers."

Something I should have done.

Karma shifted her gaze from Anarchy to a vase filled with pink roses. "They're my favorite."

I bet Anarchy already knew that.

A very safe bet since his cheeks had managed to blanche and flush at the same time.

"How pretty." My voice sounded funny. Too high. Too tight. And my face—my lips had curled into a rictus grin. They were stuck there.

The two of them exchanged a look.

For an instant, the same green-eyed emotion Mother had experienced roared through my blood. It was quickly replaced by a hole in my stomach. I swallowed into emptiness then brought my hands to the sides of my face. That damned grin made my cheeks hurt. "Looks like you two have some catching up to do and I'm interrupting." I backed toward the door. "Karma, I'll check on you later."

I slipped out the door and bent over at the waist, holding my arms across my stomach, just to make sure none of my shredded intestines fell out.

After a few seconds, I stood. I couldn't be here. Could not. I flew down the hospital's corridors, jumped into my car, and raced away. Away. Getting away from Anarchy and Karma (even their names went together well) was the most important thing ever.

I was a fool. I knew what men were like. I'd been married to a man for eighteen years. Why had I expected Anarchy to be different?

My skin felt too small to contain the storm raging inside me.

I pulled over to the side of the road and stared blindly through the windshield.

I had two options. I could go home, crawl into my bed, and never come out, or I could find Libba and drink. Okay, there was one option.

I parked in front of Libba's building, got out of the car, and smiled with taut lips at the doorman. "Good afternoon, Lincoln. Is Libba in?"

"Mrs. Russell, you're in luck. She got home a few minutes ago. Should I tell her you're here?"

"Please."

I walked with leaden feet to the elevator and jabbed the up button.

When the elevator arrived on Libba's floor, she was standing in the hallway waiting for me with a wrinkled brow. "What's wrong?"

"How do you know something is wrong?"

"You never show up here without calling. What happened?"

"Where do I start?" Tears welled in my eyes and I swiped them away.

My best friend's gaze softened. "You start with a drink." She led me into her living room with its spectacular view of the Plaza. "Gin or vodka?"

"Vodka."

"Soda or tonic?"

I wavered. "Soda."

"Lime or lemon?"

"Lime. Two if you have them."

"I always have bar fruit."

Of course she did. I sank onto the couch and ran a finger across velvet upholstery. "New?"

"I suppose." Libba walked over to the bar and mixed the drinks. "I've had it for at least a month. The last one was so dark." This one was white. White velvet. A couch for a woman with no children or pets.

She brought me my drink.

My hand closed around the glass and I sipped gratefully. A large sip. Then I coughed. Libba made drinks strong enough to strip paint. Had she done more than pass the soda bottle over the glass?

She sat across from me. "So, what's wrong?"

My jaw ached and my throat tightened. "Everything."

"Everything?"

I took another sip and searched Libba's uber-chic living room for a box of tissue. "Daddy invited Karma to stay at my house. I've found two bodies this week. Grace adopted a cat. Mother is furious. And Anarchy and Karma knew each other in San Francisco."

She blinked. "*Knew each other*, knew each other?"

"I think so." Where were the damned tissues? I opened my handbag and dug out a handkerchief.

"Have you asked him?"

I shifted my gaze to my lap and kept it there. Seeing pity on Libba's face would do me in. "I walked into Karma's hospital room and he was holding her hand." Every insecurity I'd ever had joined me on the couch. Not-Pretty-Enough? That one plunked down and pushed against my thigh. Not-Smart-Enough leaned back and crossed its legs. Too-Boring actually put its feet up on the coffee-table.

"I thought Karma was staying with you." There wasn't a hint of pity in Libba's voice.

I looked up and wiped my eyes. "She is. She was. Tonight she's staying in the hospital."

"What happened to her?"

"She fainted when we found Frank Wallace's secretary at The Nelson with her neck broken."

Libba screwed up her face and wrinkled her nose

"What?" I snapped.

"I don't like Frank Wallace. Never have."

"I don't like him either." Especially now.

"I don't know why Celine puts up with him."

"Yes, you do."

Libba shook her glass and the ice tinkled against the crystal. "You're right. Marry for money and you earn it every day."

"I don't want to talk about Frank and Celine." My voice shook.

"Right. Anarchy and your half-sister." Libba raised her left brow and pursed her lips. "You can't get mad at him until you talk to him."

Yes, I could. And since when was Libba the voice of reason? "You don't mean that."

"I do. I know it looked bad—"

Bad? I snorted. He'd been holding her hand.

Don't forget, said Not-Pretty-Enough, *they were gazing into each other's eyes.*

"But—"

I scowled at the insecurities crowding around me. "Do you remember how Marjorie stole every boyfriend I had in high school?"

"You had bad boyfriends."

She's right, said Not-Smart-Enough.

"Pish."

"Pish?" Libba looked almost stern. "Karma is not Marjorie. And Anarchy is not Henry. You need to give them the benefit of the doubt."

I pished under my breath.

"I mean it, Ellison." She actually smiled. "The way that man looks at you—" she shook her head "—no way is he straying. Not for an instant. Especially not with your sister."

"But—"

"No buts. I know men. Anarchy wouldn't think of stepping out on you." Libba took a long sip and leaned back into her chair. "If I'd been married to Henry, I'd have trust issues too. But Anarchy Jones is a straight arrow. He would never, ever hurt you like this."

Maybe she was right. Anarchy was nothing like Henry. I wiped my eyes and lifted my near empty glass to my lips.

"I'll get you a fresh drink." Libba took the glass from my hand.

"You might actually add some soda to this one."

"There's the Ellison I know and love."

A moment later, she handed me a fresh vodka soda (with almost no soda). "So we've decided. You're going to talk to Anarchy."

We'd decided that? When?

"What do I say?"

"He and Karma obviously have a past. Ask him about it."

She made it sound so easy.

"That's settled. Now—" she reclaimed her chair and tucked her feet beneath her knees "—why on earth did you let Grace get a cat?"

I woke the next morning to a mouth filled with cotton and a dull headache. Oozing out of bed made the room spin. I grabbed the edge of the mattress and breathed through my nose.

Never again.

I pushed myself to standing and stumbled downstairs to the kitchen.

Mr. Coffee didn't judge, didn't point out how late I'd come home, didn't tell me I looked like fifty miles of bad road. I closed my hand around his pot and filled a mug with coffee. "Thank you," I whispered.

"Who are you talking to?" Aggie stood in the doorway from the front hall.

Why had I never noticed her voice was so loud?

"No one."

"Do you want some eggs and bacon? They might help."

"Please." I sat down at the counter and sipped my coffee while she cooked.

"Do you want to talk about it?"

"Libba mixed the drinks."

"Ah." She did not ask why I'd downed so many of Libba's drinks. Instead, she opened a cupboard, pulled out a bottle of aspirin, opened the lid, and shook out two pills. "Here you go."

"Thank you."

"You look as if you need them."

"I do." I swallowed the pills.

A few moments later she put a plate of fried eggs and crispy bacon in front of me.

My stomach flipped. Triple flipped.

"Eat a few bites. I guarantee you'll feel better."

I lifted a forkful of egg to my mouth and chewed.

Aggie refilled my coffee cup.

Maybe it was the eggs or the aspirin or the coffee or a combination of the three, but I felt marginally better. I took a second bite.

"Why were you drinking with Libba?"

In the morning light, telling her that Anarchy had hurt my feelings seemed childish. "Poor choices."

She snorted—a fine-don't-tell-me snort. "You need to take that ham over to Ruth Marshall's this morning."

Ugh.

I ate my eggs and bacon slowly (Max left off sitting in front of the closed door to Grace's room to watch the bacon move from the plate to my mouth), stumbled up the stairs, and stood in the shower until part of my headache washed down the drain.

Ruth Marshall's. There would be people. I would be expected to converse. I glanced with longing at my bed.

Tap, tap.

"Come in."

Aggie stepped into my bedroom. "I brought you another cup of coffee."

Gratitude welled in my eyes.

"You don't drink often."

"I don't."

"You don't cry often."

That too was true.

"Did that detective do something to hurt you?" Aggie's late husband had been a private investigator. I'd often wondered if she'd been the brains behind Al DeLucci's operation. How else could she jump from a hangover to Anarchy?

"I don't know."

"If he did, it's not too late to—"

I held up my hand. "Hunter deserves a woman who's over the moon for him." If things went sideways with Anarchy, I wouldn't use Hunter Tafft as balm for my wounds.

Aggie sighed. Of the two men, she much preferred Hunter.

"I'd better get ready."

She left me but I heard her voice in the hall. "You leave that cat alone."

Max didn't reply.

I donned a navy blue suit (Bill Blass), stockings (leaning over to put them on nearly did me in), conservative pumps (Ferragamo), and pearls (Grandmother's).

Aggie had the ham (slathered in a brown sugar and mustard

glaze, studded with cloves, and baked in Coca-Cola) wrapped and waiting for me. I carried it out to the car, settled it into the passenger seat, and drove to Ruth's.

Ruth and Winthrop (now just Ruth) lived in an enormous house a block from Mother and Daddy's. I parked at the curb and made my way up the front walk, carrying the ham with both arms.

Ruth opened the door before I got there. "Ellison."

"I brought you a ham." A needless statement. There was no way she could miss the enormous aluminum-foil swaddled bundle in my arms. I stared up at her (she had a good seven inches on me— even in heels) and added, "I hope you like ham."

"How thoughtful of you. I love ham." Her voice was a piano wire stretched too tight. "Come in."

Mine was the only car at the curb. Coming in meant a one-on-one conversation with Ruth. A conversation that would be difficult if I felt halfway decent. I felt only ten-percent decent and that last percentage point was iffy. "You must have a million things to do. I don't want to impose."

"Actually, I'd like some company."

Drat. "In that case, I'd love to come in."

She held open the door and led me to the kitchen where I settled the ham onto a counter already laden with Bundt cakes. The Bundt Cake Brigade had been here in force.

"Would you like coffee?"

"Please."

She poured a mug and handed it to me. "Cream or sugar?"

"Cream, please."

She opened the refrigerator, revealing shelves filled with casseroles. "I think I've received at least five Pyrex dishes of funeral potatoes." She looked over her shoulder and a tight smile lifted her lips. "That alone makes this all worthwhile."

All this—her husband's murder. "They are tasty."

She took the cream out of the refrigerator door, stacked a few things, and shoved the ham in the fridge.

I spilled some cream into my mug and returned the container

to her.

"Do you mind sitting in the family room?" she asked. "I feel as if I've spent too much time in the living room."

"Of course not."

Ruth led me to a cozy room with a brick fireplace, French doors that opened onto a generous patio, and plaid couches.

She waved me toward a wingback chair, waited until I sat, then claimed my chair's twin for herself.

"I'm so sorry for your loss."

Ruth snorted. "You found him. You know what kind of man he was."

There was no response to that—at least not one I could think of.

"I know you understand how I feel," Ruth continued. "Your husband had the morals of a tomcat."

"True." I stared into the coffee mug in my hands. "But Henry and I planned on divorcing."

"Winthrop wouldn't give me a divorce. A wife kept him protected from getting too involved." The lines in Ruth's neck were taut. "My only choice was to hire an investigator, prove adultery, and go through the public humiliation of a trial." She leaned back and sipped her coffee. "This way is much better."

No trial. No embarrassment. No paltry alimony payments. With Winthrop dead, Ruth got everything.

Was I having coffee with a murderess?

I shifted my gaze from the view out the window to Ruth. She was still an attractive woman. Fit. Still tanned from six weeks spent in Palm Springs. Pretty blue eyes. With Winthrop gone, she could move on.

Ruth Marshall wasn't the sort of woman who'd kill her children's father—even if those children were grown and out of the house. "Ruth—"

"I know. I shouldn't speak ill of the dead." Her mouth moved as if it was chewing on all the things she wanted to say. "But I feel as if I can be honest with you. Your husband cheated. Your husband was murdered. You understand."

I hadn't thought about that. I did understand. I also understood that as the wronged wife of a murdered man, Ruth was probably the prime suspect.

With anger radiating off of her in waves, I couldn't blame the police for considering her a suspect.

"You know people will be talking...wondering."

She shrugged. "I got some of my own back but I didn't kill him."

Some of her own back? What did that mean? "Ruth—"

Ding, dong.

She sighed and stood. "That'll be the well-meaning horde. I've got more Bundts than a woman could eat in a lifetime."

"Maybe someone brought you more potatoes."

She brightened and looked down at me. "You are coming to the funeral?"

I swallowed a sigh and rose from my chair. "Of course. I'll see you tomorrow morning."

THIRTEEN

Daddy brought Karma home that afternoon.

My father, who never fussed—who'd barely noticed when at fifteen I broke my arm falling off a horse, who'd worked late the night a twelve-year-old Marjorie was hospitalized with pneumonia—fussed around Karma like a maiden aunt. "Are you comfortable? Is it too warm in here? Ellison turn down the furnace. Would you like something to drink? Are you hungry? Ellison, what does Aggie have in the fridge? Do you need another blanket?"

Karma stretched out on the couch in the family room with an amused half-smile on her face. "I'm fine, Dad."

Daddy sat on the coffee-table and held her hand. Tightly. "You've had a head injury. Is it too bright in here?" He scowled at the sunlight pouring through the windows. "Ellison, pull the curtains."

"It's not too bright and I like the view."

"Do you want some fresh air? Ellison, open a window."

"Dad. I'm fine. Stop."

The corner of Daddy's eyes drooped and his lips bowed downward. "This hasn't been the trip you hoped for."

No way had Karma hoped to find a body or end up in the hospital or take on Mother.

"I'm fine," she murmured.

He should be more worried about me. I was the daughter who'd have to deal with Mother when Karma was safely back in San Francisco.

"I just need some rest."

"Of course you do. Remember, the doctor said no TV or reading."

"I remember."

Daddy leaned forward and kissed her forehead. "Ellison will take good care of you."

Oh dear Lord. The woman had been here a matter of days and already she had Daddy wrapped around her little finger and Anarchy holding her hand. From what I'd seen, she was fully capable of taking care of herself.

Daddy looked at me expectantly.

"Of course, I'll take good care of Karma." I didn't sound grudging. Not a bit. "Daddy, I'll see you out."

He stood, dropped a second kiss on Karma's forehead, then walked out of the room.

When we reached the kitchen, I leveled my best death-glare his way. "You told me that you'd told Mother about Karma."

His cheeks flushed. "I meant to tell her but the timing wasn't right."

I stared at him. Gaped, really. "Daddy, she found out Karma was in Kansas City from a friend. Not from you. Not even from me. Has she had the locks changed?"

"Not yet." His expression darkened. "I'd like to get my hands on whoever called her."

"You can't shoot the messenger."

His drawn brows, thin lips, and clenched fists said he could and would. "What a mess."

I took a deep breath. "You need to clean it up."

His brows rose. At my tone? At my message? At the idea the mess belonged to him?

"Fix things. With Mother. Today."

"But—"

"She's your wife. The woman you promised to love, honor, and cherish till death do you part. I guarantee you she's not feeling honored or cherished right now."

"But Karma—"

"Karma is a grown woman who put you in the soup. I would have been happy to go to San Francisco but she insisted on coming here."

"This isn't her fault."

"Not entirely," I nodded my agreement. "You're equally to blame."

"Me?"

"You. You should have told Mother. You promised you'd tell her. This is your mess and you need to fix it."

"How? I can't send Karma home. The doctor said she couldn't fly for a few days."

"Find out how Mother wants to handle this...situation. Then do whatever she asks."

"But—"

"Karma can stay here as long as she needs to."

"But—"

"No buts, Daddy. If you value your marriage, you should be at home with Mother not fussing over Karma."

His gaze flitted back to the family room where Karma lay on the couch.

"I'll take care of Karma. You should go."

"Ellison—" he sounded as if he had arguments at the ready.

"Whatever you're about to say, I don't want to hear it."

Daddy's chin dropped to his chest as if he was a little boy who'd just been scolded.

"Go. Talk to Mother. She needs you."

Daddy shuffled out of the kitchen and into the front hall. I almost felt sorry for him. Almost. Dealing with Mother wouldn't be easy. But, he'd brought this on himself.

I returned to the family room. "Do you have everything you need?" My voice was concierge-at-a-five-star-hotel polite. And just as remote.

"If it's not too much trouble, could I have a cup of coffee? Please?"

I couldn't withhold coffee, not after everything she'd been through. "I'll make a fresh pot."

"Ellison."

I stopped on my way to the kitchen and looked over my shoulder. "What?"

"There's nothing between me and Anarchy."

"But there was." And something told me she wouldn't object to revisiting the past.

She didn't deny it. "I want you to know, I'm sorry."

"For what?" Was she apologizing for their shared past? Or for wanting a reprise?

"I just wanted to meet you and see what Dad's real life was like. I didn't consider how my coming here would affect your family."

She wasn't apologizing for all that hand-holding in the hospital. She was apologizing for the elephant-sized wrench she'd tossed into our family dynamics.

I didn't much feel like accepting apologies. "If you knew what would happen, would you have come anyway?" My brief acquaintance with my sister had convinced me she was a woman who usually got what she wanted.

"No." She shifted her gaze to the view of the backyard. "Yes." Her eyes closed. "I don't know."

"Well, you're here now. And you're not going anywhere anytime soon. Mother and Daddy will have to work things out."

"What if she tells him it's her or me?" Karma's voice was small. And sad.

Unwelcome pity tugged at my heart. "She won't do that. Mother is many things but she's not cruel. And Daddy would never cut you out of his life. It's obvious he adores you."

Karma nodded. Once. Not a convinced nod. "About Anarchy—"

"Don't." Whatever the story was, whatever their history was, I didn't want to hear it. Not from Karma. At that moment, my beleaguered emotions couldn't take anymore sisterly bombshells. I headed to the kitchen. "I'll get you that coffee."

* * *

Winthrop Marshall's funeral was scheduled for eleven o'clock the next morning. I arrived at half past ten to a church already near full.

Winthrop might have been a horrible human being but he'd made a lot of people a lot of money and they'd come to pay their respects.

I slipped into a pew, nodded at the friends and acquaintances who caught my eye, then opened the prayer book in front of me and pretended to read.

I'd dodged Anarchy's phone call. What did that say about me? Maybe I wasn't ready for a relationship? Maybe I was afraid of falling in love? Maybe I wasn't ready to trust?

I'd also left the house without saying goodbye to Karma. What kind of sister was I?

"May I join you?"

I looked up from the prayer book. Gaye Hardy was waiting for an answer.

"Of course."

She settled in next to me. "Quite a turn out."

"Quite."

"Poor, Ruth. She must be devastated."

"I think she's managing."

"Hmm." Her tone told me she thought I was wrong.

"How was your movie?"

"My movie?" She tilted her head as if she had no idea what I was talking about.

"The one you saw with Hunter."

"Oh, that movie. Good, I suppose."

"What did you see?"

"*Shampoo.*"

"You liked it?"

She wrinkled her nose. "It was a bit risqué for my tastes. All sorts of cheating and drinking."

Sounded like life in Kansas City. "You didn't like it?"

"Hunter liked it."

"But what did you think?"

"It was just a movie, Ellison." She glanced around the church. "Tell me about you and the Detective."

"There's not much to tell." And if there was, I wouldn't tell Gaye. She was nice enough, but I hardly knew the woman.

"That's not what it looked like to me."

I offered her a weak smile.

The organ's first notes silenced any further questions.

Ruth and her children, along with their spouses, walked down the center aisle and sat in the first pew.

Gaye might think Ruth was devastated, but there was a bloom on the widow's cheeks that said she was not remotely saddened. She even looked over her shoulder and whispered to the people in the pew behind her.

I squinted. Ruth was talking to Frank Wallace. I'd assumed Detective Peters had arrested Frank.

Obviously, I'd assumed wrong. Frank had his arm draped around Celine as if he didn't have a care in the world.

The priest walked down the aisle. The choir sang. We stood and knelt and sat at all the right times.

And then it was over and the congregation was invited to the undercroft for cookies and punch and a word with the family.

Gaye slipped away and I took my place in the line snaking down the stairs.

"Ellison?"

I turned. "Hester, what a surprise."

"We decided to stay for the funeral. This is my husband, Chauncey Nelson. Chauncey, this is Ellison Russell, the woman who was kind enough to take me shopping."

Chauncey Nelson extended his hand. He looked exactly as I'd expect a man named Chauncey to look. Spoiled and slightly soft around the middle and beautifully dressed. A slightly younger version of Frank Wallace. "You cost me an awful lot of money, Mrs.

Russell."

The line inched forward.

"Oh?"

"You took my wife shopping."

"Hester bought some beautiful things. Things she'll use for years." Except for that fuchsia number. I bet that was good for one season.

He grunted. "If you say so."

It was my turn to say something. What did one say to a puffed suit? "I understand we have a mutual acquaintance."

"Oh?"

"Karma Michaels."

He cocked his head. "Who?"

Why did I get the feeling he knew exactly who I meant? "Karma Michaels from San Francisco."

Chauncey Nelson wrinkled his nose and the corner of his mouth lifted in a tiny sneer. "That's right. She runs a brokerage out there."

"You don't approve?"

"Managing investments requires steady nerves." He held up a finger. "A certain acumen." A second finger lifted. "And a feel for the markets." A third finger rose. "I've yet to meet a woman who has all three."

Oh dear Lord. I forced a smile. "Winthrop had all that?"

"In spades. A good man. A good money manager. A real loss to this community."

What drivel.

I stood on my tiptoes and surveyed the line. "You know, I think I'll give you my spot in line."

"You're not going to pay your respects to Mrs. Marshall?" asked Hester.

"Not until after a trip to the powder room. It was nice to meet you, Mr. Nelson, and lovely to see you again, Hester." I left them. With their eyes on my back, there was no place to go but the powder room, so that's where I went.

I stepped inside, put my handbag down on the shelf in front of the mirror, dug my compact from the purse's depths, and powdered my nose.

"Eeeep."

The sound came from one of the stalls.

"Are you all right?" I asked.

"Eeeep."

"Can I get you anything?"

"This stall is out of toilet paper."

"Just a minute." I went into the second stall, unspooled a length of paper, and held it under the partition.

Whoever was in there, took it from me and blew her nose.

A long hard blow.

I returned to powdering my nose. I touched up my lipstick. I licked the tips of my fingers and smoothed a few stray hairs into place.

Finally, the door to the stall opened. The woman who stepped out had a blonde bob, pointed chin, and red-rimmed blue eyes.

"You're Joanie." I stared at her reflection in the mirror.

"Do I know you?"

"We met the other day. At the office."

"You were looking for Bonnie."

"Yes."

"You found her?"

"I did."

Fresh tears welled in her eyes.

"Are you okay?"

"It's hard. Mr. Marshall dying."

It was probable that many of the people who'd populated Winthrop's funeral grieved for the stockbroker who'd achieved double-digit returns for them. But, aside from his children and maybe Frank Wallace, there was no one who grieved for him as a man. No one but Joanie.

"You had a relationship with Winthrop?"

She looked at me with her red-rimmed eyes and lifted her chin high. "He loved me. He was going to leave his wife. I agreed to leave my husband."

Winthrop leaving Ruth seemed highly unlikely, but he wouldn't have been the first man to trade in decades of marriage for a woman half his age.

"You told your husband you wanted a divorce so you could marry Winthrop?"

Her chin quivered. "I was going to. It's just that Larry gets so upset and jealous and I didn't want to rock the boat until—"

"Until Winthrop left Ruth," I finished for her. "But he didn't."

"He didn't have a chance! He was going to leave her. He said she'd done something unforgivable and they were through."

Really? "Did he say what Ruth did?"

She shook her head. "He wouldn't tell me. But, the very next day, he was dead."

What had Ruth said? That she got some of her own back? What had she done?

Joanie pressed the back of her hand against her lips. Fresh tears welled in her eyes. Her cheeks were as white as the walls.

"Are you all right? Don't you think you should sit down?" I led her to a bench covered in pink Naugahyde.

She sat and lowered her head to her hands. "My husband suspects I cheated. Winthrop's dead. And the firm is in trouble. I could lose my job."

I could solve one of her problems. "The firm will be fine. Buzz will be back at work in no time. And I understand Frank is just as good at picking stocks as Winthrop."

She raised her head and somehow managed to look down her nose at me even though she was seated and I was standing. "You don't know anything."

"What is it I should know?"

"There's trouble. Big trou—"

The door to the powder room swung open and Celine Wallace strode in. Her face was pale but furious dots of red colored her cheeks. She blinked when she saw me. "Ellison—" she kissed the air near my cheek "—how nice to see you."

"You too."

Celine dug a compact out of her handbag and covered the redness on her cheeks. "Such a sad day."

"It is."

Neither of us meant a word of it.

Joanie gave Celine and me a look that clearly said we were harpies then dashed out of the powder room.

"Who on earth was that?"

"One of the firm's employees. I think Winthrop's death has been hard on her."

"She's the one?"

"The one?"

"Winthrop's latest dalliance. Frank told me the latest girl had Winthrop in a twist."

Had Joanie been right? Had Winthrop really considered divorcing Ruth?

Celine looked in the mirror then pulled a lipstick out of her bag. "Those girls positively throw themselves at the brokers."

Not the story I'd been told.

"They wear short skirts and tight sweaters. They're positively begging for attention."

Or they felt they needed to wear them to keep their jobs.

Celine applied her lipstick. "It's a good thing Frank is immune."

Did she not know about Frank and Marcy?

I thought it best to keep my mouth closed.

FOURTEEN

The line to pay respects was much shorter when I emerged from the powder room. Not the blessing one might think. Not after Joanie's revelations. Not when I wasn't sure what to say to Ruth. *Did you know about Winthrop's mistress?* hardly seemed appropriate. I took my place at the end of the line behind a beefy man who'd opted to wear a sports jacket and a plaid tie to a funeral. He regarded me with hooded eyes. "Sad day."

"Indeed," I replied. My tone did not invite further conversation.

Either the man didn't recognize my reluctance to chat or he didn't care. "Barney Wilson." He extended a calloused hand which swallowed mine whole.

"Ellison Russell."

"How did you know Mr. Marshall?" Barney pumped my hand with enthusiasm.

"I was a client." It was the easiest explanation—the shortest explanation. I extracted my crushed fingers.

"Me too. Winnie was a great broker." Barney shook his head with evident regret.

Winnie?

"He did seem to have a golden touch."

"Ain't that the truth? These past few years, he hasn't picked anything but winners. I'm gonna miss him." Barney waved his hand at the line in front of us. "All of his clients will miss him."

"How long have you been investing with him?" The words

slipped out unbidden. I wasn't in the mood for plaid-tied strangers and my question was an invitation to chat.

"Going on fifteen years. We got off to a rocky start, but, like I said, these past few years, ole Winnie hit his stride."

"I've never heard him called Winnie."

"Winnie and Barn."

Sometimes lines inched. Sometimes they jumped. Now, when I wanted a slow-moving line, the dratted thing leaped forward as if a whole slew of people had given up waiting for Ruth and opted for the cookies.

"What about you?" asked Barney. "How long have you been investing with Winthrop?"

"To be honest, I'm not exactly sure. My husband handled our investments until he died last summer."

Barney's face fell. "I'm sorry for your loss."

"That's kind of you, Mr. Wilson."

"Barney. Mr. Wilson was my father."

"Barney," I corrected.

Ruth was within spitting distance.

"It's good you had Winnie as your broker when your husband passed. If something happened to me, I'd want a broker like him taking care of my wife."

Given everything I knew about Winthrop, I sincerely doubted that.

We were just steps from Ruth. The bloom on her cheeks had faded and exhaustion seemed to pull at her jaw line. She looked twenty years older than she was.

Barney took a giant stride and thrust his hand at Ruth. "Sorry for your loss, Mrs. Marshall."

Ruth searched his face with tired eyes. "So kind of you, Mr.—"

"Wilson. I was one of your husband's clients."

"It's nice of you to come." Even Ruth's lips sagged.

Barney Wilson looked back at me, the last person in line, then returned his gaze to Ruth. "If you don't mind my saying, Mrs. Marshall, you ought to sit down."

"Ellison—" she glanced my way "—do you mind?"

"Of course not. Sit." After the things Joanie had told me, not talking to Ruth was a relief.

Barney led Ruth to a chair and hovered until she sat. "I'm gonna get you some punch and a cookie."

Barney returned with a glass of punch and a little glass plate filled with cookies faster than one would have thought possible. He must have cut the lines.

I leaned over and kissed the air next to Ruth's cheek. "Call me if you need anything."

"Thank you. I will."

I slipped away without having to say anything substantive. I even managed to escape the undercroft without anyone stopping me.

I drove home with Ruth Marshall on my mind. What had Ruth done to make Winthrop angry enough to throw her over for a secretary?

And once she knew he was leaving her, had she decided being a widow was better than being a divorcée?

My fingers tightened around the steering wheel and the tension in my neck had me rolling my shoulders. I knew firsthand, when it came to murder, everyone suspected the surviving spouse. I also knew having long-time friends suspect you of murder was a horrible feeling. Until there was conclusive proof otherwise, I had to give Ruth the benefit of the doubt.

What of Joanie's husband? He certainly had an axe to grind with Winthrop Marshall. Had the police looked at him?

Lost in thought, I pulled into the drive, and slammed on the brakes.

Anarchy's car was parked right outside the front door.

I hadn't been ready to talk to Ruth nor was I ready to talk to Anarchy. Especially not with Karma in the house.

Was it too late to throw the car in reverse?

The front door opened and Anarchy stepped outside and gazed at me.

It was too late.

With a sigh that reached from the top of my head to the tip of my toes, I put the car in park, turned off the ignition, and got out of the car. Slowly. Slow enough for the weight of dread to settle in my stomach.

"You're home." Anarchy shoved his hands in his pockets and offered me a heart-stopping aw-shucks smile.

"I am."

"Aggie said you went to Winthrop Marshall's funeral."

"Yes." I had no intention of making small talk.

"I've been waiting for you."

"I'm sure Karma kept you entertained." That sounded catty. A soul-deep wound and the tattered remains of a hangover could make the nicest of women sound catty—and, on my best day, I was not the nicest of women.

Anarchy's cheeks flushed. "About Karma—"

My stomach did a sideways maneuver and I covered my mouth in case the cookie I'd cadged on my way out of the church decided to reappear. "Please. I don't want to talk about you and Karma. Not now."

"I know things at the hospital looked—"

I held up my hand and shook my head. What part of *I don't want to talk about it* did he not understand?

Anarchy descended the front stoop and strode across the drive, stopping directly in front of me. "It was a long time ago."

La-la-la-la-la. I don't want to talk about it. My heart couldn't take another hit. Nor my stomach—I really should not have eaten that cookie.

"Ellison." One hand closed around my left arm. The other hand tilted my chin until I had to look into his coffee-brown eyes. "The past is past. There's only you."

His expression was serious. His eyes beseeched.

I searched his face for a lie and didn't find one.

This was Anarchy Jones, the man who followed rules, the man who was nothing like Henry. If we were going to move forward, I had to trust him.

"What you saw at the hospital looked bad but—"

"It looked awful." Even now the wave of hurt threatened to drown me.

"It wasn't what it looked like. I'm sorry." His voice overflowed with sincerity. "I didn't think about how things might appear. Forgive me? Please?"

I sniffed.

"Please? We've got something here. Something special. I'd kick myself—forever—if I messed it up.

Staying angry would be a lot easier if I didn't have to look into his eyes—and if he didn't sound so damned earnest. And trustworthy. And genuine.

"Ellison." He touched my cheek with the tips of his fingers. "I want this to work."

I could send him away or I could take a risk. There had been very few risks in my well-orchestrated life until I found my first body. Since then, I'd been a tightrope walker without a net. But trusting was the biggest risk of all. If I wanted Anarchy in my life, I had to trust him. And I had to be honest. "I was jealous. And hurt." I turned my face away from his steady gaze. "I know that sounds pathetic."

"Are you kidding? If I walked into a room and saw Tafft holding your hand, I'd lose my mind. I should have explained right away. Please, forgive me."

"It doesn't sound as if there's anything to forgive."

"Forgive me anyway."

"Done." The anvil in my stomach disintegrated and I leaned my head forward until it rested against his chest.

His arms circled me and his chin rested atop my head. "Do you think Marian Dixon is watching us?"

Marian Dixon, nosy neighbor extraordinaire, spent her days watching the goings-on at my house.

"I'm sure of it."

"Damn."

"Why?" I lifted my head and gazed up at him.

"Because I'd really like to kiss you."

My heart did a triple-flip in my chest. "We could give her a thrill."

The grin on Anarchy's face made my bones melt.

He leaned down.

I raised up on my tiptoes.

Our breath mixed.

Our lips parted.

"Mom!" Grace stood in the front doorway. "I need you! Now!"

A teenage daughter who thought she didn't need her mother calling for help was as good as a cold shower for killing a romantic moment. "What's happened?"

"McCallester got out."

Meeeow!

Woof! Woof, woof, woof!

Crash!

Oh dear Lord.

I took off running.

The foyer was eerily quiet. Calm-before-all-hell-broke-loose quiet.

"How did the cat get out of your room?"

Worry furrowed Grace's brows. "I thought if I just introduced them..."

"Grace." I used one word to say everything. Max wasn't interested in cat friends, he was interested in cat pelts. She'd promised to keep the two separated. She'd broken her promise.

"I know but—"

Crash!

"Where are they?"

"They might be in your studio,"

"My studio?"

"McCallester ran down here, then he ran back upstairs. The door to the attic was the only one open."

I bounded up the stairs. There were paints and paint thinner and finished canvases and things I cared about in the studio.

Woof!

Meow!

I ran faster.

I turned the corner at the top of the attic stairs and stopped.

Grace ran into me and my knees collapsed. We tumbled onto the hardwood floor.

All the better to see the upset drafting table, the pool of cold coffee on the floor, and McCallester on the top of an unanchored bookcase filled with notes and sketchbooks and favorite (heavy) art books.

Max stood on his hind legs, his two front paws resting on a shelf, and grinned.

McCallester hissed.

Woof! Max leaned back for a better view and the book case leaned with him.

The cat shifted its panicked yellow gaze to Grace.

I hauled myself up off the floor and lunged for Max's collar. "No! You leave that cat alone."

I was too late. I blame slipping in the pool of coffee.

The bookcase tilted. And fell. Hard enough to shake the house.

Max, who had as many lives as the cat he was chasing, somehow avoided being turned into a pancake. Thank God.

"Max!" I grabbed his collar.

He looked over his shoulder and grinned as if amused by my futile attempt to stop the madness.

McCallester grabbed his chance for escape. He leapt to a table covered by my palette and tubes of paint.

Unfortunately, he landed on an imperfectly closed tube of Napthol red. Paint squirted across the table and the cat ran through it.

Then the red-pawed cat made a break for the stairs.

With super-canine effort, Max pulled free of my grasp on his collar and ran after him.

They were easy to follow, McCallester left a trail of red acrylic paw prints.

I raced down the stairs with Grace at my heels.

McCallester was nothing but a blur of ginger and a trail of red paint.

Max ran so fast he tripped over his paws, completed a somersault, and never broke stride.

They ran toward Anarchy who stood at the top of the stairs.

"Grab Max," I called (begged).

Anarchy hurled his body across the top of the stairs.

With cat-like reflexes (imagine that) McCallester changed course. McCallester leapt.

Off the landing.

For a moment, the cat hung in space. Then, he twisted, wrapped a paw around the chandelier, and hung there.

At the top of the stairs, Anarchy, Grace, and I stared in horror. Max grinned like an evil genius whose plot for world domination has just succeeded.

At the bottom of the stairs, Aggie and Karma gazed up at the swinging cat with slack jaws.

"What are we going to do?" asked Grace.

Max knew. He snaked through our legs and shot down the stairs, taking a position directly below McCallester.

"Aggie, can you get Max to the backyard?" I called (begged).

Aggie stepped forward, her eyes still on the dangling cat. She closed her hand around Max's collar and dragged him down the hall. "Bad dog."

Max was unconcerned with her scolding.

"Do you have a ladder?" asked Anarchy.

"Not one that will reach up there."

"I've got an idea." Karma disappeared into the living room. A moment later she reappeared, dragging one of a pair of Scalamandré-covered club chairs behind her. She positioned the chair beneath the cat.

Just in time.

McCallester fell, landing on four paint-covered paws.

I groaned. Why couldn't Karma have chosen one of the ugly chairs from Henry's office?

Grace ran down the stairs and wrapped the ginger-haired devil in her arms.

"We can't keep that cat." I spoke under my breath.

But Anarchy must have heard me. His brows rose.

I looked down at my coffee-soaked suit, down at the trail of red paw prints on the carpet, down at the ruined upholstery. "Either my house will be rubble or Max will kill the cat. Possibly both. Grace was supposed to find it a home." That cat might be the straw that broke the camel's back. I covered my eyes with the heels of my palms. Keep the cat and ensure destruction of everything I owned or return the cat to the shelter and break Grace's heart.

"I'll take it."

I took my hands away from my eyes. "What?"

"I miss having a pet and having a dog wouldn't be fair to the dog. I'm not home enough. But cats—they're independent."

"You mean it?" Hope fizzed like champagne.

"I wouldn't offer if I didn't."

"You just got yourself a cat." Then, with Grace and Karma and McCallester watching, I threw my arms around Anarchy's neck and kissed him.

FIFTEEN

"Anarchy took the cat?" Libba smirked at me from across the bridge table. "I told you talking to him was the right thing to do."

Discussing Anarchy over the bridge table was such a bad idea. I glanced out the window. The golf course was showing the first signs of green, and, given the mild weather, there were sweatered golfers taking full advantage.

"Why exactly did you have a cat?" Jinx shuffled a deck of cards. "I'd think that dog of yours would object."

Ruined carpet, ruined upholstery, and a disaster-area studio all flashed through my mind. "He did object. Strongly. And, believe me, I had nothing to do with bringing that cat into the house. Grace brought it home from a shelter."

One of Jinx's brows raised slightly. "Why was Grace at an animal shelter?"

"She was volunteering."

"How many more animals is she going to bring home?"

"None. She promised." Famous last words.

Jinx chuckled. "Maybe she should volunteer as a candy striper instead."

Daisy exploded into the card room, late as usual. "Am I late? I'm sorry."

She was late but it was a surprise when Daisy was on time. She had more children than the little old woman who lived in a shoe. And just when she thought the end was in sight, she and her husband had been blessed with a surprise. She wasn't showing yet, but she also wasn't drinking and she'd somehow prevailed upon Jinx to forego smoking when we played cards.

"How are you feeling?" I asked.

"There's a reason women get pregnant when they're young." She sat, dropping her handbag, which, thanks to all the things her children stuffed inside, usually weighed upwards of ten pounds (I knew, I'd swung it once) on the carpet next to her chair. "Just a little morning sickness."

I made a sympathetic noise.

Jinx merely fanned the cards.

We each drew.

"I guess I'm dealing." Libba threw her high card, the queen of spades, back into the deck.

As Libba distributed the cards, Jinx leveled an I'm-cranky-because-I-need-a-cigarette look my way. "You've had quite a week."

"That's right!" Daisy leaned forward. "Tell us about your latest body."

"It's not my body."

"Oh, pooh!" Daisy's face scrunched. "You know what I mean."

"I found Winthrop dead."

"And Frank Marshall's secretary," added Jinx. "Don't forget her."

As if I'd ever forget finding a body at The Nelson.

"Is that the woman Frank was fooling around with?" Libba finished dealing.

Remembering Celine's flushed cheeks, I replied, "No idea." I wouldn't add fuel to that fire. I picked up my cards and counted ten middling points.

"Well—" Daisy rearranged the cards in her hand "—I heard he was carrying on with one of Celine's friends."

"Where did you hear that?" I hadn't heard so much as a whisper about Frank and someone we saw socially.

Daisy waved her free hand with an airy (ditsy) lack of concern. "Someone told me. I can't remember who." She scrunched her face again and shifted a card. "Maybe Bea? I stopped by yesterday with a casserole."

"Can Buzz eat casseroles?" asked Jinx.

"I didn't think about dietary restrictions." Daisy chested her cards and her brow wrinkled. "Can he eat bacon or cheese?"

"I'm sure Bea appreciated your thoughtfulness." I wasn't remotely sure of that. "What did she say about Frank?"

"I honestly can't remember. I had Janie with me." Janie was Daisy's six-year-old. A tornado impersonating a little girl. "I had to keep an eye on her."

Libba looked at me from across the table—a look fraught with meaning. "One spade."

"Pass."

I glanced at my hand. "Two spades."

"Pass."

"Four spades."

I hoped Libba had enough points for game because I did not.

Daisy played the ace of diamonds and I put down my hand.

Libba tsked as if her four spade bid was my fault.

"I stopped at two."

"I know," she groused.

"Ellison, what are you wearing to the gala?" Daisy winced as Libba trumped her ace.

"A jade green silk gown."

"Sounds pretty."

"It's too conservative." Libba played the ace of spades from her hand.

"This isn't the party to be daring."

"Yes, it is." Libba curled in satisfaction as Daisy threw the queen of spades. "Do you have any other ideas?"

"Well, I did see a dress at Swanson's."

"Oh?" Libba looked up from her study of the board. "And?"

"Chinese red Ultrasuede from Halston."

"We'll go look at it when we're done here. That jade gown looks like something Frances picked out."

"Mother has exquisite taste."

Libba played the king of spades. "And she's a generation older than you."

There was no point in talking when Libba got like this—I couldn't win—and all because she'd overbid our hands. "I'm going to run to the ladies' room while you play this. Good luck."

Libba grunted and stared at the club Daisy had sloughed.

I walked toward the ladies' lounge wondering if maybe I should buy the red dress after all.

"I can't believe you asked her." An outraged voice floated down the hall from the lounge.

"Ellllison Russell is a lovvvvely woman."

My steps faltered. Whatever was happening, I didn't want to walk in on it.

"She finds dead people," said the voice I couldn't identify.

"She's a luuuuvely woman." Nan Roddingham's drawn out syllables were unmistakable.

"Oh, please. She finds dead people. All the time. And you invited her to join the book club."

"Not just me. All the posssssible members were on a balllllot. Ellison won the most votes."

"More than me? I can't believe it. I can't believe so many people would vote for her. She's not book club material." Whoever Nan was talking to, the woman wasn't one of my fans.

"She is book club material and there will be annnnother opening in a few months."

"The spot you gave to Ellison should be mine. I'm a legacy. Ellison Russell is—well, she's a Bohemian."

I was?

"She's dating that cop."

I was.

"She's not our kind."

I wasn't? My hands fisted. I should go in there and say something. I took a step forward but a horrific choking sound stopped me—someone in the lounge was doing an impersonation of a cat ridding itself of a hairball.

"Our kind? What kind is that, dear?" Mother's voice was chilly. "The jealous kind? The petty kind? The little-people-have-little-minds kind?"

There were days I adored Mother. This was one of them.

"Mrs. Walford, I didn't realize you were in the water closet."

"Obviously." Mother's tone could freeze a swimming pool in mid-July. "My daughter is smart and accomplished and one of the pre-eminent women artists in the country. She knows interesting people. She has interesting thoughts. She's a fabulous addition to book club."

I pressed my hands to my heart.

"As for that detective she's seeing, his father is a professor and his mother is a respected artist."

How did Mother know that? I didn't remember telling her.

"Correct me if I'm wrong, but doesn't your father own a hardware store?"

Ouch!

"At least my father doesn't have any illegitimate children." The woman's voice was small but filled with venom. Whoever she was, she had a death wish. It was one thing to insult me, another thing to insult Frances Walford's husband.

"Are you referring to Karma?" Mother's tone cooled well beyond freezing a swimming pool. She could freeze a lake. A large one. Michigan and Superior combined.

"Is that her name?" The woman was foolish enough to allow a sneer in her voice.

"It is. Karma Michaels. She has an MBA from Stanford. She's charming, well-respected, and has better things to do than belittle people who are better educated and smarter than she is."

Wow. Mother was owning the story.

"I don't care if she becomes the first woman president of the United States. She was still born on the wrong side of the blanket." The woman in the lounge would rue those words. Forever. She'd just earned a lifetime of poor committee placements (if she was even asked to be on a committee). She would never chair a gala, never run the Junior League, never join the book club she cared so much about.

"You know, Dear. On reflection, I think you're right. Ellison isn't your kind. Neither is Karma." There was a moment of silence and I could picture Mother patting a hair into place before she wielded the killing blow. "I'm rather pleased about that."

Another moment of silence. I'd bet anything Mother was tapping her lips with her index finger before she swung her axe. "Remind me, what committees you're working on."

If she was smart, the woman would apologize and run. Not that running would do her any good. She'd picked a fight with Frances Walford, insulted her daughter and her husband. Those committee jobs would disappear before the end of the day.

Whoever she was, I didn't want her catching me listening at the door. I slipped into a phone booth but left the door cracked so the overhead light wouldn't come on.

A second later, Gaye Hardy fled the ladies' lounge.

Gaye Hardy? Really? When she'd sat next to me at the funeral I'd thought we might be moving from acquaintances to friends.

As soon as she was out of sight, I abandoned the phone booth and hurried down the hallway. I slipped into my seat as Libba took the last trick. "Did you make it?"

"I did." She glanced up at me. "What's wrong? You look as if you've seen a ghost."

"No ghosts. Mother's here."

"Ah." Libba needed no further explanation. "Are you going to Veronica Crawford's engagement party on Saturday night?"

Veronica Crawford. I'd watched her grow up. It seemed impossible she was old enough to get married.

"I am."

"By yourself?" Libba would rather walk naked down Nichols Parkway than go to a party alone.

"Why not?"

"Who's she marrying?" asked Daisy.

"Kate and Bill Matthews' son, Chip. I give it a year. If that."

Apparently the need for a cigarette had made Jinx cranky. She usually allowed young people at least a few years of happiness before she foretold divorce.

"Why just a year?" asked Daisy.

"Have you seen them together? They're getting married because that's what people do not because they're madly in love."

"Maybe shared goals are more important than love," said Libba.

"Nope," said the cranky, jaded woman at the table. "Love is what matters."

We played cards until half past two when Daisy looked at her watch and gasped. "I have to leave for carpool."

"Let's drive to Swanson's together," Libba suggested.

I'd forgotten all about her plan to have me buy yet another dress. Given that the Halston gown still lurked in thoughts, trying it on was a sound decision. "Fine."

"I'll drive."

We said goodbye to Jinx at the door to the clubhouse and climbed into Libba's 450sl.

"How are things going with your house guest?"

"I feel a talk coming on."

"I'm just asking," Libba snapped.

"I mean I feel a talk coming for me and Karma."

Libba glanced at me out of the corner of her eye. "I'm here if you need me."

"Thanks."

"I bought more vodka."

I reached across the seat and squeezed her hand. "Thanks."

Libba pulled into the parking garage next to Swanson's, slotted her Mercedes across two spaces, and walked toward the entrance. "Hurry up." She was always eager to shop.

I'd already spent enough at Swanson's. I trailed behind her.

We'd entered on the second floor. Couture was to our left. Libba strode that direction. I followed more slowly, pausing to feel a fabric and inspect a seam (I loved lower-priced clothing lines—I didn't feel as bad when blood soaked the cuffs or spattered the collar).

Libba looked over her shoulder. "Are you coming?"

I dropped the sleeve of a silk blouse, turned, and bumped into someone.

The someone dropped her purse.

We both bent to retrieve the bag and knocked our heads.

"Ouch." I took a step backward. "I'm so sorry."

"My fault." Hester Nelson straightened. "Ellison!" A caught-with-her-hand-in-the-cookie-jar expression blossomed on her long face.

"You're still in town."

"Chauncey's business kept him here a few more days." Her gaze traipsed across Swanson's lovely offerings. "I thought I'd shop."

"Ellison—" Libba had doubled back "—are you coming?"

"Libba, this is Hester Nelson from New York. Hester, this is my best friend, Libba."

Aside from the obvious—they were both women—the two were polar opposites. Libba, dressed in wide-leg black pants, killer heels, and an apple green silk blouse, wore full makeup and not a hair on her head was out of place. Hester wore a wrap skirt, sensible pumps, and a twin set. Her face was free of makeup and her hair hung limp around her cheeks. The two might have come from different planets.

"Nice to meet you." Libba extended her hand.

"A pleasure."

They shook.

A shadow crossed over Libba's face. "How do you know Ellison?"

"She was kind enough to take me shopping earlier this week. The day it was so cold."

"Ah. What brings you to Kansas City?"

"I came with my husband. He's here on business." Hester looked over her shoulder as if Chauncey might be monitoring her spending. "I really should go. Ellison, it was nice to see you again. Libba, nice meeting you.

"Nice to meet you too." Libba grabbed me by the arm and dragged me toward couture.

"Goodbye, Hester. Have a safe trip back to New York." I turned to Libba. "That was incredibly rude."

"Pish."

"Pish?"

"That woman had a limp fish handshake. My father told me never to trust anyone whose hand felt like a three-day-old flounder."

"You can't judge a woman on her handshake."

"What am I supposed to judge her on? Her clothes?" Libba's silk-clad shoulders shuddered.

"Her accomplishments?"

"What has that woman accomplished?"

I didn't have an answer.

"Come on. Let's take a look at the Halston. You need something to wear."

SIXTEEN

After pussy-footing around for nearly an hour, Libba bought the Halston. For herself.

"You're sure you don't mind? You saw it first." Libba's brow wrinkled with concern as Esme slotted a well-worn charge plate into the swiper and made an imprint of Libba's card.

"I'm positive." Chinese red looked far better on her than me and the daring neckline was better suited to a woman who invited attention. I peeked at my watch.

"Someplace to be?"

"Errands." A lie, but far easier than explaining the complicated family dynamic upending my life. The truth: Daddy was spending the afternoon with Karma and I'd promised to be home early so he could get home to Mother.

Mother. My heart warmed when I thought of the dressing down she'd given Gaye.

I could not be late.

Esme presented Libba with a receipt and Libba signed, pausing mid flourish. "Esme, Ellison needs a different dress for the gala—a real showstopper."

Oh dear Lord. The jade gown I'd decided upon was fine. I said as much.

"You deserve better than fine. You should look amazing. It's your gala. Your night." Libba's heart was in the right place, but she should mind her own darned business.

"I like the jade dress. Ignore her, Esme."

"'Like' isn't good enough. I want you to have a dress you can't wait to wear."

"That's sweet of you, but—"

"Don't tell me the gown is fine."

"All right, I won't." I glanced again at my watch. Daddy. Karma. Mother. "I have to go."

Libba scrunched her face at me then she opened her index and middle fingers into a "v," touched her eyes, and waved her v'd hand at the fabulous clothes in the couture salon. "Esme, I'm counting on you."

Being caught between two of her best customers was not an ideal spot for Esme. She offered us a vague smile. "I'll talk to the buyers."

"Libba, we have to go. Now."

We hurried back to her car and she sped to the club.

"Are you all right?" She glanced at me. I wished she wouldn't. As fast as she was driving, her glances should be reserved for the road.

"I'm fine." My fingers clutched the door handle.

"Did something happen earlier? While we were at the club?"

Apparently some part of me was piqued about the things Gaye had said about me. I didn't want to repeat them. "Other than almost running into Mother? Do you have any idea how angry she is about Karma?"

Libba pursed her lips, not entirely buying my explanation. "You left for the ladies' lounge in one mood and came back in another. A mood change like that—you'd have to actually run into Frances."

Libba knew me well.

I slumped against the seat. "Can I tell you about it later?"

"I suppose." She glanced my way again. "I won't forget."

Libba had a memory like an elephant (I knew her as well as she knew me).

"I know you won't. I promise, I'll tell you later."

"I'm worried about you." Libba took a corner at top speed.

"You seem tense. I think you should come to yoga with me."

My nail prints permanently embedded in her door handle.

"Yoga? Since when do you do yoga?"

Libba ignored my question. "Yoga will help with your stress."

In the past several days, I'd found two bodies, welcomed my half-sister as a houseguest, sat in a ringside seat for one of Mother's implosions, watched helplessly as a cat destroyed my home, and questioned my relationship with Anarchy. "The only thing causing me stress is your driving like Evel Knievel."

She eased off the accelerator. Slightly. "Yoga works miracles." She spoke with the zeal of the newly converted.

"We'll see." I wasn't making any promises. If I put her off long enough, she'd move on to something new.

Libba zipped up the long drive to the clubhouse and parked in the space next to my Mercedes.

I swung out of her car and set grateful feet on the pavement. "I'll talk to you later."

She gave me a you'll-tell-me-what-happened-when-you-went-to-the-lounge-or-I'll-camp-on-your-front-lawn look. "Remember, I want the story. And we're going to yoga."

I settled into the front seat of my car. The blue suit I'd worn when I slipped in the puddle of coffee was bundled onto the passenger's seat. Why hadn't I asked Aggie to run to the dry cleaners?

I did have an errand to run before I entertained Karma.

I motored to the dry cleaners and ran the suit inside.

A woman already stood at the counter. I waited behind her, staring at her back and breathing in the scent of dry cleaning chemicals mixed with freshly laundered linen and starch.

The woman accepted a handful of men's shirts and turned.

"Nan!"

Nan Roddingham squinted at me and donned a polite smile. "Hello."

As far as I was concerned, Nan could squint all she wanted. She'd stood up for me when Gaye Hardy said I wasn't book club material. "So nice to see you."

"You, too. Listen, I musssst run. Talk soon?"

"Of course."

Nan and her husband's shirts hurried out the door. I stepped up to the counter with my suit.

"She can't see a thing without her glasses," said the clerk, an older woman with a cotton-candy spin of white hair, violently pinked cheeks, and a soft blue sweater.

"Pardon me?"

"Mrs. Roddingham. She can't see without her glasses. She didn't know who you were."

I glanced over my shoulder. Nan stood next to a car, digging in her purse, presumably for her keys.

She could dig all she wanted. The keys wouldn't work. She was standing next to my car.

"Truth is—" the clerk, whose name was Betty, reclaimed my attention, looking at me from behind the rhinestone-speckled rims of her own glasses "—she can't see all that well with them. I only mention it in case you were offended. Some people expect to be recognized."

"Thank you for telling me." I handed over my suit. "I'm afraid I landed in a pool of coffee."

Betty *tsked.* "This will take a few days. Is next week all right?"

"Fine. Thank you."

I glanced again over my shoulder. Nan must have found her keys. She and her Mercedes were gone.

I drove home with the radio on. Dan Fogelberg sang, "Part of the Plan." As if there was an actual plan. As far as I could tell, the world was held together by women like Mother—strong-willed women who held the line against chaos.

Daddy and Karma and Max waited for me in the family room.

Karma was ensconced on the couch with her feet up. A black watch plaid blanket covered her legs.

Daddy perched on the arm of a club chair

He rose when I entered. "How was your afternoon?"

"Interesting." Mother could tell him about Gaye Hardy. I wasn't about to admit to eavesdropping.

He glanced at his watch. "I'll see you girls tomorrow."

"We're not girls." Karma's tone was pleasant, but her brow wrinkled and the expression in her eyes was serious.

Daddy glanced at the ceiling. For an instant. "I'll see you ladies tomorrow."

"I'll walk you to the door."

Together, Daddy and I ambled to the front of the house, as if he wasn't in a hurry to get home to Mother. Max trailed behind us.

"I'll talk to you soon." I raised up on tiptoes and kissed his cheek.

He gave me a quick hug. "Be careful. Your sister is in a mood."

I was in a mood. Mother was in a mood. Moods were going around.

"Thanks for the warning." I opened the front door and watched Daddy walk to his sedan. The potshots life had recently lobbed at my father didn't seem to bother him. His back was straight and his stride confident.

I closed the door, resting my head against the wood. What a day.

Max nudged me.

And the day wasn't over yet. I lifted my head and returned to the family room and Karma. "It's five o'clock. Do you want a drink?"

"The doctor said no alcohol, but you go ahead. You look like you could use one." Karma winced. "That didn't come out right."

"It's okay. It's been a long day."

"What did you do this afternoon?"

"I played bridge then went shopping."

Her brows rose. When I put it that way, my day didn't sound terribly long.

"I overheard someone talking about me at the club."

She tilted her head.

"Mother heard it too."

"Oh."

"And my studio. It's going to take a week to put it back together." Now I sounded whiny.

"Aggie's been up there for most of the day."

Of course she had.

"She's spectacular. My mother never approved of hiring help around the house but, having met Aggie, I can see the appeal."

"Aggie keeps me sane. If you're sure you don't mind, I think I will have a glass of wine."

"Of course I don't mind."

"Back in a jiff." I hurried into the kitchen, pulled the wine from the fridge, and took the bottle back to the family room. There, I poured myself a generous (over-the-top generous) glass.

Karma regarded the level of wine in my glass. "We should talk."

I'd rather not. "Oh?"

"We should talk about Anarchy and me."

I'd *really* rather not. Surely there was a limit to the number of difficult conversations one had to endure. "I think it's time for the evening news." I walked toward the television.

"I know things looked bad at the hospital when you walked in, but—"

"Let's just watch for a few minutes." Maybe Walter Cronkite could distract her.

"Our history isn't what you think."

My hand hovered above the dial. "Your history with Anarchy is none of my business."

"We both know that's not true. I've seen the way you look at each other." And she'd still held his hand.

I took an extra-large sip of wine.

"When I was at school—"

"With Anarchy."

"With Anarchy," she conceded. "There was an economics professor who guided me toward a finance degree. He encouraged me to think about finance as a career. He challenged my beliefs in what I could and couldn't do." She looked up from her lap. "I thought of him as a mentor. A second father."

I had a sinking feeling about this story. I tightened my grip on my wine glass.

"When he hit on me, I didn't know what to do. I was shocked and hurt and my confidence was shaken." She regarded me with sad eyes. "Had he said all those things because he believed in me, or was it all part of some elaborate seduction?"

That sinking feeling had been right.

"When I turned him down, told him no, he failed me."

"What did you do?"

"I cried for three days then I asked the person who'd witnessed some of Professor Crosbie's behavior to step forward and back up my story. It was a huge risk for him. It put relationships at risk. Maybe even his future."

I sank onto the couch. "Anarchy was your witness."

"Like I said, we have a history. Just not the one you thought."

This news called for another extra-large sip of wine. "What happened to the professor?"

"Nothing."

"Nothing?"

"Not one thing. He had tenure." There was enough bitterness in her voice for two or three disillusioned co-eds. "The administration had another professor grade my final project. I graduated and tried not to look back." She brushed a strand of hair away from her face. "Anarchy and I lost track of each other. Seeing him here was a surprise."

"I bet."

"We should have told you—I should have told you—but that chapter of my life isn't something I talk about easily. At the time, I second guessed everything I'd ever said to my professor. Did I bring his attention on myself by laughing at his bad jokes or smiling when I said hello? It took me years to realize it wasn't my fault."

The look on her face—furrowed brow, deep frown, haunted eyes—suggested she still wasn't one-hundred percent convinced.

"Thank you for telling me."

"You know what?" She smiled at me. "To hell with doctor's orders. Half a glass of wine won't kill me."

"You're sure?"

"I've never been more sure of anything."

I got up, poured a scant half-glass, and took it to her.

She lifted the glass to her lips. "I'm sorry I didn't tell you sooner."

"I understand."

We drank in silence.

"I met Chauncey Nelson."

"Oh?"

"At my broker's funeral." Another sip of wine. "He said he knew you."

"No." Karma's voice sounded too loud in the family room. "We've never met."

Max lifted his head from his paws and stared at us.

I wasn't about to argue.

Brnng, brnng.

I stood and crossed the room to the phone on my desk. My fingers closed around the receiver. "Hello."

"What did you say to Buzz Bisby?"

"Pardon me?"

"You heard me. What did you say to Buzz?"

"Who is this?"

"Frank Wallace. What the hell did you say to Buzz?"

There was only one thing I'd said that could make Frank this angry. "I told Buzz, if he didn't stand up for his employees, no one else would." I'd hinted Buzz was a coward. I'd hinted Frank was little better than a rapist.

"What happens at my firm is none of your damned business."

"Be that as it may, I—"

"None of your damned business."

"Frank, those women deserve your respect."

He snorted. "Keep your nose out of my affairs."

"Are you threatening me?"

"No. I'm warning you. Stay away from the firm."

SEVENTEEN

I handed the clerk the paperback copy of *Postern of Fate*.

"I love Tommy and Tuppence, don't you?" The clerk smiled at me, eager to discuss Agatha Christie with another reader.

My answering smile was vague. "Of course." Presumably Tommy and Tuppence were the sleuths.

"Although, Miss Marple is my absolute favorite." The clerk wrote my name and address along with *Postern of Fate* and its price on a sales pad. "Will there be anything else today, Mrs. Russell?"

"Just the book." I looked down at the cover. An angry horse face looked back.

The young woman used the tip of her finger to trace a line on a sales tax chart then added the amount to the sales pad. "Two dollars and ten cents, please."

I pulled my billfold from my handbag and handed over a five-dollar bill. "If you'll give me a moment, I'm sure I have a dime."

With the book and three dollars in change in hand, I glanced out the window onto Nichols Road. The Plaza sidewalks were busy with shoppers taking advantage of the mild weather.

I pushed open the door and stepped outside.

"Ellison."

I glanced over my shoulder. Celine Wallace, dressed in a navy wrap skirt embroidered with yellow umbrellas, a twin set, and light coat, stood on the sidewalk impeding the flow of foot traffic. Did she know her husband had threatened me? Her smile was friendly.

I doubted she knew. "How nice to see you."

"You, too. Shopping for books?" Her gaze rested on the yellow paper bag with orange medallions tucked under my arm.

"Yes. A book club read."

"I ordered a book." She nodded at the bookstore. "The clerk called and told me it's in." She shifted her gaze to the concrete beneath her feet. "Such a sad day yesterday."

"It was. Ruth will need all her friends." I rearranged my handbag in the crook of my arm and took a tiny step.

"May I ask you something?" The edge in Celine's voice stilled my feet.

"Of course."

"Do you have time for a cup of coffee?"

I always had time for coffee. I nodded.

"Shall we walk over to Putsch's Coffee Shop?"

Now? She meant now?

"Is there a problem?" Maybe Celine did know Frank had threatened me. Maybe she felt the need to apologize. If so, we could get it over with immediately. "If this is about Frank, I'm sorry I made him so angry—" I wasn't the least bit sorry "—but he shouldn't treat the..."

Celine's chin was wobbling and her eyes were filled with tears

"It's not about Frank being annoyed with me."

"No, it's not. I need your advice."

"Of course." I swallowed a sigh. "Let's go."

We walked side by side. A southerly breeze ruffled my hair. I stole a glance at Celine. Her eyes were red-rimmed. We needed a distraction. "Such a nice day. I hope spring is finally here."

Celine merely nodded.

"What are your plans for Easter?" I asked.

"Easter?" Celine sounded as if I'd introduced a foreign concept. "Easter. I don't know. You?"

"The usual. Services. Brunch. Then, if the weather is nice, Grace and I will play golf with Mother and Daddy." That part of the day was the longest. Long enough that I prayed for rain. There was a reason Mother and Daddy seldom played golf together. Daddy was much better than Mother and he offered advice. Lots of advice. Advice Mother didn't appreciate.

"That sounds nice."

If she only knew.

A gust of wind pulled at the hems of our skirts and we hurried inside the coffee shop where a hostess led us to a table.

We sat and Celine pulled off her gloves and stashed them in her purse. She pressed her lips together. She lit a cigarette and blew smoke toward the ceiling.

"What did you want to talk to me about?" I didn't have all day and Celine looked as if she might take hours before she broached her subject.

"You and Henry had problems." She fixed her gaze on the passers-by outside the window.

"Yes." There was no denying it. Everyone in town knew my husband had cheated on me. With verve.

"And you knew? I mean about the other women?"

"I knew." Poor Celine. Had she just now realized Frank was unfaithful? "Henry, for all his faults, was a good father. We agreed to stay married until Grace went to college. To me that meant a modicum of decorum. To Henry that meant permission to bed as many women as possible."

Celine nodded. Once. At the window. "Frank is—" yet another plume of smoke "—cheating on me."

That I knew.

She crushed out her cigarette in the glass ashtray. "I don't know what to do."

"Do you want to stay married?"

"Yes." She lit another cigarette. "No." She shifted her gaze to me. "I don't know."

"You should decide before you do anything."

She nodded and her shoulders sagged. She planted an elbow on the table and sank her forehead into her hand. "I've known for a while." Celine's voice was hardly a whisper.

I leaned forward, close enough to hear her cigarette burning.

"There have always been girls but they didn't mean anything. I looked the other way." She lifted her head and returned her gaze to the busy sidewalk. "But, there's someone new." A bare murmur.

"I'm sorry."

"He sings in the shower." She patted under her eyes with her free hand then took a deep drag on her cigarette.

How to respond?

"He locks himself in his office and talks on the phone. For hours."

Oh, dear. My heart ached for Celine.

"He's in love."

"I'm so sorry." What had Libba said? Frank was having an affair with someone we knew. "Do you know who it is?"

"I thought it might be Marcy, but Frank doesn't seem upset about her death." She shook her head. "No. That's not true. He's upset. But it's because he was identified as a suspect."

I'd been there when Nan told the police.

"It's a good thing he was with Chauncey Nelson at the time of the murder or he'd be in deep trouble."

So that was why Detective Peters hadn't arrested Frank.

She leaned back, lifted her chin, and gazed at the ceiling. "I never thought this would happen to me."

"It sounds as if you want to keep him."

She kept her focus fixed on the ceiling. "I don't want to be alone."

"It's not so bad."

She snorted and smoke shot from her nose. "You weren't alone for five minutes."

That's not how being widowed and suspected of murder had felt. I'd felt isolated and alone and scared.

"Hunter Tafft and that cop were competing for your attention before Henry was in his grave."

I didn't argue the point. "How long have you known about Frank and this woman?"

"A few months." The weight of her gaze settled on me. "I followed him once." She looked down at her lap and a dull flush colored her cheeks. "More than once. He goes to The Alameda on Thursday mornings." She crushed out her cigarette and looked at the waitress who'd appeared at our table. "Coffee. Just coffee."

"Two, please."

The waitress jotted on her pad. "Do you need cream?"

"Please." I offered the woman a smile and a nod.

"Coming right up." She walked away.

Celine lit another cigarette. "It's funny. Frank met Chauncey Nelson at The Alameda the morning Marcy was killed. One slight change in his routine and Frank gets lucky. He doesn't have to tell the police about his mistress."

Frank had an alibi. That meant Nan and her terrible eyesight had made a mistake about the man in the Asian gallery. Who had she seen?

I reached across the table and squeezed Celine's hand—the one without the cigarette. "What can I do?"

"I don't know. There are mornings I want to cry till I drown in my tears and there are mornings I want to kill him."

"I understand." When Henry died, I'd mourned Grace's father and not my husband. "Maybe you should talk to a lawyer. Find out what your options are."

"That's good advice. Thanks for listening, Ellison. I appreciate it." Her mouth was tight and drawn. Her eyes were narrow and angry. As if she was contemplating murder and not divorce.

We finished our coffee, paid the tab, and stood.

"I need to pick up my book. Thank you for taking time to listen to me."

"Of course."

We stepped out onto the sidewalk.

"Celine, I left my book inside."

"I can wait."

"No, no. You go run your errands. I'll talk to you soon."

With a sad little nod, she replied, "Thank you again." Her

shoulders hunched against the breeze as she walked away.

I dashed back inside.

The hostess was waiting for me. "I have your book right here, Mrs. Russell."

"Thank you."

"Ellison," Bea Bisby had joined us at the hostess stand.

The blessing and curse of the Plaza was that one ran into everyone. Messy hair? In need of fresh lipstick? Run in one's stocking? One was guaranteed to see half of one's circle. "How are you? How's Buzz?"

"Better. I'm just waiting on a prescription." Bea waved in the general direction of Bruce Smith Drugs. "I stopped here for a cup of coffee. I wanted to thank you."

"Thank me?"

"For sending Aggie over with that wonderful meal. It fit exactly within the doctor's guidelines and Buzz enjoyed it. He actually said he might be able to follow the diet."

"Aggie deserves all the credit." All of it. I didn't know a thing about this meal.

"Well, you were kind to think of us." Obviously Bea didn't know how angry I'd made Buzz, how the machines monitoring his heart had beeped, how the nurse had kicked me out of his room. If she did, she wouldn't be telling me I was kind.

"I will pass that on to Aggie."

She smiled bravely. "I won't keep you. Again, thanks so much."

I kissed the air next to her cheek. "You're welcome."

I met Anarchy for lunch at Winstead's.

He slid into the booth and said, "Hi."

"Hi." I couldn't keep a stupid smile off my face. "How's the cat?"

"Grateful to be alive."

"Grace better not bring home more animals. I don't think I can take it." I lifted my coffee cup to my lips and sipped. "I know I can't." The vision of McCallester hanging from the chandelier would haunt my dreams.

"Have you put your studio to rights?"

"Aggie's been working on it. I plan on spending the afternoon up there."

Ruby, Grace's favorite waitress, appeared at our table. "What'll it be?"

"A steakburger, hold the onions, an order of rings, and more coffee when you have a moment."

"And you, sir?"

"Double steak burger with cheese, fries, and a frosty malt."

"You want everything on that burger?"

"Please."

Ruby headed to another table and I returned my attention to Anarchy. "I ran into Celine Wallace this morning."

"Oh?"

"She told me Frank has an alibi for Marcy's murder."

"He does."

"Nan seemed so sure." I took another sip of coffee.

"Eyewitnesses aren't always reliable."

"At least you know it was a man."

"We don't know that."

The hand holding my coffee mug froze halfway to my mouth. "Nan couldn't mistake a man for a woman."

"One of the guards said he saw a woman in the Asian gallery. It's possible she was in the temple and Mrs. Roddingham didn't see her."

"Marcy's neck was broken." That didn't seem like something a woman would do.

Anarchy shrugged. An I've-seen-worse shrug. "Did you learn anything interesting at Wallace's firm?"

"The men in the office prey on the women. The general consensus is that Marcy and Frank were together."

"You don't sound convinced."

"Talk at the bridge table is that Frank's been carrying on with a woman we know."

"Who?"

"No idea. And Celine doesn't know either. Apparently Frank and this mystery woman have their trysts at The Alameda."

"Trysts?" His eyes sparkled.

"Trysts," I repeated. Trysts sounded so much better than the sordid reality.

"I'd think The Alameda would be a great place to get caught."

I considered. "Maybe. Maybe not."

Ruby appeared and put paper-wrapped burgers on tiny plates and sundae dishes overflowing with onion rings and French fries in front of us. "Anything else?"

Anarchy gave her one of his melting smiles. "My frosty?"

"More coffee?"

"Comin' right up."

"What do you mean maybe not?" Anarchy asked.

"It's easy to get to the rooms in The Alameda without going through the lobby. And if someone is seen, it's a lot easier to explain being there than at some no-tell motel."

Anarchy took a bite of his steak burger and groaned.

My fingers snuck across the table and stole one of his French fries.

"I saw that."

"You can have a ring." I pushed the dish toward him. "Half a ring. The going rate for a whole ring is two fries."

We grinned at each other and our gazes caught.

We might have stared at each other all afternoon if Ruby hadn't appeared with Anarchy's frosty.

She put it down on the table in front of Anarchy, shook her head as if we were teenagers mooning over each other, and walked away.

"Did you learn anything about Marshall?"

"He was sleeping with a woman named Joanie."

"Joanie Wilson?"

"That's the one."

"She didn't say anything to us."

"I ran into her in the powder room at Winthrop's funeral. She was distraught over his death. She claimed he was going to leave Ruth."

"Really?"

I nodded.

"Maybe Mrs. Marshall preferred being a widow to a divorcée."

"Ruth?" Doubt colored my voice. "I can't see it."

Anarchy helped himself to an onion ring.

"That'll cost you two fries."

"Deal." He bit into the ring and chewed.

I took a bite of my burger.

"You talked to Karma?"

I choked on my burger. "She told you?"

"No. You just seem..."

"Calmer?"

"I guess."

"You helped her."

"Anyone would have done the same."

"No. They wouldn't."

"It wasn't like there was much on the line for me. It was easy to do the right thing."

"That's not how she tells it."

He shook his head. "The professor who put moves on her—he was one of my father's best friends. The only fallout for me was making my father angry."

"Was he? Angry?"

"Very. He told me I should have minded my own damned business. I told him his principles meant nothing if he'd let a young woman be victimized. We didn't talk for a year."

"That must have been hard."

"My father can be very rigid."

Saying nothing seemed the smartest course.

"I'm glad Karma told you."

"Me, too."

Again our gazes caught.

Ruby chuckled as she poured me more coffee.

I sneaked my fingers across the table and grabbed a fry. "Thief."

"Nope. You still owe me one."

We were too old to smile like idiots. We did it anyway.

Finally, Anarchy shifted his gaze to his steakburger. "You're putting your studio back together today?"

Did he have a better offer? "That's the plan."

"I don't suppose you'd talk to Joanie Wilson again?"

"About what?"

"About her relationship with Winthrop Marshall and anything else that was going on at the firm."

"You think Joanie killed Winthrop?"

"If I did, I wouldn't ask you to talk with her." He picked up his spoon and sank it into the frosty. "The way you found him—"

Pants around his ankles and his—no. I wouldn't ruin a wonderful lunch thinking about Winthrop's equipment.

"The way you found him suggests someone wanted to humiliate him. Even in death."

"I'll talk to Joanie." I'd also talk to Ruth. Of all the people who might have wanted to humiliate Winthrop, his widow was the first in line. Second in line were the husbands and boyfriends of the women Winthrop had harassed. Well, maybe. Maybe the actual women were second in line. There were also former employees and probably an ex-mistress or two. There was no shortage of people who might have wanted to kill him.

"Take Aggie with you."

"Aggie?"

"I don't want you going alone."

"Promise."

Our gazes caught and this time we didn't let go.

EIGHTEEN

When I arrived home, I went straight to the kitchen where Aggie was rubbing seasoning on a roast as Max supervised. Carefully supervised. "You took dinner to the Bisbys?"

"I did." She nodded her head and her earrings bobbed like crazy. "I remember what it's like to have an ailing husband."

I crossed my arms. "You gave me credit."

She shrugged and returned her attention to the roast. "You sending a meal made sense. A meal from your housekeeper seemed odd."

I looked for an argument and couldn't find one. "Bea is very grateful and Buzz enjoyed everything you fixed. So much so, he thinks he can stick to a low-sodium diet."

Aggie's grin was as bright as the afternoon sunshine. "I'm glad they liked it."

"Is Karma here?" Daddy had taken her on that promised tour of the Board of Trade.

"Not yet." Aggie put the well-seasoned roast in a pan and tucked carrots, potatoes, and pearl onions around it.

We were alone. Now was the perfect time to ask for her help. "I had lunch with Anarchy."

"Oh?" She nestled a potato closer to the roast.

"He'd like me to talk to Joanie Wilson."

"Who?"

"The woman who was sleeping with Winthrop. According to Joanie, he was going to leave Ruth."

Aggie turned the pan, checking the roast from all angles. "He wants you to get involved?" Doubt cooled her tone. She adjusted a potato and slid dinner into the oven.

"He'd like you to go with me."

She looked over her shoulder. "Really?"

"Really."

The corners of her lips curved and her brows rose. "And he doesn't think we're interfering?"

"Joanie has already talked to me once. The police got nothing from her."

"When?"

"How about tomorrow? The only thing on my calendar is an engagement party tomorrow night. Which reminds me, I need to call Vicky Crawford."

"Tomorrow is fine." She grinned and adjusted the temperature dial on the oven. "As long as you're going to be on the phone, I put your messages on your desk."

"Thanks. Let me get through these calls then we'll put together a strategy for talking with Joanie."

Max followed me into the family room and rubbed his head against my leg.

"I love you, too." I scratched behind his ears as I shuffled through the messages with my free hand. Mother had called. Twice. And Ruth Marshall. And Grace's pre-calculus teacher.

I ignored the messages and called Vicky.

"Crawford residence."

"May I please speak with Mrs. Crawford?"

"Who may I say is calling?"

"Ellison Russell."

"One moment, Mrs. Russell." Vicky's housekeeper put down the phone.

A few seconds later, Vicky was on the line. "Ellison, how are you?"

"Fine, thanks, but I have a favor to ask."

"Oh?"

"Would it put you out if I brought a guest?"

Vicky didn't reply.

"You see, I have a houseguest and I can't just leave her at home alone. May I please bring her with me tomorrow night?"

"Of course. The more the merrier." Vicky sounded relieved. Had she thought I wanted to bring Anarchy? Why was that a problem?

"Thank you. I'm so thrilled for Veronica and Chip."

"Hard to believe my little girl is old enough to get married."

"She'll be a beautiful bride." No lie. Veronica was a lovely young woman. "I won't keep you. I'm sure you've got a million things to do."

"I do. I'll see you and your houseguest tomorrow night."

"Looking forward to it." I hung up the phone and considered my options. Mother. Ruth. Ms. Divestri.

Eeny, meeny, miney, moe? None of them promised a pleasant conversation.

I sat down at my desk and dialed the school's number. "This is Ellison Russell calling for Ms. Divestri."

"I'm sorry, she's in class right now."

"Please tell her I returned her call. I should be at home for the rest of the afternoon."

"Of course, Mrs. Russell."

"Thank you." I hung up the phone, wadded up the phone message, and threw it in the trash. Hopefully, the other two calls would be as painless.

I dialed Mother's number.

The phone rang three times before Mother's housekeeper picked up the extension. "Walford residence."

"Penelope, it's Ellison. Is Mother at home?"

"I'm sorry, Mrs. Russell. She's not in."

I leaned back in my chair and allowed myself a smile. I'd picked the perfect time to return calls. "Will you please tell her I phoned?"

"Yes, ma'am."

I put the receiver back in the cradle. One more call. Could my luck hold?

I dialed.

"Hello."

"Ruth, it's Ellison Russell returning your call."

"Oh. Ellison. Thanks for calling."

"How are you?"

"Holding up."

"You will let me know if there's anything I can do?"

"Actually, there is something."

Uh-oh. "Name it."

"Um...well...the thing is..."

I waited.

And waited.

Oh dear Lord. If Ruth couldn't just tell me, whatever she wanted had to be enormous. I rested my head on the back of the chair and closed my eyes.

"The firm..." she began.

I waited a good fifteen seconds for more. "The firm?"

"With Winthrop's death, and then that secretary's, the firm is on shaky ground."

"Marcy."

"Pardon me?"

"The secretary's name was Marcy."

"That's right. Marcy." The sound of her swallow carried through the phone line. "The firm doesn't need more bad publicity."

I waited.

And waited.

Another swallow. "I know the men there haven't always behaved—"

I snorted.

"—but those girls need their jobs. If you keep talking about Winthrop and Frank's indiscretions, the firm will lose business."

"They were more than indiscretions, Ruth."

"You're right. You're right. But Winthrop's ownership in the firm is my biggest asset. I can't afford for the firm to be the subject of gossip."

Ruth owned a third of the firm.

"You could change things."

"What?" Ruth didn't actually say *Ellison, you've lost your mind,* but I heard it in her voice.

"You could."

"The girls at the firm are pretty and young and they dress to attract attention. It doesn't matter where they work, men are going to show an interest."

"Right now, if they say no, they can be fired."

"There's nothing I can do."

"Of course there is. You just told me you owned one-third of the business."

"Do you really think Buzz and Frank will listen to me? Especially about how they treat their staff? All they want is to buy me out. Assuming the firm is worth anything after all this."

"Right now, you own a third. You should have a say in how things are run."

"I can't change things."

"Then I can't stop talking about those girls."

Ruth's answering silence was chilly. And long.

"You could change things, Ruth. Someone has to."

I waited.

And waited.

"If I talk to Frank and Buzz about this, you'll stop talking?" Ruth's voice was chilly enough to cool the receiver in my hand.

"For now. If things change for the better, I won't ever mention it again."

"I'll talk to them."

"Then I'll keep quiet."

"Are they worth it?" Icicles formed on the edge of the phone.

"What do you mean?"

"Are women you hardly know worth ending a friendship?"

"The friend I know would never stand for what's been happening at that firm."

"High-minded ideals are wonderful things for those who can afford them."

I'd promised I'd ask her more about Winthrop's death but, perhaps, now wasn't the best time.

The click of a receiver meeting its cradle made the point moot.

I didn't sleep. Ruth's last words ran like ticker-tape through my brain. Was she right?

Maybe. It was easy for me to tell her what she needed to do. Was I sure the same thing wasn't happening to the women who worked for the bank Grace had inherited from her father?

I threw off the covers, got out of bed, and paced.

Max, raised a single eye-lid. Why was I disturbing his rest?

"Fine," I huffed. I pulled on a bathrobe and went in search of Mr. Coffee. He didn't care if I woke him up in the middle of the night.

Except, when I got to the kitchen, Mr. Coffee wasn't alone.

Karma sat at the kitchen counter, staring at one of my paintings. She shifted her gaze to me and her mouth curved in a wry grin. "I couldn't sleep."

"Me neither."

"Something bothering you?" she asked.

"The way women are treated at the firm where my money is invested. What about you?"

"Believe it or not, I was missing my mother."

"Do you want to talk about it?"

Karma stared at me for a long second then nodded her head.

"Shall I make a pot of coffee?"

"Decaf?"

Ugh. "Sure." I filled Mr. Coffee's pot with water then poured the water into his reservoir.

"I never could have come here while she was alive."

"Why not?"

"She would have taken it the wrong way."

I raised my brows and scooped decaf coffee into the filter.

"It's hard to explain."

I pressed Mr. Coffee's button. "How so?"

"Wanting to know more about Dad's other kids—she would have seen coming here as a repudiation of her choice."

"I think most daughters have a hard time living up to the lives their mothers want for them."

"You and Frances don't seem to have any problems."

I simply stared at her. Gobsmacked. When I regained the ability to speak, I said, "We have plenty of problems."

"Really?"

"She disapproves of my job, the man in my life, and my habit of finding bodies. She seems to think I find them on purpose. For the express purpose of vexing her."

"My mother hated what I do for a living. Making money for people who already had enough—that's what she called it."

I winced on Karma's behalf.

"Mother sees the way I run my life as a reflection of her and the way she raised me. That's why the finding bodies thing is such a problem." I pulled two mugs from the cabinet and poured cream into the creamer. "Do you take sugar?"

"Just cream." Karma rested her arms on the kitchen island and lowered her head. "If my mother saw things the way yours does, she would be terribly disappointed."

"In you? I don't believe it. You succeeded in a man's world. I bet she was proud."

"If so, she never told me."

"I know Daddy is proud of you."

Karma's smile was wistful.

"And I am."

She lifted her head and looked at me as if I'd sprouted a set of horns. "You are?"

"I am. I've seen how the women are treated at the brokerage

firm where I do business—did business—here in Kansas City. For a woman to thrive in that kind of environment she has to be strong and smart and driven."

"Thank you."

"You're welcome." I grabbed Mr. Coffee's pot, filled two mugs, and pushed one across the counter toward her. "I'm glad you came."

"You are?"

"Absolutely, I am." I added cream to my coffee then pushed the little pitcher towards her. "We're going to a party tomorrow—" I glanced at the clock on the wall "—tonight. I'll introduce you to some of my friends."

Karma poured cream in her coffee then wrapped her hands around the mug. "You've been nicer than I dared hope."

I shrugged. "We're family. Sisters." She probably didn't want me to see the tears welling in her eyes, so I picked up a tea towel and wiped off Aggie's immaculate counter.

"Do sisters hug?"

Now there were tears in my eyes too. Dammit. "All the time."

"What are you two doing?" Grace looked at us with an adults-are-whacky expression.

Maybe we were—hugging in the kitchen in the middle of the night.

"Having coffee."

My daughter rolled her eyes.

"Do you want a cup? It's decaf."

"Nope."

"Do you want to tell me why your math teacher is calling me?"

"She wants me to tutor some kids."

"So you're not failing math?"

That earned me another eye roll. While I could manage arithmetic, Grace's ability to do serious mathematics was inherited from her father. "Of course not." Her tone said *duh*.

"Good." One less unpleasant phone call in my future. "Do you want to tutor other kids?"

"It could be cool." Grace shrugged as if tutoring didn't matter but I saw the light in her eyes. She pulled a stool away from the kitchen island and sat. "Why are you guys up?"

"We couldn't sleep."

"And coffee helps with that."

When had Grace become so sassy?

"I think it's cool you found each other." Her gaze traveled between Karma and me. "I'd love to have a sibling."

For all I knew, she might have one—a secret sibling like Karma. With Henry having been Henry, the possibilities were good.

"The sister I grew up with borrowed my clothes, my lipsticks, and my boyfriends—all without asking."

"But you had an ally. Someone who was always on your side."

I choked on a sip of coffee. "Do you have any idea how many times your aunt sold me out to your grandmother?"

"Yeah, but she stood up for you at school and the club and other places."

"True." My sister Marjorie had reserved the right to make my life miserable for herself.

Both Karma and Grace sighed as if having a sister to defend them was the missing piece in their lives.

"But that's what families are for, not just sisters."

I reached for Karma's hand. "We're your family now."

"Does that mean we can go to San Francisco and visit?"

"Absolutely."

Grace's eyes lit with enthusiasm. She was making a mental list of the things she wanted to see and do—Fisherman's Wharf, Ghirardelli Square, Chinatown, Gump's (she was definitely my daughter). "That's so cool." She settled her gaze on Karma. "And you'll come for holidays?"

Karma opened her mouth as if she meant to answer but didn't know what to say. I didn't know Karma well—yet—but it was easy to see thoughts of Mother floating through her mind.

"If Karma wants to come, she'll be most welcome."

That earned me a sharp glance from my new sister.

"Welcomed by the whole family," I added. What had Mother said about her? Karma was charming, well-respected, and smarter than Gaye Hardy (that praise might be faint but it was still praise).

"You're sure?" Karma didn't sound convinced.

"Positive. Although, given our recent holidays—" a disastrous Thanksgiving dinner came to mind "—you may want to stay in California. It's safer there."

"I'd love to come."

It was her funeral. And, depending on Mother's response, quite possibly mine.

NINETEEN

Aggie and I stared out the car window at the little bungalow.

"Cute neighborhood," said Aggie.

"Yes." Waldo was cute, a neighborhood filled with sweet bungalows and scaled down Tudors.

"Anarchy really wants you to do this?"

"He gave me the address." For the third time I matched the number on the slip of paper to the house number. "This is it."

"Well, let's get this over with." Aggie opened the car door.

I climbed out of Aggie's bug (she'd convinced me the Mercedes would draw unwanted attention) and took a few steps up the front walk.

Aggie followed, her hands stiff at her sides in an attempt to keep her kaftan from blowing above her head. "Where did this wind come from?"

A rhetorical question. March was always windy.

We paused in front of the bright blue door.

"You know what you're going to ask her?" Aggie's finger hovered about the doorbell button.

"I think so. Isn't Mac coming?"

Aggie glanced over her shoulder. "He should be here soon but he's going to stay in his car."

"Oh?"

"He can be a little intimidating."

The new man in Aggie's life was roughly the size of a rhinoceros.

She jabbed at the button.

A moment later, Joanie cracked the door. She spotted me and her eyes widened. "What are you doing here?"

"I was hoping we could talk for a few minutes."

"Who are you?" She directed her gaze at Aggie.

"A friend," I answered.

Joanie's eyes narrowed as if squaring "friend" and a redhead wearing a cerise kaftan was difficult.

"Aggie DeLucci." Aggie thrust out her hand.

Opening the door wider, Joanie took Aggie's fingers in her own and shook. "You'd better come in."

The front door opened into a room nearly overwhelmed by a shag carpet the color of paprika. To this, Joanie had added harvest gold sofas. A television rested on a stand in the corner. On the wall hung a Margaret Keane print of big-eyed children. From the ceiling hung a macramé sling holding a sad fern. All in all, an oh-dear-Lord sort of room.

"Have a seat." Joanie waved toward the sofas.

I sat next to Aggie.

"What do you want to talk about?" Joanie's eyes were red-rimmed and she clutched a crumpled tissue in her hand.

"Winthrop."

She sniffled and wiped her nose. "What about him?"

"Who wanted him dead?"

She sat down across from us. Poor woman. Not only was she grieving, but she had to look at Aggie's cerise kaftan. The color wasn't playing nicely with the paprika and gold of the living room. Joanie blinked a few times than fixed her gaze out the window. "His wife. His wife wanted him dead."

"Anyone else?" I crossed my ankles, ignoring the way Joanie's carpet grabbed at my heels.

"There were people he fired. Some of them might have wanted him dead."

"You told me your husband suspected you were cheating. Did he suspect it was with Winthrop?"

"No!" Bright spots of color livened her cheeks. "Of course not."

"You did say Larry was suspicious. It would be natural for him to think it was someone at the office."

Joanie shook her head. "Ruth Marshall is the one with the motive. Winthrop was going to divorce her."

"Obviously, Mr. Marshall adored you." Aggie offered Joanie an encouraging smile. "But, were there other girls? Girls he might have tired of?"

"Of course. Winthrop was a very attractive man."

If I couldn't say anything nice, it was best to say nothing at all.

"Who?" asked Aggie. "Which girls?"

"Winthrop had flirtations with half the girls in the office before we realized we were meant to be together." She rubbed her knuckle beneath her eyes.

"Were any of the girls upset about you and Winthrop?"

"Lots of them."

I swallowed a snort.

"Are you all right?" asked Joanie.

"Just a tickle in my throat. Allergies."

Now Aggie snorted.

Joanie wiped her eyes then held her palm against her lips as if her hand could contain her grief.

"What are you going to do?" Aggie's voice was gentle. "About your marriage?"

Joanie slid her palm from her mouth to her throat. "I haven't decided. Larry has an awful temper and—" something outside the window had caught her attention.

Aggie and I turned and looked over our shoulders.

"It's my husband. It's Larry." Joanie's voice was an octave higher. "He can't find you here."

A man even bigger than Mac was striding up the front walk. Huge biceps strained against the arms of his blue shirt. His feet, encased in work boots, were the size of anvils. And, unlike Mac, this man didn't look as friendly as a Labrador puppy.

"Why can't we be here?"

Joanie's answering look made it evident she thought I had rocks for brains. "He'll want to know why you're here."

She was obviously an adept liar, surely she could make something up.

Joanie leapt to her feet. "You have to hide."

Hide?

"Now! You have to hide now!" Another octave higher still. She opened the door to the coat closet. "Please. He'll kill me."

Aggie and I exchanged a look and bundled into the closet. Joanie closed the door after us.

The coat closet was a small one and it was already full of coats and boots and mufflers, a set of golf clubs, and a galaxy of dust motes. Aggie and I pressed close together. Her elbow lodged somewhere in my rib cage, a wire hanger poked at the back of my neck, and rough wool scratched my arms.

"What are you doing home?" Joanie's voice was new-penny bright.

"Checking on you. You've been so upset."

"Of course I'm upset, Larry. Two people from my office have been murdered."

"Quit." The man offered a simple solution.

"What?"

"You heard me. Quit. Get a different job. Or, stay home and make babies. You don't need that place."

"But—"

"Ain't no buts about it, Babe. That place hasn't been good for you. For us."

"It's not that easy to find a job."

"I'll take care of you. You don't need to work." Larry didn't sound like a suspicious man with a temper. Not at all. He sounded like a caring husband.

Joanie didn't strike me as the kind of woman for whom a bungalow in Waldo would be enough. She'd set her sights on Winthrop and easy street. Larry in his work shirt and boots wasn't going to land her in the lap of luxury anytime soon.

"I don't want to quit. I like working."

"Then find a new job."

"But—"

"No buts. I'll support whatever you want to do. Work. Stay home. But my wife isn't going to work with that bunch of clowns anymore." Larry sounded adamant. "It's not safe. You said it yourself, two people have been murdered."

Aggie shifted slightly and the tip of her elbow dug deeper into my side.

Not that I could complain—I was fairly certain I was standing on one of her feet.

"You been out of the house today?"

"No."

"Well, put on some lipstick and I'll take you out for lunch."

Oh, thank God. Aggie's elbow was pressing against my bladder resulting in a sudden, urgent need for a bathroom.

"But—"

"No buts! If I didn't know better, I'd think you don't want to go out with me."

"That's not it. Not at all. I look a mess."

Seriously? If they left, Aggie and I could escape the closet. I could find a bathroom.

"You look good to me. Better than good." There was a new tone in Larry's voice. A bedroom tone.

Oh dear Lord.

"I'm going to sneeze." Aggie's voice was so low it barely registered as sound. A sneeze would be much louder.

"You can't."

There was silence in the living room.

Silence then a woman's sigh. "Oh, Larry."

Aggie's impending sneeze would definitely kill the mood.

"Hold your nose."

"I can't reach it."

I could. I grabbed Aggie's nose and squeezed.

"Ouch," Aggie breathed in my ear.

I loosened my grip. Slightly.

If there was such a thing as karma (there was—she was staying at my house), I must have done something truly awful to deserve this.

"Oh, baby." Larry's voice overflowed with amorous intent. If I didn't wet my pants, I might vomit.

Bzzzzzzzz.

"You expecting anyone?" Now Larry sounded suspicious.

"No," Joanie squeaked.

Next came the sound of a door opening.

"What do you want?" Larry's voice was the opposite of welcoming.

"I'm looking for Aggie DeLucci."

Aggie exhaled. Mac, her knight in shining armor had arrived.

My fingers searched for a doorknob and found nothing.

"Sorry, bud. She ain't here." The door closed.

Bzzzzzzzz.

"That guy won't give up." A hint of menace had crept into Larry's voice. "You know him?"

"Never seen him before in my life."

Again the door opened. "I told you. She ain't here."

"I know," said Mac. "I must have written the address down wrong. May I please use your phone?" Mac must have seen Aggie's car. God love him.

"We don't let strangers in the house. There's a gas station couple blocks west. They got a payphone."

Again, the door closed.

Dammit. My bladder throbbed. I shifted my weight and Aggie swallowed a gasp. I was definitely on her foot.

"Can you move your elbow?" I whispered.

She shifted and the pressure increased.

"You sure you don't know him?" Larry demanded.

"Positive."

"He's sitting in his car out front."

"He's checking the address."

"I don't like it."

"He's just got the wrong house. Let's go get something to eat."

Hallelujah!

"Yeah. Fine. But I'm not going anywhere while that guy is parked in front of our house."

I pressed my knees together. *Mac, drive around the block. Please. Please.* Telepathy had never worked for me before but desperate times called for desperate measures.

"He's leaving," said Joanie. "What do you want for lunch?"

"Smaks."

"Really?"

If they argued over where to eat lunch I was going to find and fill a rubber galosh.

"You asked," said Larry. "I want a burger."

"Fine." Joanie's tone said a burger was the opposite of fine. Was she crazy? Did she want her husband to discover us in the closet? He might notice the puddle expanding from underneath the door. "I'll grab my purse."

For the love of Pete.

A moment later, we heard Joanie and Larry exiting the front door.

I pushed on the closet door. "Can you find a knob or a handle?"

Aggie shifted her elbow away from my bladder and I nearly sobbed in relief.

"What's wrong?" she asked. "Your voice sounds funny."

"I need a powder room in the worst way." My teeth-were-floating-away worst way.

"Uh-oh."

"Uh-oh?" I *eeped.*

"I can't find a door handle. We're locked in."

Where was that galosh?

"Mac wouldn't leave you. He'll be back." Hopefully, he'd be back soon. I pressed my knees together.

"But how is he going to get inside to open the door?"

Details. I didn't have time for details. I bounced on the balls of my feet.

"What are you doing?" One might think, from Aggie's tone, that she was locked in a closet with a fractious toddler.

"Thinking of deserts."

"There's no room for bouncing."

"There's no room for a lake."

"We need to get out of this closet."

She'd get no argument from me. I leaned against the golf clubs, ignored the nine-iron boring a hole into my back, and thought of the Sahara.

"Aggie?" Mac's voice should have been followed by a choir of angels.

"In here!" Aggie beat her hand against the expanse of wood keeping us from light, clear air, and a powder room.

Mac yanked the door open.

Aggie and I stumbled into Joanie's living room, blinking at the light.

Aggie stumbled right into Mac's arms.

I stumbled toward the back of the house. There had to be a powder room nearby.

Tiny, with lavender tiled floor and lavender and green tiles on the wall, a sink that needed scouring, and limp towels hanging from a hook on the back of the door, it was the most beautiful bathroom I'd ever seen.

I emerged a moment later feeling like a new woman.

"We need to get out of here." Mac glared at me. "Now."

If I didn't know better, I'd almost imagine he thought visiting the powder room after breaking and entering was a bad idea. Maybe so, but the other options were worse.

Mac wrapped a mammoth arm around Aggie's shoulders and propelled her toward the door. "Let's go."

She looked up at him with a Mac-hung-the-moon expression on her face and nodded.

I followed the two of them onto the front porch. "Aggie, you go with Mac. I'll drive your car home."

With the Mac-hung-the-moon expression still on her face, she handed me the keys.

I climbed into her VW bug and sat behind the wheel, thinking. Why had Joanie left us in the closet? Why was she so sure Ruth had killed Winthrop? Who decided mint green and lavender was a good color combination for a bathroom?

I slid the key into the ignition. Were those sirens in the distance?

I shifted into first gear and pulled away from the curb.

Just in time. The lights of a patrol car pulling up to Joanie's house filled my rear-view mirror.

Anarchy was waiting in the driveway when I arrived home. He leaned against his car with his arm crossed and a serious wrinkle creased his brow.

"Tell me you didn't break into Joanie Wilson's house." His tone was serious too.

"I didn't."

"But you were there?"

I nodded.

Anarchy pinched the bridge of his nose between his fingers.

"Joanie locked us in a closet. We broke out."

Anarchy dropped his hand to his side and stared at me. "She locked you in a closet?"

"With coats. And galoshes."

"Why did she lock you in a closet?"

"Because her husband came home and she didn't want to explain our presence."

"You escaped the closet."

"Joanie and her husband went out to lunch."

Anarchy waited for more.

Nope. I wasn't saying another word. Aggie and I had not broken any laws but it was possible Mac had. "Joanie thinks Ruth killed Winthrop."

Anarchy relaxed. Slightly. "Does she have any other theories?"

"Maybe a disgruntled ex-employee."

"Like Tim Vanderlay?"

Now my forehead creased.

"I found him on my own. You didn't betray any confidences. And, if it makes you feel better, he has an alibi."

That made me feel much better.

"What about Joanie's husband? Could he have killed Marshall?"

"She was scared. Scared enough to lock Aggie and me in a closet and leave us there."

"How did you get out?"

"Pardon?"

"If you were locked in the closet, how did you get out?" The twinkle in his eye was the only thing keeping my stomach from plummeting.

"We just did. Do you want coffee? I want coffee." I took a step toward the house.

"Ellison—"

I stopped walking.

"Where's Aggie?"

"Aggie?"

"You're driving her car." Anarchy grinned at me and his eyes sparkled.

"Um..."

"I'm glad Mac was there to rescue you. It was smart to take him as back up."

In my chest, my heart beat double-time. I swallowed a stupid grin. "Mac? I have no idea what you're talking about."

TWENTY

Anarchy followed me into the house—to the kitchen where Mr. Coffee sat on the counter, steadfast. I filled his pot with fresh water, scooped coffee grounds into a filter, and started the process that yielded heaven in a cup.

Anarchy settled onto a stool. The serious expression in his eyes told me we wouldn't be flirting. "Do you think it's possible Ruth killed Winthrop?"

No flirting. I hated it when I was right. "Anything's possible but I have a hard time thinking of Ruth as a killer."

"She's the most likely suspect."

"But why would she kill Marcy?"

"You think the two murders are related?"

"It seems impossible that they're not."

"Agreed."

"It must be something related to the firm. Somehow. Maybe Winthrop was preying on some girl who expected Marcy to protect her." I shook my head. "Except Joanie says Winthrop had eyes only for her." The whole thing was a convoluted mess.

"Maybe Ruth thought Marcy was the one having an affair with her husband."

It was the more probable explanation but it didn't make sense to me. "Why kill Marcy after Winthrop's dead?"

"To hide the affair?" Anarchy rested his forearms on the counter and leaned toward them. "Or, could be Ruth wanted them both gone."

"I can't see it. Ruth might have killed Winthrop. Lord knows he gave her plenty of reasons to want him dead. But Marcy—" I shook my head "—why bother? What do you know about Marcy?"

"She was single. She'd been at the firm four years. She paid her bills on time. She had a cat named Nora."

"Boyfriend?

"No one serious. There's nothing about her that invited murder."

Except there was. People didn't get murdered for no reason.

Mr. Coffee made that wonderful gluggy sound that meant he'd completely filled a pot.

"Coffee?"

"Sure."

I pulled two mugs from the cabinet, poured coffee, and handed a mug to Anarchy.

Our fingers touched and we paused, murder temporarily forgotten. At least by me. Maybe Anarchy was imagining crime scenes.

Or not. His coffee-colored eyes were as warm as the ambrosia in his cup.

The back door swung open and I jumped away from him.

Max and Karma had caught us mooning.

Max wore a huge grin.

After seeing Anarchy and me, a grin spread across Karma's face as well. She hid it by bending and unhooking Max's leash.

Freed of his tether, Max trotted over to me and rubbed his head against my leg.

I scratched behind his ear.

"It was too pretty to stay inside." Karma shrugged off a light jacket. "We walked to the park."

"Max loves that. Thank you."

"He likes squirrels."

"He likes chasing squirrels." I was fairly certain if Max actually caught a squirrel, he wouldn't like squirrels at all. "Coffee?"

"Please."

Brnng, brnng.

"Would you mind helping yourself?" I nodded at Mr. Coffee, walked toward the phone, and picked up the receiver. "Hello."

"Are you sitting down?" Libba had something juicy to tell me; I could tell from her tone.

"No. Why?"

"Sit down."

"Fine. I'm sitting." I wasn't.

"You won't believe what I heard." How long was Libba going to ring around the rosie?

"What?" Impatience edged into my tone.

"Guess."

"Daisy is pregnant."

"That's an open secret."

"Prudence Davies got run over by a bus?" A woman could dream.

"Not even close."

"What?" My patience was at an end. I stretched the phone cord and picked up my coffee.

"You're sure you're sitting down?"

"Positive."

"Ruth Marshall is having an affair with Frank Wallace."

I sprayed hot coffee halfway across the kitchen. "What?"

Anarchy and Karma regarded me with wide eyes and dropped jaws. Libba's announcement deserved more than mild surprise. Libba's announcement deserved sprayed coffee. Of course, they hadn't heard the news. Yet.

"Where did you hear that?" I demanded.

"Jinx told me."

"How does Jinx know?"

"She saw them."

"Saw them?"

"Together at The Alameda."

I grabbed a tea towel off the oven handle and wiped my face with a tea towel. "What was Jinx doing at The Alameda on a

Thursday morning?"

"How did you know it was a Thursday morning?"

Whoops. "Lucky guess."

"Lucky guess?" Libba didn't believe me.

"I'm a good guesser."

"Hmmph." Libba's hmmph that said I was NOT a good guesser and we'd return to that point in a moment. "Jinx was meeting with the hotel's special events manager and saw them."

Jinx hoarded gossip like a dragon hoarded treasure. Libba must have offered her something good for Jinx to tell her about Ruth and Frank.

Realization hit me and I put down my coffee and the towel and clutched the counter "You told Jinx about Karma. The whole story."

Karma's brows rose.

"It was only going to keep another day or two," said Libba.

If that long. Gaye Hardy had known about Karma.

"You're not too mad are you?" Worry colored Libba's voice.

"It's not me you need to worry about. It's Mother."

"What happened?" mouthed Karma.

"Libba." It was a complete explanation in one word.

"What?" asked my best friend.

"Nothing. I was talking to Karma."

"I don't suppose you'd run interference for me with Frances?" I could picture Libba, perched on her white couch, wrapping the phone cord around her finger. Maybe even catching the corner of her lower lip in her teeth. Taking on Mother was no small thing.

"Today is your lucky day."

"Oh?" Cautious optimism bled through the phone line.

"I'm taking Karma to Veronica Crawford's engagement party."

A few seconds of silence followed. "You are?"

"I am."

"Does Frances know?"

"No. Not yet. But I can almost guarantee Mother will approve."

That was met with a few seconds of silence on Libba's end. "What makes you so sure?" She of little faith.

"Karma is part of the family and you know how Mother feels about family." Mother stood up for family in ladies' lounges. I smiled at Karma.

She smiled back—a tenuous, tremulous smile.

"Does Vicky Crawford know you're hijacking her daughter's engagement party?"

"I asked Vicky if I could bring her." Sort of. I asked Vicky if I could bring a guest. I hadn't explained she was my half-sister.

"Now I wish I hadn't declined the invitation."

"You'll just have to hear about it later." My thoughts returned to Libba's news. "Did Jinx tell you how long ago she saw Ruth and Frank at the hotel?"

Anarchy's gaze sharpened.

"No," Libba replied. "But it couldn't have been more than a few months ago. That dinner she planned for George's clients was right after she got out of rehab."

"And she's positive they were together and not just in the hotel at the same time?"

"Jinx wouldn't tell me if she wasn't sure." Jinx hated being wrong. "Do you think Ruth and Frank knocked off Winthrop so they could be together?"

"Divorce would have been easier," I insisted.

"Not in this case. Ruth divorcing Winthrop to be with Frank would have destroyed the firm."

Libba had a point.

But, if Libba was right, Celine, not Marcy, should be dead.

"Are you free for brunch tomorrow?" Libba demanded. "I'll want to hear about the party and we can solve your detective's case over bloodies. Bring Karma. I've been dying to meet her."

"Fine. Where and when?"

"The Monastery at noon." The Monastery was a dark little restaurant with a stellar wine list in Brookside.

"See you then."

"Bye." Libba hung up the phone.

I dropped the receiver back in its cradle and turned to

Anarchy. "You heard?"

"Ruth Marshall and Frank Wallace?"

I nodded.

"I wouldn't have guessed that. How good is your source?"

Jinx was never wrong. Not about gossip. "Excellent."

"What's this about Thursday mornings?"

"Celine told me Frank was having an affair with a woman he met on Thursday mornings." Poor Celine. "She had no idea who it was."

"Ruth Marshall's motive just got a lot better."

I couldn't argue.

Karma and I paused on the Crawfords' front stoop.

"Vicky and Bob, right?"

"Exactly. Their daughter is Veronica and she's marrying Chip Martin."

"Got it." Karma smoothed the fabric of the silk dress she'd borrowed.

I pressed the doorbell.

A few seconds later Bob Crawford opened the door. "Ellison—" he leaned forward and brushed a light kiss across my cheek "— we're so glad you could come." He turned to Karma and his brow wrinkled. "Marjorie?"

"Bob, may I introduce you to Karma Michaels? Karma, this is my dear friend, Bob Crawford. I dated his younger brother in high school."

"Which means we've known each other forever." Bob's lips were moving but his gaze was fixed on Karma's face. "Longer than forever. I have to say, you look just like Ellison's sister, Marjorie."

Karma smiled at him. "I've been hearing that a lot."

"How do you and Ellison know each other?"

Karma looked my way—waiting for my lead.

"Karma is my half-sister."

Bob's eyes widened. "I didn't know you had a half-sister."

Neither did I. "Karma grew up in California."

"You're moving to Kansas City?"

"Just visiting."

"Karma runs a brokerage firm in San Francisco."

"Well, we're glad you could join us tonight." He looked over my shoulder where the Olivers were waiting to be welcomed.

"Thank you for having us." Rote responses. So useful when my stomach was fluttery. Had bringing Karma been a mistake?

"The bar is set up in the living room."

"Thank you."

Karma and I moved in that direction, but a young woman stopped us. "Hi, Mrs. Russell."

"Veronica, how lovely you look." Veronica Crawford was clad in happiness. She gave new meaning to walking on air.

"Thank you. I'm so glad you could be with us tonight."

I glanced around Vicky's elegant living room and the chattering guests. "I wouldn't have missed this for anything. Veronica, this is Karma Michaels who's staying with me. Your mother was kind enough to let me bring her this evening. Karma, this is Veronica Crawford, she was Grace's favorite babysitter when she was little."

Veronica extended her hand. "Pleased to meet you Mrs. Michaels."

"Best wishes to you."

Veronica positively glowed. Girls shouldn't fall that deeply in love—not when men cheated and lied and chased their assistants around their desks.

"Tell me about the wedding, Veronica. What are your colors?"

"Yellow chiffon for the bridesmaids' dresses. It's such a sunny, bright color."

A color few people wore well. Her bridesmaids wouldn't thank her.

"They'll carry bouquets of daisies." She looked over her shoulder then lowered her voice. "Chip and I really wanted an outdoor wedding but Mother wouldn't hear of it."

"Isn't the wedding in July?" Thank God Vicky had a modicum of sense—July in Kansas City was only a few degrees cooler than hell.

Veronica offered me a charming shrug. "Summer is my favorite season."

She might enjoy melting, but her guests were accustomed to air-conditioning. "Well, inside or outside, I know you'll make a beautiful bride."

"Thank you." She waved toward the corner of the living room. "We've hired Chester to bartend, you must get drinks."

"We will. Have a marvelous time tonight and enjoy this special time."

Veronica glowed even brighter.

Karma and I made our way toward the bar. "People are staring." She spoke without moving her lips.

"They'll get over it." They would. Eventually. We stood in the short line at the bar. "I've been meaning to ask you, would you consider taking me on as a client?" It wasn't as if I could leave my portfolio where it was.

"We should probably review investment strategies before you ask that."

I stepped up to the bar. "May I please have a vodka soda with two limes, Chester."

The man behind the bar waited for Karma.

"Just a glass of wine, please."

"Coming right up." Chester scooped ice into an old-fashioned glass. "Nice to see you, Mrs. Russell."

"Nice to see you, too. How's your family?"

"Doing fine." He poured vodka then soda into the glass and added two large lime wedges.

"Thank you." I lifted the drink to my lips. "Give your wife my regards."

"I sure will, Mrs. Russell." Chester turned to Karma. "Would you like red or white wine, ma'am?"

"White, please."

Chester poured Liebfraumilch into a glass and put it down in front of Karma.

I turned to my half-sister. "What do you mean investment strategies? The strategy is for the portfolio to grow."

"How much risk are you willing to assume?"

"Risk?"

"Didn't you have this conversation with your last broker?"

"Never."

"What kind of returns were you getting?"

"Fifteen to twenty percent."

Her brows rose. To her hairline. "Tell you what, let me review your statements and I'll tell you what I think."

"Fair enough."

We surveyed Vicky's living room. Built-in bookcases flanked an impressive fireplace topped with a gilt mirror. A brass and glass coffee-table held books, ashtrays, cigarettes, and a sterling lighter. The furniture was covered in shades of harvest gold velvet. The walls were creamy and filled with art.

"A pretty room," said Karma.

"Yes." The pretty room faded when I spotted Jinx marching toward us with a determined look on her face. "Prepare yourself."

"For what?"

"Ellison!" Jinx kissed the air next to my cheek. "And you must be Karma." Jinx latched onto Karma's arm. "I've been dying to meet you. I'm Jinx, one of Ellison's dearest friends." She shot me an I-shouldn't-have-had-to-learn-about-Karma-from-Libba look then returned her focus to Karma. "We need a get-to-know-you chat."

The whites of Karma's eyes seemed to take over her face and her jaw went slack.

"Don't worry. Jinx is friendly." Usually. I shot Jinx a be-nice-to-my-sister-or-else look.

Jinx responded with a predator's grin before she led Karma away.

I nursed my drink and studied a Modigliani print.

"How's the book?"

I turned away from the art. Oh dear Lord. Celine. I wished I didn't know about Frank and Ruth. Keeping life-changing secrets made small talk difficult. "What book?"

"The one you bought at Bennett Schneider."

That book. "The Agatha Christie? I haven't started it yet."

Celine stepped closer to me and whispered, "I'm sorry I unloaded on you the other day."

"I was happy to listen."

Her gaze traveled the crowded room. "Things have been so unsettled with Winthrop's murder, then Marcy's, and with Buzz in the hospital."

"I understand."

"I'm sure everything will be fine." She held up her glass and regarded the room through the liquid in the bottom.

I did not share her certainty. Not when her husband was sleeping with his partner's widow. "Of course."

"Do you ever come to these things and want to warn the young people?"

I raised my brows.

"I mean it!" She raised the near empty martini glass to her lips. "Don't you want to tell them love fades, men change, and the things they hold as certain will crumble to dust."

"An engagement party probably isn't the best place for those pearls of wisdom."

She snorted and held her empty glass out to Chester. "Another please. Extra dry."

"Right away, Mrs. Wallace."

"Are you married, Chester?" Celine asked.

"Going on forty years, Mrs. Wallace." Chester swirled ice and gin and a drop of vermouth in a pitcher.

"Are you happy?"

"I am, Mrs. Wallace." He poured the martini into a glass then picked up a tiny fork and reached into a jar of olives.

"Mrs. Chester is a lucky woman."

"Dibble," I corrected.

"Dibble?" Celine's brows furrowed.

"Chester's last name is Dibble."

"Ah." Celine accepted a full martini glass complete with olive. "Mrs. Dibble is a lucky woman."

"I'm the lucky one," Chester replied.

The world needed more men like Chester.

Celine sipped her drink and sighed. "Perfect. Thank you."

"You're welcome, Mrs. Wallace. May I fix you another, Mrs. Russell?"

"Not right now, thank you."

Celine and I stepped away from the bar.

"Frank's here somewhere," she scanned the crowded living room. "Why have the party here? Why not the club?" She glanced back at Chester. "It's because Bob is tighter than a tick and he didn't want to pay the liquor bill at the club." How many martinis had Celine had? Insulting the host while at the party was very bad form.

I kept my voice mild. "He does have a wedding reception to pay for."

"*Pfft.*"

Oh dear.

"Frank is the goose."

"Pardon me?"

"The goose that laid the golden egg," she explained. "Frank and his partners have made piles of money for almost everyone in this room."

"The three of them have been remarkably good at picking stocks."

"*Pftt.* That's what they want you to think." Celine swayed slightly.

She might be mad at Frank but she couldn't argue with his results. "Why don't we sit?" I took her elbow and guided her to a loveseat.

Celine didn't so much sit as collapse. Gin sloshed onto the harvest gold velvet. She didn't notice.

"Stay here. I'll see if I can't find Frank."

"Frank. *Pfft*." Poor woman. How many people knew Frank was cheating on her with Ruth? How long till she knew?

"I'll be right back."

She lifted her glass and something malicious glinted in her eyes. "Take your time. I'm here all night."

I paused. And stared. Did she already know about Ruth? If Celine confronted Ruth, Karma would be second-page news. And Veronica's engagement party would be spoiled.

"Stay put."

I searched the living room and the dining room and the sun porch (where Jinx was whispering to Karma) and (with growing dread) the veranda overlooking the golf course, but Frank was nowhere to be found.

TWENTY-ONE

"Vicky, have you seen Frank Wallace?" I hated to disturb my hostess but, given my track record, the likelihood Frank was dead and stuffed behind the boxwood hedges was high.

"He just left."

At least he wasn't dead.

"He took Celine home. She had one too many martinis." There was no judgment in Vicky's voice. Some hostesses would have alluded to the sad fact that Celine had been at the party less than an hour before she needed to be taken home. Not Vicky. "Poor woman. I think the murders have been hard on her."

Hard on Celine?

I was the one who'd found both bodies.

I tried for a smile and failed. Mother was right. I was the woman who found bodies. So old hat that no one remarked on it anymore. "As long as she's taken care of."

"Frank has it handled. Would you excuse me, please?" Vicky glanced at the simple gold watch on her wrist. "I need to check with the caterer. The buffet should be out by now."

"Go."

I circulated. I made small talk. I ate a canapé—two (the cheese puffs were delicious). And, I thought. *Frank has it handled.* Frank was a more likely murder suspect than Ruth. He had a reason to want Winthrop dead. Marcy had worked for him. Had she known his secret? Would Celine be all right?

"You're deep in thought."

Startled out of my musings, I looked up into Whit Broderick's craggy face.

"I've been meaning to call you."

"Oh?"

"I need a table for that gala you're hosting." He made it sound as if I was throwing a gingham cloth on a picnic table and ordering BBQ.

"Of course. I'll put a sponsor sheet in the mail to you tomorrow."

"I heard all the thousand-dollar tables are gone."

"True."

"And the five thousand-dollar tables."

"Also, true."

"Sounds to me as if you're doing a bang-up job."

"I have a wonderful committee."

"What level tables do you have left?"

"Ten thousand." It was an enormous amount to spend on one evening.

"Sold."

Really? I should attend more cocktail parties. I pressed a hand to my chest. "Thank you."

"Seats ten?"

"Yes."

"Do you want a check right now?"

"If you have your checkbook, I'd be delighted to take your money." Fundraising one-oh-one, if someone offers to write you a check, take it.

"Got it right here." He patted his breast pocket.

He walked me toward a covered radiator and put the checkbook down on its surface. "Who do I make it payable to?"

"The museum."

He wrote the check and signed his name with a flourish.

"Thank you." I accepted the slip of paper.

"For ten thousand dollars, I'd better have one of the best tables in Kirkwood Hall."

"You will. I promise."

He glanced over my shoulder. "Looks like they're putting out the buffet. I'd better find Enid."

I stepped out of his way. "Enjoy your supper. And, thank you."

"Selling your services?" That snide tone could only belong to one woman.

I could rise above. I could. "Whit bought a table for the gala." Prudence and her horsey face and horsey teeth would not ruin my evening.

"I hear you brought your half-sister tonight."

I did my best impression of a Mona Lisa smile.

"Your sainted father isn't so saintly after all."

I could rise above.

"Has Frances filed for divorce yet? Or maybe your father's will be the next body you find."

Why, oh why, couldn't I find Prudence's body? "Your slip is showing."

She glanced down at her hemline where not a hint of a slip showed.

"I meant metaphorically. All that ugliness you keep inside is peeking out."

It was at that moment that Karma appeared at my side.

Prudence curled her lip. "You look just like Marjorie. You must be Harrington's bastard."

Nearby, someone gasped.

I'd told Mother to own the scandal. It was time I took my own advice. "Karma, let me introduce you to Prudence Davies, one of the many women my husband was—" I searched for a word that wouldn't make Tilly Draper (who was obviously eavesdropping) faint "—boffing before he died. Prudence, this is my half-sister, Karma Michaels. Karma went to Stanford and manages one of the most successful brokerage firms in San Francisco."

"Boffing?" Karma asked.

"It was the nicest word I could think of."

Prudence didn't speak, she just opened and closed her mouth

like a goldfish.

We left her there.

The rest of the evening passed quickly. Karma explained her parentage thirty times. I found zero dead bodies. All in all, a successful party.

It wasn't till we were driving home that Karma said, "You have nice friends."

"I do."

"What's the story with the woman who looks like a horse?"

"She was in love with Henry. Deeply in love."

"And he cheated on you with her?" Karma shook her head as if she couldn't quite believe Henry's taste.

"He cheated on me with any woman who'd say yes."

"I'm sorry."

She was sorry? "It's not your fault."

"No. I mean it must be hard for you to trust and I made it seem as if there was something between Anarchy and me. I'm sorry."

A lump rose in my throat. "Water. Bridge."

"Still. I'm sorry."

"I appreciate that." Then, keeping my gaze firmly fixed on the road ahead of us, I added. "I'm glad you came to visit."

"Me, too."

I peeked out of the corner of my eye. Like me, Karma's gaze was fixed on the road.

I woke up early, tiptoed down the stairs, let Max outside, and pushed Mr. Coffee's button.

By the time Max was ready to come inside, a full pot of caffeine awaited me. I found the largest mug in the house, poured myself a cup, and climbed two flights of stairs to my studio. The past few days had been overwhelming and fraught with emotion; I needed the comfort of my studio, if only for an hour or so.

Aggie had done a bang-up job cleaning after the McCallester

incident. The books were back on the shelf (alphabetically instead of by art movement—I'd have to fix that). The floor was spotless. Even the bits of paper I'd rescued from the trash bin were in a neat stack on the corner of my drafting table.

Idly, I moved a few around as if they were pieces of a jigsaw puzzle.

"I thought I'd find you up here." Grace held a fresh cup of coffee.

"Good morning."

She handed me the new cup. "So—"

Uh-oh. "What?"

"Did you really call out Ms. Davies last night?"

News traveled fast. Mother had probably heard about it too.

"I did. She deserved it."

Grace's brows rose.

"She called your aunt a bastard. To her face." I finished my first cup of coffee and started on the one Grace had brought me.

"She's awful." Presumably Grace was referring to Prudence.

"True. But you have to give her credit. She's up front about it. She's not nice to my face while she trashes me behind my back."

"She's still awful."

"No argument."

"What are those?" Grace pointed to the scraps of paper.

"A puzzle of sorts. Me being nosy." With the tip of my finger I slid one piece next to another and got gibberish. "What are you doing today?"

"Homework."

"Karma and I are having brunch with Libba."

Ding dong.

"What time is it?" Surely it was too early for someone to be dropping by.

"Eight thirty."

Definitely too early. Mother? Who else would ring the doorbell before church on a Sunday?

I sighed and drained my second cup of coffee. "Whatever it is, it can't be good."

Grace followed me to the second floor then disappeared into her bedroom.

"Coward," I called after her.

"I live to be criticized for my hair or my clothes or my makeup another day."

"Hmmph."

At least Max stuck by me. Together we descended the front stairs. It wasn't till I was standing in front of the door that I remembered Mother had a key. If she wanted to excoriate me for taking Karma to the Crawfords' party, she wouldn't ring the bell. She'd plan a sneak attack so I couldn't escape out the back.

I peeked outside.

Celine Wallace waited on the stoop.

I opened the door.

Celine looked awful. Crimson rimmed her eyes—her extremely puffy eyes. Her skin was wan. Her hair was a mess. And, she had on the cocktail dress she'd worn last night.

"Are you all right?" An inane thing to ask her. Obviously, she was the opposite of all right. "Come in." I stepped out of her way. "What can I get you? Coffee?"

Her chin wobbled.

I chose to interpret that as a nod.

"Let's go to the kitchen. There's coffee and Aggie made a Bundt cake."

Another wobble.

I led her to the back of the house, sat her on a stool, and put a piping hot cup of coffee in front of her.

She wrapped her hands around the mug and stared into space.

"Cake?" I cut two thick slices, put them on plates, and positioned one of the plates in front of her.

Celine didn't react.

I poured myself a cup of coffee and settled on the stool next to hers. "Celine, what's wrong?"

"Did you know?" Her voice was as raw as a morning in early

March.

"Know what?"

"Frank." She covered her mouth with her hand. "And Ruth."

"I heard, but I didn't know if it was true." A lie. As soon as I heard, I'd believed.

"When?" she demanded. "When did you hear?"

"Yesterday."

"You didn't tell me. You could have told me last night and you didn't."

"No."

"Why not?"

"Parties aren't the best place to receive news like that."

Celine released the coffee mug and lowered her head to her hands. "How could she? We've been friends for years."

"I don't think it was about you."

Celine lifted her head and glared at me as if I was the one having an affair with her husband.

"What I mean to say is I think Ruth was getting back at Winthrop."

"Oh." She closed her eyes and her head moved from side to side like a metronome. A single tear ran down her cheek. "Getting even with him was more important to her than our friendship."

"I'm so sorry."

"Do know what it's like to be stabbed in the back?"

"I do." I picked up my fork and cut a bite of cake. "Eat something. Drink your coffee. You'll feel better."

"I just found out one of my best friends is sleeping with my husband and the only advice you have is to drink more coffee?"

When she put it that way, I sounded shallow. But the advice was sound.

"You will feel better if you eat." And who didn't feel better after a cup of Mr. Coffee's magic brew? "As for advice, I can give you the number of a good divorce attorney."

"I don't want a divorce." She wrapped her fingers around her fork and stabbed the poor, unsuspecting Bundt cake. "I want to kill him."

"I have a second piece of advice."

"What?" she snapped.

"Don't say that out loud. If Frank turns up dead, it'll make you suspect number one."

I sat with Celine for three hours. I listened as she wondered again and again how her friend could betray her. I watched as she ate half of Aggie's Bundt cake. I closed my fingers around the powdered softness of her hands. And I pretended not to notice the whiff of desperation that surrounded her like a moth-eaten wool coat.

At half past eleven, she looked at her watch and said, "I should go."

"You're welcome to stay."

"No. I should go." She gathered her purse and her gloves and wrap and stood—swayed.

"Did you drive? Should I call you a cab?"

"I drove and I'm fine." She spoke with such tragic dignity I didn't dare argue.

"You'll call if I can do anything?"

"Yes." She sounded as if life had beaten her to a pulp.

I walked her to the door, hugged her, and said, "Remember, call if you need me."

"Thank you, Ellison. You're a good friend."

Libba would not agree. Karma and I were going to be late for brunch.

I closed the door on Celine and got myself ready in record time before Karma and I positively flew to Brookside.

Libba stood in front of the restaurant with a scrunchy look on her face.

I waved as we drove past her.

She beckoned and I slowed the car.

Karma rolled down the window.

Libba stuck her head in the car. "There's something wrong with their water line. They're closed." She shifted her head and stared at Karma. "I'm Libba."

"I guessed that. Nice to meet you."

The car behind me honked.

"Get in," I said. "We'll go someplace else."

Libba pulled her head out of the car then put her whole self into the backseat. "Where do you want to go?"

"The Pam Pam Room?" It was nearby, had plenty of tables, and poured a delicious cup of coffee.

"Fine. I'm starving."

I drove us to The Alameda Plaza Hotel and let the valet take the car.

The three of us stepped into the lobby then walked toward the hotel's first-floor restaurant.

"I don't believe it," I muttered.

"Don't believe what?" Libba asked.

"That's Chauncey Nelson."

"Where?" Karma turned her head, looking.

"Over at the front desk. I can't believe he hasn't gone back to New York." Chauncey and Hester stood stiffly, as if the young man behind the desk had somehow annoyed them.

"He's heavier than I remember. Older." Karma's voice was off. "Which way to coffee?"

Without comment, I pointed us toward the Pam Pam room. Why was Karma avoiding Chauncey Nelson?

TWENTY-TWO

We sat at a table overlooking the Plaza. The cutlery shone like freshly silvered mirrors. The linen was crisp. The air was laden with the smell of coffee and cinnamon.

I smoothed a napkin over my lap and looked at Karma. "Spill."

Libba raised her brows.

Karma colored a pretty shade of rose.

"What are you talking about?" asked Libba.

Karma, who knew exactly what I was talking about, admired the view.

"Spill," I repeated.

Karma kept her gaze fixed on the Spanish-style buildings across the creek. "It was a long time ago."

"You had an affair? You? With Chauncey Nelson?" It boggled the mind.

"I wouldn't call it an affair. I was brand new in the business. He offered to be my mentor."

Poor Karma, two predators in a short period of time. "And he behaved like your professor?"

Karma answered with a grimace and a nod.

Libba, who'd been following our exchange like a spectator at a tennis match, beckoned the waitress. "We'll need a round of screwdrivers."

I speared my friend with a look. "You do realize liquor isn't the answer to every question?"

"This isn't every question. This is a man question. Trust me, liquor is the answer."

Who was I to argue with Libba's vast experience?

The waitress jotted on her pad and disappeared.

Libba reached across the table and patted Karma's hand. "Do you want to talk about it?"

The flush on Karma's cheeks faded to bone white. She shook her head.

"So that's a no?"

Karma squirmed in her chair. It was a no.

It was time for a new subject.

"Celine Wallace was at my house all morning. I felt so sorry for her."

"Now there's a woman who needs a drink." Libba leaned back in her chair and looked for the waitress and our vodka and orange juices.

"She cried. A lot."

"Her husband had an affair with her friend." Libba scrunched her face—a judgment of friends sleeping with each other's husbands or of Frank and Ruth in particular? "As far as I'm concerned he's pond scum. They're both pond scum. Ruth, too."

"She had no idea?" Karma asked.

"None," I confirmed. Libba should have ordered coffee with the screwdrivers. I needed coffee more than I needed vodka.

"How old is their firm?"

"Old," I replied. "Buzz's father was an original partner and I think Winthrop's as well. Buzz and Winthrop added Frank. Why do you ask?"

"I looked at your statements this morning."

"Oh?"

"They're very good at picking stocks."

"Where is that waitress?" Libba scanned the restaurant.

"How good?" It was really too bad I had to fire them.

"You don't have many losers in that portfolio."

"They've always been good at picking winners."

"There she is!" Libba announced the arrival of our drinks.

The waitress set the three screwdrivers on the table. "Are you ready to order?"

"We need a few minutes," I replied. "We haven't had a chance to look at the menus. But, in the meantime, would you please bring me a cup of coffee?"

The waitress nodded and went to take another, speedier, order.

Libba lifted her drink. "To us, girls." She sipped her drink and sighed. "Tell me about the party last night."

"The usual," I replied.

"Chester at the bar, passed rumaki, and a buffet featuring things we've eaten fifty times already this year?"

She was very close. "They passed cheese puffs. They were delicious."

"I heard Veronica wanted an outdoor wedding."

"She did," I confirmed. "Vicky won't let her have it."

Libba pursed her lips. "Vicky has all the sense in that family."

"What does Bob do?" asked Karma.

"He's a doctor." Libba glanced at the ceiling as if being a doctor and an inability to change a light bulb were somehow connected.

"I see." Karma's tone suggested she agreed. "A few of my clients are doctors. They insist on picking their own stocks then complain when their portfolios don't perform."

Libba nodded. "It's not as if you try and do their job. Why do they try and do yours?"

"They're very smart men and they think that intelligence translates to everything they touch. They're often wrong." Karma opened her menu. "What's good here?"

"Everything." Fortified by her drink, Libba turned her attention my way. "I've been meaning to ask you, how did you know Jinx spotted Frank and Ruth on a Thursday morning?"

"Celine told me he met someone on Thursday mornings." I watched a car zip down Ward Parkway. "Frank was lucky he was with Chauncey on Thursday morning instead of Ruth or his affair would have become common knowledge even sooner."

Karma tilted her head to the side. "Frank Wallace was meeting with Chauncey Nelson? On a Thursday morning?"

"Yes. Chauncey was Frank's alibi. It's why Frank wasn't arrested for Marcy's murder. Nan was sure she'd seen him."

Karma's lips thinned and her eyes glazed. She looked as if she was figuring out a complex equation—one with a vexing solution.

I lost my appetite. "What? What do you know?"

"Chauncey has a girl in every city. He usually reserves Thursday morning for them."

"Chauncey was with a girl and not Frank? He lied to the police?"

"Possibly. If Frank is a good enough client, Chauncey would definitely lie."

"Wait." Libba actually released her drink and held up her hands. "Didn't he bring his wife on this trip? Didn't you take her shopping?"

"I did."

"He takes his wife on a business trip and still finds a way to cheat." Libba reclaimed her glass and held the rim just below her lips. "That's a new low."

"Hester has worn blinders for years." Karma flushed as if she'd revealed too much.

"You were one of his Thursday girls?"

I was glad Libba asked the question instead of me.

Karma's nod was miniscule. Her sip of screwdriver enormous. "And Monday, and Tuesday, and Wednesday..."

"How did it end?" Libba asked.

"I came to my senses. I left New York—" Karma twisted her napkin into a rope "—I got fired, left New York, and went back to San Francisco."

"And became hugely successful," I added. Karma looked as if she needed a pep talk.

She offered me a grateful smile.

I smiled back. "If Chauncey lied for Frank, I need to tell

Anarchy."

Libba jerked her chin toward the entrance. "Isn't that Bea Bisby?"

I glanced over my shoulder. "It is."

Now Karma looked. "The third partner's wife?"

"Exactly."

"Who is she here with?" asked Libba.

"I can't tell. Her back is turned."

"Hester Nelson." Karma sounded as if she wanted to crawl under the table.

The hostess led Bea and Hester to a table—a window table as far from us as was possible to be.

Karma breathed a sigh. A relieved sigh.

"Did she know about you?" asked Libba.

"Not about me specifically but she had to know—has to know—Chauncey cheats on her."

"Do they have children?" Teeth gritted, I'd put up with Henry's antics. The moment Grace was out of the house and settled into a college dorm room, I'd planned on filing for divorce. His death had saved me the trouble.

"Their children have to be grown and gone by now," said Karma.

"Why does she stay?" I wondered out loud.

Libba shot me a you-must-be-kidding look and went so far as to put down her drink and hold her hands palms-up in front of her as if she were weighing options. "Wife of a successful businessman." One hand went up "Or divorcée living in a walk-up apartment." The other hand went down. "You do the math."

"Maybe she loves him," Karma ventured.

"*Pfft.*" Libba and I *pffted* in harmony.

"Is that him?" Libba asked.

Again, I glanced over my shoulder. "Yes."

Libba narrowed her eyes. "Nothing special."

She was right. Chauncey Nelson had the expanding waist-line, receding hair-line, and air of self-importance of many of the men his age. "How old is he?"

"Pushing sixty," Karma replied.

"Hester doesn't seem that old." I'd put her age closer to fifty.

"She's younger."

"Hmmph." Libba opened her menu. "What are we having?"

I pushed open the front door and stepped into the foyer with every intention of calling Anarchy but Aggie was waiting for me with a fistful of phone messages in her hand.

"Celine Wallace has called eight times."

"Eight?"

Aggie's hair sproinged every which way as she waved the messages in the air. "She's been calling—regularly—since ten minutes after you left for lunch."

Poor Celine. Poor Aggie.

Brnng, brnng.

"I bet that's her."

"I'll get it." I left Karma and Aggie in the foyer and answered the phone in Henry's study. "Hello."

"Ellison!" Breathless, raw, panicked—Celine sounded as if she was falling apart. "Would you come over? Please?"

"What's wrong?"

"Please come."

"Celine, what's wrong?"

"I need you—" her voice cracked and she sobbed in my ear.

"I'm on my way." I hung up the phone and returned to the foyer. "I have to run over to the Wallaces' house." My shoulders sagged—all I wanted to do was put my feet up and enjoy a lazy Sunday afternoon. "I don't know how long I'll be. I'm sorry—" I'd been leaving Karma alone. A lot.

"Take care of your friend. I'll be fine."

"Thanks for understanding." I headed back out the front door and climbed in the car.

What was wrong now? Had Celine found out about additional

women? Had Ruth rubbed her nose in the affair? I took a deep breath, turned the key in the ignition, and wished the Wallaces lived farther away than they did.

Five minutes later, I parked at the curb in front of Frank and Celine's Georgian home, only a few houses away from Mother and Daddy's. The boxwoods were neatly trimmed. The lawn was carefully manicured and already greening. The front door hung open.

Oh, dear.

I got out of the car and hurried up the walk. "Celine?" I poked my head into the foyer.

No one answered.

Dread weighed heavy in my stomach.

"Celine!" Louder now.

Again, no one answered.

I stepped inside. "Celine, it's Ellison. Are you here?"

"Ellison." Celine, looking very much as if she'd been dragged through a hedge backward, appeared in the hallway leading to the back of the house. "I'm so glad you're here."

"What's wrong?"

"This way." She turned her back on me.

The weight in my stomach quadrupled and, for an instant, running out the front door seemed the wisest plan. I swallowed a sigh and followed her down the hall, through the kitchen, and into the family room.

I should have run.

Frank Wallace sprawled across the floor with what looked like an icepick handle rising from his chest.

"Did you—" my voice cracked.

"Of course not. He was like this when I got home."

"From my house?"

Celine nodded.

"But that was hours ago."

She nodded again.

"You didn't call the police?"

She shook her head and tears welled in her eyes. "Frank always handles the unpleasant chores." Handles not handled.

Calling the police and telling them your husband had been murdered was more than an unpleasant chore.

Celine gave me an encouraging smile. "I figured you'd know what to do because—"

"Because I find bodies so often?"

"Exactly!" If Frank couldn't handle her unpleasant chores, I could.

"You need to call the police." My voice was gentle.

"They'll make a fuss."

This wasn't a speeding ticket her lawyer could have fixed. This wasn't a citation from the homeowners' association because her trees needed trimming. This was murder. "Your husband is dead."

"I know that," she snapped. "It doesn't mean I want a fuss."

She was going to get a fuss. A huge fuss.

"Will you call? Please? You know what to say." She looked so lost and helpless and vague I caved.

"Where's your phone?"

She pointed to a black telephone not three feet from Frank's body.

Not in a million years was I getting that close to him. "Is there one in the kitchen?"

She nodded.

I turned on my heel, hurried into Celine's avocado green kitchen, and grabbed the receiver. My fingers knew the number.

I focused on the ceiling while the phone rang. Celine had a pot rack suspended over her kitchen island—a pot rack positively dripping with copper pots and molds.

"Jones." Just the sound of Anarchy's voice lifted some of the weight pressing down on me.

"It's me."

"Are you all right?"

"I'm fine." Better now that he was on the phone. "Why?"

"You have that sound in your voice."

"What sound?"

"That I've-found-another-body sound."

"Oh." I wrapped a loop of the phone cord around my ring finger. "That sound."

"You haven't, have you?"

If I narrowed my eyes just-so, the loop around my finger looked like a ring. "Found another body? Not exactly."

"Ellison—" There was a storm warning in his voice.

"Celine found the body." The words came in a rush. "She called me to come over."

Anarchy's silence was long. And fraught. Why-can't-I-find-a-girlfriend-who-finds-deals-on-dress-shirts-instead-of-bodies fraught.

"Are you there?" I finally asked.

"Yeah." Resigned. Anarchy sounded resigned. "Where are you?"

I gave him Celine's address.

"Are you safe?"

"I think so."

"Stay that way. I'm coming."

I hung up the receiver and returned to the family room where Frank lay on the floor and Celine smoked a cigarette.

I stared at her for a long second. Smoking? Now? Really? "Celine, do you have a lawyer?"

She turned her gaze my way. "A lawyer?"

"Yes."

"Why?" She blew a plume of smoke at the ceiling.

"I think you should call him."

She blinked a few times. "Why?"

"The police are going to have questions."

"Frank was dead when I got home." The woman was obviously in shock. Or denial. Or both.

"You left my house at half past eleven."

"Yes." She didn't see the problem.

"It's two thirty."

Celine glanced at her watch. "Closer to a quarter till three."

"The police are going to wonder why you didn't call earlier."

"I couldn't."

"Why not?"

"I was waiting for you."

Who was I to argue?

TWENTY-THREE

Anarchy arrived at the Wallaces' house in a matter of minutes.

I answered the front door. I let him in the house. I resisted, barely, the temptation to fall into his arms.

Mainly I resisted because he'd brought Detective Peters with him.

Detective Peters, clad in a trench coat so wrinkled it would embarrass Columbo, curled his lip at me. "You ever think of staying home with the doors locked?"

"All the time."

He squinted as if he suspected I was being flippant.

I wasn't.

"Who's the stiff?"

"Frank Wallace. He's one of the suspects in the murders of Winthrop Marshall and Marcy—" I didn't know Marcy's last name. I'd found her body and I didn't know her name. Suddenly I needed to sit down.

Anarchy led me to one of the straight-backed chairs that flanked a chest and mirror in Celine's foyer. "You okay?"

"I'll be fine. I just need to sit a minute." I waved toward the back of the house. "Frank's in the family room."

"Do you want coffee?"

More than anything. "I'm fine. Go."

Anarchy's brows drew together, doubt writ across his face. I never turned down coffee.

"Go." I shooed him toward Frank's body.

With one last worried glance, he went.

I sat. And watched a half-dozen uniformed officers tromp through Celine's house. And thought. I thought hard.

Someone had murdered Frank. Celine? Was she in shock or a phenomenal actress? Or had the killer who'd murdered Winthrop and Marcy visited the Wallace house? Three people dead in the same firm in a matter of days. It couldn't be a coincidence. But why? All those young women victimized. Had one of them opted for revenge? Maybe one of their husbands?

I planted my elbows on my knees and lowered my head to my hands. There were too many suspects.

If Frank killed Winthrop over Ruth, would Joanie kill Frank in revenge? That seemed a stretch.

Maybe Marcy had a secret boyfriend.

Maybe Celine had snapped.

Maybe I should leave the whole convoluted mess to Anarchy and Detective Peters.

Maybe a Mr. Coffee lived in Celine's kitchen.

I rose from my chair.

"Ellison Walford Russell, what in the world is going on?" Mother stood at the front door, ready to flatten the uniformed police officer who barred her entrance.

"Frank Wallace was murdered."

"And you found the body?" The officer's blue-clad shoulder was a wisp, easily wiped away by the stiff wind of Mother's delivery.

I straightened my spine. "I did not. Celine found him."

"Then why are you here?"

"She called me."

"And you came?" Mother's expression clearly equated me with the village idiot.

"She didn't tell me he was dead. She said she needed me, so I came." Which explained my presence but not Mother's. "What are you doing here?"

"I saw your car out front."

"I'm going to have to ask you to leave, ma'am." It was cute that the officer thought he could tell Frances Walford what to do.

Mother ignored him. "How many bodies in the past week, Ellison?"

Three. "You make it sound as if it's my fault."

"You could have asked Celine what she wanted."

"She was at my house all morning crying because Frank was having an affair with Ruth Marshall. I thought she was calling about that."

"Frank and Ruth?" Mother's eyes narrowed. "Isn't Ruth a bit long in the tooth for him?"

"Pardon me?"

"Everyone in town knows Frank cheats but it's usually with younger women. Women who make him feel likes he's in his twenties, not pushing sixty-five."

"Frank and Ruth," I confirmed. "They're—they were—a thing."

"Shame on Ruth."

Shame on both of them.

Mother, tiring of talking over the uniformed officer's shoulder, pushed him aside and marched into the foyer. "You look exhausted."

"It's been a stressful week."

She snorted. "This has to stop."

"No one would like that more than I would."

"You have a daughter. Responsibilities."

"I know that, Mother."

"You can't expend all your energy on dead bodies."

I looked up and studied Celine's chandelier. Brass and glass. Not my favorite.

"You think you're strong, that you can take all this on. But let me tell you something about strength, it's not a constant. One day nothing can stop you, the next you're brought low by a broken nail." Mother wagged a perfectly manicured nail under my nose. "Some people think strength is like an oak tree—a seedling that grows and grows. They're wrong. Strength is a well. You find a bucket and draw what you need. For some of us, the well is deep—" she indulged in a satisfied smile "—for others it's shallow." She stared into my eyes. "No one gets a bottomless well, Ellison. Pick your battles. Save your strength for the things that matter."

"Mother, I don't find bodies on purpose. There are things I can't control."

"And there are things you can."

"Finding bodies isn't one of them." It was as if we were speaking different languages.

"Now you're just being stubborn."

I blinked. Repeatedly. I was the one being stubborn?

"How did he die?"

I blinked some more. "Someone put an icepick through his heart."

Mother wrinkled her nose and her lips drew back from her teeth.

I closed my eyes and reminded myself of the nice things she'd said about me in the ladies' lounge when she didn't know I was listening.

"Are you free to go?"

I opened my eyes. "I'm not sure."

"You're not a suspect, are you?"

"No."

"Then why are you here?"

"Because the police may have questions. Because Celine may need me."

"Oh, please. That woman has probably taken so many Valium she doesn't even realize he's dead."

Valium. That explained so much. Why hadn't I realized?

"Tell the police you're leaving." She looked over my shoulder as if she could see the family room from the foyer. "That detective is here, isn't he? He'll let you leave. I'll stay with Celine."

That detective. Anarchy.

"Ellison—" Mother looked straight into my eyes "—your reputation can't take too many more murders. Go."

Because of the nice things she'd said about me in the ladies' lounge when she didn't know I was listening, I nodded. "Fine."

I walked toward the kitchen.

"Where are you going?"

"To get my purse and to tell Anarchy I'm leaving."

Mother merely sighed.

I ignored the put-upon-ness of her sigh, went to the kitchen, and picked up my handbag from the counter. "Excuse me," I said to one of the uniformed officers. "Would you please ask Detective Jones to step out for a moment?"

"Yes, ma'am."

It was only a few seconds before Anarchy appeared in the kitchen. "What's wrong?"

"Mother's here." Two words that completely answered his question. "She's going to stay with Celine. I'd like to go home."

For one crazy instant, he looked disappointed. "I'll come by later."

I smiled up at him. "I'll see you then." I draped my purse over my shoulder and scurried out of the kitchen before I did something stupid like kiss him in front of the uniformed officer.

Mother lurked in the foyer. "You're going?"

"I am."

She nodded. Once. A regal I-got-my-way nod. "I'll call you later."

Because of the nice things she'd said about me in the ladies' lounge when she didn't know I was listening, I kissed her cheek. "Thanks, Mother."

I drove home with the radio on. An O'Jays song played.

I parked in the circle drive.

Before I'd even opened the car door, Aggie had the front door open. What now? Another fistful of messages? Another disaster? Another murder?

I got out of the car and lurched toward her. "What's happened now?"

"Nothing. I just wanted to know what happened at Mrs. Wallace's."

"Someone murdered Frank."

"Mrs. Wallace?"

"I don't think so. Mother's sitting with her."

I stepped into the foyer. "Is there any coffee?"

"I'll make a pot."

Together we walked to the kitchen.

"Where's Karma?" I asked.

"She's poking around your studio."

Normally that would give me hives but, thanks to McCallester and Max, everything was already out of place. I merely shrugged. "I'll go find her in a few minutes."

"Coffee first," Aggie noted.

She knew me well.

Aggie filled Mr. Coffee's reservoir. I scooped coffee grounds into a filter. And, in no time, Mr. Coffee was doing what he did best.

"Who do you think killed him?" Aggie settled onto the stool next to mine while we waited for Mr. Coffee to brew.

"There's something going on at that firm."

"But what?"

"No idea. It must have something to do with the way Winthrop and Frank treated their employees but I can't make the pieces fit. If it's about preying on the girls, why kill Marcy?"

Brnng, brnng.

What fresh hell was this?

Brnng, brnng.

"We could let it ring," Aggie suggested.

"It could be Mother. If I don't answer, she'll come over."

Brnng, brnng.

I sighed and stood. My fingers closed around the phone. I lifted the receiver. "Hello."

"Ellison? Is it true?"

"Who's calling?" I asked.

"It's Bea. Is it true?"

"Bea, I didn't recognize your voice. Is what true?"

"Did someone murder Frank Wallace?"

News traveled fast. "Yes."

"Oh, my. Oh, my. Oh, my." Her pitch was one normally reserved for bats or dog whistles.

"Bea, take a breath."

"Take a breath! Buzz could be next!"

"What?"

"First Winthrop, then Frank. Buzz is the last partner."

She had a point. In her shoes, I'd be worried too.

"Where is Buzz?"

"He went to the office."

"Shouldn't he be resting?"

"Yes! That's exactly what I told him but do you think he listened to me? No! He insisted on going. There's some report Marcy didn't finish, and the regulators are coming."

"Couldn't Bonnie do it?"

"Exactly what I asked him. But he said he had to make sure it was done right." She took a giant gulp of air. "Now he's down at the office by himself and there's a murderer on the loose."

"Call him and ask him to come home."

"He's not answering the phone." Bea rasped another breath. "I'm going down there."

Oh dear Lord. "Bea, you can't go by yourself."

"Thank you! I knew I could count on you."

She could?

"I'll be there in ten minutes."

"Bea—" I was too late. She'd already hung up the phone. "Dammit."

"What?"

"Bea Bisby is on her way over here. She wants me to go to Buzz's office with her. Apparently he's not answering the phone."

"You shouldn't go alone."

"Exactly what I told her."

"Call Anarchy." Anarchy. Not that detective. Was Aggie thawing?

I picked up the phone and dialed Celine's number.

The line rang busy.

I hung up. "The number is three-six-one-oh-eight-nine-four, would you keep trying?"

"Where are you going?"

"If I'm going to that office with Bea, I'm taking my gun." I raced up the backstairs, threw open my bedroom door, and pulled the gun out of the top drawer of the nightstand.

When I returned to the kitchen, Aggie was still trying the line. She hung up when she saw me. "I'm going to call the police station and have him paged."

"Good idea." I slid the gun into my purse.

"A better idea would be for you to wait until he can go with you."

She wasn't wrong, but a little voice was telling me Buzz didn't have much time.

Ding dong.

"She's here." I glanced toward the front hall. "Get in touch with Anarchy. Have him meet us there."

Ding dong.

"Coming," I called.

Less than a minute later I was in Bea's car with my hands clenched on the dashboard. "If we get in an accident, we can't save him."

Bea eased up on the gas pedal. Slightly. "What if something has already happened?"

"I bet Buzz spread all his papers on the conference table and didn't hear the phone."

"If you really thought that, you wouldn't have come with me."

Bea was right. I did think Buzz was in terrible danger and I'd chosen to involve myself. If she found out, Mother would have a hissy fit.

On a Sunday afternoon, the building's parking lot was empty. Bea parked right in front of the door and jumped out of the car.

"Bea," I called after her. "Slow down."

She waited for me at the door, a look of supreme impatience

on her face. She slotted a key into the lock and we rushed into the lobby. She rushed past the elevators that could carry us to the seventh floor. She rushed into the stairwell.

"Bea, why not take the elevator?"

"They turn them off on the weekends."

"Buzz just had a heart attack and he climbed seven flights of stairs?"

"The man won't listen."

We were breathless on the fifth floor when the sound of the elevator moving vibrated through the wall. We exchanged a look.

Leaving Bea, who was holding her side as if one of her ribs had pierced a lung, I ran up the last two flights, pulled my gun out my purse, and pushed open the door to Bisby, Marshall & Wallace. Just Bisby now.

"Buzz?" The shout I had planned escaped my lips as a whisper.

The office was filled with shadows. And quiet.

I tiptoed forward. Where was I in relation to the partners' offices? There was the reception area, which meant Buzz's office was in the far corner.

Glad of the thick carpet on the floor, I crept toward his office. My fingers tightened on the .22 in my hand. "Buzz?"

Silence answered me.

There was the door to his office.

I closed my hand around the knob and turned. Nothing happened. The door was locked. I should have grabbed Bea's keys before I sprinted up the steps. I tapped softly. "Buzz?"

Nothing.

I tapped again.

Still nothing.

"I have keys."

I jumped three feet in the air and my heart ricocheted around my chest like a pinball.

I turned and glared at the woman who'd snuck up on me. "You're lucky I didn't shoot you."

Bea looked at the gun in my hand and her eyes widened.

"Give me the keys."

"I'll do it." She pushed past me.

Fine by me. After the fright Bea gave me, my hands were shaking too much to fit a key in a lock.

Bea's hands shook too. It took her three tries to slide the key into the lock and turn it.

"Buzz?" She pushed open the door.

Buzz's office was filled with afternoon light. Light that illuminated the man on the carpet all too well.

"Buzz!" Bea raced to her husband's side and fell to her knees. "Buzz!"

"Is he breathing?"

"I can't tell."

Oh dear Lord. I hurried toward them.

"Ellison!" Anarchy's voice echoed through the empty offices.

"Back here!" I rushed back to the door. "Buzz's office!"

Anarchy emerged from the shadows and pulled me hard against his chest. "Are you all right?"

"Fine. But Buzz—" I pulled away from the safety of Anarchy's arms and pointed.

The cop look settled into Anarchy's eyes and he rushed past me, dropped to his knees next to Buzz, and felt for a pulse. "Call for an ambulance."

I grabbed the receiver of the phone on Bonnie's desk, pushed the button for an outside line, and called for help.

Needing an ambulance had to be a good thing. If Buzz were dead, Anarchy wouldn't have sounded so urgent. At least that's what I prayed was true.

TWENTY-FOUR

Anarchy and I watched the ambulance carrying Bea and Buzz to the hospital drive away then he turned to me. A tight, angry expression darkened his face. "What were you thinking coming here by yourself?"

"I was thinking Buzz needed help."

"You could have waited. You should have waited."

I shrugged. "Maybe. Maybe not."

His lean face was serious. "You're not supposed to take risks like this."

It wasn't as if I was completely helpless.

"You're not trained for this. You're not—" he fisted his hands and crossed his arms over his chest "—you're not Pepper Anderson."

Police Woman. Poor Pepper. She had to go undercover all the time—as a nurse, a model, a prostitute, a moll, an exotic dancer, a teacher, a secretary, a masseuse. It sounded exhausting.

"I don't want to be." It was the truth.

"Then leave chasing bad guys to the police."

"I wasn't chasing a bad guy, I was helping a friend."

He scowled at me. "Is that why you brought your gun?"

He could scowl all he wanted. If a friend needed me, I would help. And his scowl would be a thousand times deeper if I hadn't brought the gun. I raised my chin, ready to argue.

We stared at each other for the longest ten seconds ever. Then Anarchy sighed as if I was a lost cause. "Come on, I'll take you home."

As we walked to his car, I asked, "Do you think Buzz will be all right?"

"The EMT seemed to think so." Then, with a grudging shake of his head, he added, "He's lucky you found him when you did."

Buzz was lucky period. Lucky he'd been brought to the carpet by another heart attack and not the person who'd murdered both of his partners and Marcy.

Anarchy opened the car's passenger door and I settled inside.

He climbed into the car and closed his hands around the wheel.

I asked, "Any idea who killed Frank?"

"None."

"How long had he been like that?" I leaned my head back against the rest, closed my eyes, and remembered Frank's body sprawled across the floor.

"You mean dead?" Anarchy turned the ignition and shifted the car into drive.

"Yes."

"The medical examiner estimates he'd been dead for around five hours when you called us."

"So Celine couldn't have done it."

"You considered her a suspect?" Anarchy sounded surprised.

"The surviving spouse is always a suspect." A fact I'd learned well when I was the surviving spouse. If Buzz had died in questionable circumstances, Bea would be a suspect. I pictured Buzz sprawled amongst all those papers and Bea's horror-stricken face.

Those papers. "I wonder..."

"You wonder what?"

"Give me a minute." An idea was coming together in my brain. Anarchy drove. I thought.

"The report."

"What report?"

"The one Marcy was working on. Could we go back to Buzz's

office? Please?"

"Why?"

"I think we should look at that report."

"Why?"

"Because we have no idea why Marcy was killed and she was working on it."

Anarchy's mouth tightened but he turned the car around.

When he pulled up in front of the building, I closed my hand around the door handle, and paused. "Darn it. How are we going to get in?"

"Mrs. Bisby gave me the keys." He held up a key ring. "She asked me to lock up."

We returned to the hushed, shadowed offices of Bisby, Marshall & Wallace and made our way to the collection of papers fanned across Buzz's desk and carpet.

"We can't take these." Anarchy followed rules. Always.

"Let me make a call." I dialed the hospital and asked to be connected to the emergency room. "Hello, this is Ellison Russell calling. Buzz Bisby was just brought in. I need to speak with Mrs. Bisby."

"This isn't an answering service."

I kept my voice polite. "I know that. And I know it's an imposition. But this is an emergency. Please, just this one time, won't you help me?" If honey didn't work, I'd pull out the big gun. Mother's name.

"Give me a minute," said the grudging voice on the other end of the line.

A moment later, Bea said, "Hello."

"Bea, it's Ellison. Anarchy—Detective Jones—and I are back at the firm. We need your permission to take a look at the report Marcy and Buzz were working on."

"Why?"

"I think it might have something to do with the murders."

"I don't know if Buzz would like that." She sounded a million miles away.

"Buzz might still be in danger."

"Fine." Her voice sharpened. "Whatever you need."

"Thanks, Bea. How's Buzz?"

"The doctors haven't told me. Ellison..."

"Yes?"

"Buzz and I can't live like this. Catch the killer." She hung up.

I dropped the receiver back in the cradle. "We have permission to review the report."

Anarchy and I gathered up the pages, glancing at numbers and graphs we didn't understand.

He looked up from a graph that looked as if it required a PhD to comprehend. "This is Greek."

"Good thing we have someone who speaks the language."

"Karma?"

I nodded. "Karma. Let's take all this back to my house."

The second time Anarchy and I left the firm, we carried a banker's box full of papers with us.

We drove through a mile's worth of silence.

"Are you sure about this?" Anarchy nodded his chin at the box in the backseat.

"Not at all. But it's worth a try." I glanced out the window. There were plenty of reasons to kill Winthrop and Frank. And, there were plenty of people who would have volunteered for the job—their spouses, Joanie's husband, the girls at the firm, people they'd fired—maybe even Buzz. "There has to be a reason for Marcy's death."

Anarchy didn't look convinced.

When we arrived at my house, Anarchy hauled the box into the dining room and deposited it on the table. "I need to get back to the Wallaces'. Call me if you find anything?"

"I will." I walked with him to the front door and paused with my hand on the knob, not quite ready to say goodbye.

"Promise me something?" He brushed a lock of my hair away from my face.

Anything. "What?"

"If you find something, you let me handle it. Don't go running off. You're not invincible."

"I know that. Lord, do I know that. Do you have any idea how many times I've been hospitalized since I met you?"

"Too many." He leaned down and brushed a kiss across my lips. "Be careful."

"You, too."

I closed the door on Anarchy, turned, and went searching for Karma. I found her in the family room. "What are you reading?"

She held up her book, showing me the cover. *You Can Profit from a Monetary Crisis.*

The kind of book I'd read to cure insomnia.

"Would you mind taking a break to help me with something? Please?"

"Of course." She dropped the book onto the coffee-table. "What?"

"A project." I led her to the dining room. "Anarchy and I don't understand what any of this stuff means. I was hoping you could look at it."

Karma lifted the lid to the box and peered inside.

"I know it's a terrible imposition..."

"Are you kidding?" Excitement danced in her eyes as if I'd offered her a treat. First the snooze-worthy book, now a love of numbers. Wow. "I love reports."

"What can I do?"

"Brew a pot of coffee?"

We really were sisters. "Consider it done."

After thirty minutes of sipping coffee and watching Karma put papers in stacks I was ready to climb out of my skin.

She looked up at me. "Don't you have something better to do? Paint? Read a book? Take Max for a walk?"

"I could put my studio back together."

"Do that!" There was a suspicious amount of enthusiasm in her voice.

I could tell when I wasn't wanted. I clomped up the stairs to my too-neat studio and scanned the books shelved alphabetically by author. I ought to fix them—reorganize them. Instead, I wandered over to the drafting table where someone had laid out all the scraps of paper I'd pulled from the trash in Loose Park. Idly I moved the pieces around.

Idly until I noticed the typeface on one tiny scrap. "...isby, Marsh..."

After I saw that, I moved the little scraps with purpose. Putting the pieces together was slow, tedious work and my back ached from hunching over the table, but it was still better than Karma's job—reviewing ledgers and graphs.

"What are you doing?" Grace appeared at the top of the stairs. "I brought you a fresh cup of coffee."

"Bless you." I straightened, stretching my back, then took the cup from her hands and drank deeply.

"Seriously." A small furrow marked the space between Grace's brows. "What are you doing?"

"Putting pieces of paper together."

"And what's Karma doing?"

"Reviewing ledger entries from a brokerage firm."

Grace yawned.

I didn't blame her.

She pointed to a small section of one page. "It looks like you've made some progress."

A tiny bit of progress. That one shredded piece of paper was coming together. The firm's name was at the top with "confidential" written in capital letters beneath.

"Where did you get all this?" Grace effortlessly moved a piece into place with the tip of her finger.

"A trash bin in Loose Park."

She snatched her finger away as if she'd catch cooties. "What? Why are you doing this?"

"I want to know what it says."

That earned an eye roll. "But why?"

"Because it might help catch a killer." There had to be a good reason shredded documents from the firm had ended up in the bottom of a trash barrel in Loose Park.

"Oh." Grace flexed her fingers, then gingerly moved another piece into place. "I'll help."

I hid a smile. "Thanks."

We worked in silence.

"Do you have a radio up here?" Grace asked.

"Nope."

"How do you stand the quiet?"

"I like it."

Another eye roll. "Have you ever heard of Plastico?"

"Maybe. I'm not sure. Why?"

She glanced down at a grouping of scraps. "This says the stock was set to rise by November 15th."

"What?" Set to rise? That couldn't be right.

"Right here." She pointed. "See?"

I read her scraps. Or tried to. I rubbed my eyes and focused. "That might be illegal."

"The price rising?"

"Knowing about an impending rise and trading on the information is."

"Mr. Wallace and Mr. Marshall were breaking the law?"

"If they used this information they were. Hold on." I raced down the stairs and pulled my most recent brokerage statement out of the file drawer in Henry's desk.

The list of stocks included the acquisition cost and the carrying price. On November 10th, I'd bought five thousand dollars' worth of Plastico at seventeen dollars a share.

I poked my head into the dining room. "Karma, have you heard of a company called Plastico?"

She looked up from a document. "Why do you ask?"

"I'm not sure. Yet."

"They were a mid-sized plastics and chemical company that was bought out by a larger competitor, SynChem."

"What does that mean?"

"Plastico shareholders, people who owned shares before—" she scrunched her face with the effort of remembering "—November 16th, received the equivalent of forty-five dollars' worth of SynChem stock for every one share of Plastico they held."

"So, someone buying before the announcement, someone buying Plastico at seventeen dollars a share, made a killing?"

"Exactly."

"Grace and I found something odd."

A pair of readers sat on her nose and she looked at me from over the top of their frame. "What do you mean?"

"Winthrop bought me Plastico on November 10th."

"He picked a good stock."

I shook my head. "There was an internal memo saying trades needed to be completed by November 15th."

Karma's gaze sharpened. "That's insider trading."

"I know."

"That's against the law."

I knew that too. "Keeping it quiet is a motive for murder."

Karma took off her glasses and put them down on the table. "Two out of three partners are dead."

"Are you suggesting Buzz killed Winthrop and Frank?"

"Someone did."

"Buzz was in the hospital when Marcy was killed."

"Maybe he has an accomplice." She waved her hand over the papers on the dining room table. "This report—" she shook her head "—it's fiction. The numbers are crazy—not even possible. He had to have known. He had to have been in on this. That or he wasn't paying a bit of attention to what his partners were doing."

Buzz willfully breaking the law seemed impossible. Although, if Winthrop and Frank had led him down a shadowy path, he might have followed them. Maybe he had traded stocks based on insider information. Maybe he'd been willing to kill to keep his crimes quiet. "I can't see it." I could see it—all too clearly—but I couldn't face another friend being a killer.

"Then who?"

"What about the person giving them the information?"

We stared at each other, realization dawning in our eyes at the same time.

"I have to call Anarchy."

Karma tapped a finger against her pursed lips. "We don't have any proof. We should wait until we have proof."

"Why? Anarchy will believe us."

"I'd just feel better if it wasn't our word against his."

I glanced down at the stacks of paper on my dining room table. "We'll find the proof. You go through the rest of these papers. I'll help Grace. We'll see what we can find."

TWENTY-FIVE

Grace and I spent the next few hours bent over the table in my studio. We pushed bits of paper around and pieced together enough to find references to another seven companies and their stocks (I checked my statement and I owned all of them). We did not find the name of the person who'd been providing the firm with insider information.

Then again, I wasn't expecting to.

"You and Aunt Karma think these murders are about hiding insider trading?" Grace tried fitting a piece of paper into the page she was working on then shifted it back to the center of the table with the rest of the unaligned pieces.

"I do." I planted my hands on my hips and stretched my back. That felt so good I reached my arms above my head and stretched for the ceiling. "I think I'm going to check on Karma. Do you want anything from downstairs?"

"A Tab, please."

"Lime?"

"Of course."

"Got it." I headed downstairs, poking my head into the dining room on my way to the kitchen. Karma wasn't there. "Karma?" I called.

She didn't answer.

I walked to the kitchen. "Karma?"

There was still no answer.

Max, who was reclining on his bed, lifted his head off his paws and yawned.

He was no help.

I wandered into the family room. "Karma?"

She still didn't answer.

Bemused, I wandered back to the dining room where Karma's neat stacks of paper lined the table.

One stack stood apart. I picked up the pages. The first sheet was a list of corporate officers for Plastico. I recognized one name. Another sheet, another list of officers—this list for one of the stocks Grace and I had identified upstairs. Again, there was one name I recognized. The same name.

My grip on the pages tightened. "Karma?" This time I yelled.

The only response was the hollow clomp of Grace's clogs on the backstairs. She burst into the dining room. "What's wrong?"

"I can't find Karma."

"Are all the cars here?"

"I haven't looked."

"I'll check." Grace was gone only an instant. "The Mercedes is gone. Where do think she went?"

I looked down at the sheets of papers clasped in my fist and my stomach twisted itself into an impossibly difficult yoga pose. "I think she went to confront a killer."

"Where?"

"We've got to call Anarchy." I dropped the pages and they floated to the floor.

"Mom, you're scaring me."

"I have to call him. I promised if I found anything I'd let him handle it."

"But Aunt Karma—"

I slipped past Grace on my way to the phone. "Anarchy can help her better than we can." My fingers closed around the receiver and I dialed his number.

A few seconds later someone answered the phone. "Detective Jones' office."

"I need to speak with him. Please."

"He's out of the office, ma'am."

"This is Ellison Russell calling."

Whoever was on the other end of the line was unimpressed.

"It's urgent I speak with him. I know who killed Frank Wallace and Winthrop Marshall and Marcy—" What was her last name?

"You know the identity of a killer?" Disbelief colored the voice.

"I do. And my sister has gone to confront the killer." Just saying the words wrapped steel bands around my chest. Tight steel bands. "I need to speak with Anarchy—Detective Jones, right now. Right away."

"I'll page him for you, ma'am."

"Thank you." Some of the tightness in my chest released

"Your number?"

"Three-six-one-oh-eight-nine-four."

"Paging him now. You should hear from him shortly."

"Thank you." I hung up the phone.

"What now?" Grace demanded.

"We wait for Anarchy's call."

"But—"

"If we chase after Karma without talking to him, Anarchy won't know where to go."

"But—"

Brnng, brnng.

I snatched the phone out of its cradle. "Hello."

"Ellison, what's wrong?" Anarchy's voice was a like a balm, soothing the worry bubbling inside me.

"Karma's gone."

"Gone?"

"I think she went after the killer."

"The killer?"

I nodded then remembered Anarchy couldn't see me. "Yes."

"Who?"

"Chauncey Nelson."

"Who?"

"He was covering up insider trading. He and his wife are

staying at The Alameda."

"I'm on my way."

"I—" I was talking into a dead telephone. Anarchy had hung up.

"Let's go." Grace had her purse over her shoulder and her car keys in her hand.

"Go?"

"You're not leaving me." She wore that stubborn I-dare-you-to-argue expression unique to teenagers.

I argued. "It could be dangerous."

"Then you shouldn't go either."

I was going. And I didn't have time to argue. "Fine. But you stay in the lobby."

The I-dare-you-to-argue expression morphed into a smirk that said where I went, she went. "Let's go."

Grace drove. I was white-knuckled and kept my mouth closed—nothing good ever came of my criticizing her driving.

"I'm not gonna crash." She sped up for a yellow light.

"I didn't say a word."

"You don't have to say anything. Your body language does your talking for you."

I released my death-grip on the door handle and forced my shoulders away from my ears. "I haven't the slightest idea what you're talking about."

Grace rolled her eyes, pulled into The Alameda's drive, and screeched to a halt inches from the terrified valet.

I said nothing. Now was not the time to argue over her driving. I merely opened the car door, said a small, silent prayer of thanks, and hurried into the lobby.

Anarchy wasn't there. Nor was Karma. I rushed over to the front desk. "I'm here to see Chauncey and Hester Nelson, would you give me their room number please?"

The young man behind the desk regarded me with polite disdain. "I'm sorry the Nelsons have checked out."

"When?" I snapped.

He blinked at my tone.

Grace, young and pretty and the owner of a thousand-watt smile, appeared next to me. "She didn't mean to be rude. It's just really important that we talk to them."

His expression softened.

I dug in my purse, pulled out a twenty, and slid it across the counter. "It is imperative."

His hand covered the bill. Discreetly. "They left for the airport about fifteen minutes ago. It's funny. You're the second woman who's asked."

Karma!

I turned away, my brain already calculating the fastest way to the airport, then turned back.

The young man raised his brows.

"A police detective should be here any minute. Would you please tell him what you told us?"

His eyes widened slightly and he nodded.

"Thank you." I turned yet again and—*whomp*—ran smack into a solid chest. I tilted my head and looked up at Anarchy. Just seeing him eased some of the tension in my chest.

"Going somewhere?" His lips quirked into a delicious smile.

"The airport."

"The airport?"

"Karma's in trouble."

"I'll drive."

"I'm coming too," said Grace.

Anarchy's expression darkened.

"I wouldn't let her leave me at home." Grace explained. Then she gave Anarchy the I-dare-you-to-argue expression.

Anarchy, a man without children, wasn't remotely equipped to withstand teenage stubbornness. The disapproval writ clear on his face stumbled and fell. "Fine. Let's go."

We hurried outside and climbed into Anarchy's car.

A moment later we were on Roanoke Trafficway speeding north.

"This is really cool," said Grace from the back seat.

I glanced over my shoulder. "Cool?"

"Yeah, cool." She grinned like a lunatic as Anarchy swerved through traffic. "Anarchy, could you give me some driving tips? When I speed, I make Mom nervous."

"Speeding is against the law." Anarchy sounded serious but his lips curled in a small smile.

We raced past downtown, flew over the Broadway Bridge (barely slowing to throw a quarter in the metal net), and hit the highway, where Anarchy put the pedal to the metal.

"How will we know which terminal?" Grace asked.

Anarchy eased up on the gas pedal. "Who has the most flights to New York?"

"When I go, I fly TWA."

"Which terminal?" Anarchy pushed the needle on the speedometer higher.

I closed my eyes and pictured the three giant rings that comprised Kansas City's new airport. If one knew the gate number, it was easy to be dropped off feet from the correct gate. We didn't know the gate number. We didn't even know the terminal. "I think it's terminal A."

Anarchy nodded.

"Why did Karma go by herself?" asked Grace.

Anarchy blew past a slow-moving car. "Recklessness runs in the family."

I opened my mouth to argue, remembered Grace's driving, and sealed my lips. Maybe Anarchy was right. Maybe we were a bit reckless.

We arrived at the airport and Anarchy pulled to a screeching halt at the curb in the middle of Terminal A's ring. We leapt from the car.

"You can't park here," said an officious little man in a blue uniform.

Anarchy flashed his badge. "Police."

The doors to the terminal opened and we ran inside, skidding to a halt in front of a baggage claim.

"Which way?" asked Grace.

The sides of the rings stretched away from us.

"We'll go that way—" I pointed to my right "—and Anarchy can go the other."

Anarchy's eyes narrowed. Almost as if I was being reckless.

"There are thousands of people here. Nothing is going to happen to us."

He nodded once—more of a jab of his chin than an actual nod.

"C'mon, Grace." I took off to the right, trusting Grace would follow me.

I ran. Chauncey Nelson was a killer. What had Karma been thinking?

The waiting areas for departing planes were separated from the public walkway by walls of glass. I scanned the waiting areas as I ran.

There!

I stopped and Grace crashed into me, sending us both careening to the floor.

I ignored the twinge in my ankle. And my elbow. And my knee. "Go." I pointed to the right. "Go find Anarchy."

Her gaze traveled to the other side of the glass where Karma stood planted in front of Chauncey and Hester.

"Go!"

Grace went.

I watched her weave through passengers dragging suitcases. When she disappeared, I pushed off the floor and limped to the check-in. "I need to get in there."

The woman checking tickets offered me an indulgent smile. "May I see your boarding pass?"

"I don't have a boarding pass. I'm not going anywhere."

"I'm sorry, ma'am. No one without a boarding pass is allowed beyond this point."

"My sister is in there. She's in danger."

The woman's brows rose in an I-always-get-the-crazies arch.

The people on the other side of the glass were stirring, gathering bags, and books, and folded newspapers, standing, stretching, shuffling towards the ticketing agent at the gate.

"You can't let that plane take off."

The woman's brows rose to her hairline.

"You can't! There's a murderer waiting to board that plane."

"Are you with the police?" Her tone said she knew I wasn't.

"No, but—"

"I'm going to have to ask you to step aside. There are people with tickets who need access to the boarding area."

Where was Anarchy?

I glanced at the concourse. Anarchy and Grace weren't there.

"Ma'am?" The ticketing agent was waiting for me to move.

"Are you getting on the plane, lady?" The man behind me sounded supremely impatient.

"You—" I channeled Mother "—are about to let a murderer escape justice. Would you like to explain that to the police?"

On the other side of the glass, Karma and Chauncey were arguing while Hester wrung her hands.

"Ma'am, I'm going to call security."

"Do it."

Chauncey grabbed Karma's arm and shook her. He'd murdered three people and now he had Karma.

"Do it, please. Call security!"

The woman's gaze followed mine to the gate where Chauncey was man-handling Karma.

Why wasn't anyone helping her? Couldn't any of the other passengers see what I was seeing?

"Ellison!"

I turned toward Anarchy's voice.

He held out his badge, ran past the woman who'd refused me entry, and pulled Chauncey away from Karma.

Chauncey fisted his right hand and swung.

The blow connected with Anarchy's jaw and his head snapped back.

"Call security!" I demanded.

The ticket agent looked blank—as if Chauncey's blow had landed on her chin instead of Anarchy's.

In the boarding area, one woman screamed. A second (Hester) fainted. A man even bigger than Mac rushed toward the fighting men.

Anarchy swung at Chauncey and the New Yorker doubled over and fell to the carpet.

Karma stepped in front of the giant's rush toward Anarchy.

The giant knocked her flat then tripped over her body.

He too fell.

Oomph.

Karma and the giant struggled to free themselves from the tangle of limbs on the floor.

A security guard with a paunch, a mustache, and a drawn gun pushed past me. Nothing good could come of that.

"Anarchy!" Just yelling his name sucked all the air from my lungs.

The detective—my detective—turned and held up his badge.

The guard lowered his gun and my lungs re-inflated.

A moment later, Karma and the giant were on their feet, Chauncey was in cuffs, and Hester was in tears.

"Chauncey Nelson, you're under arrest for the murders of Winthrop Marshall, Marcy Kowaleski, and Frank Wallace."

Chauncey leaned his head back and what looked like a smile played across his lips. "What?"

The man was genuinely surprised.

Something was wrong.

TWENTY-SIX

Anarchy, Grace, and I waited on the curb for Karma to appear with my Mercedes.

"You didn't jump into the melee." He smiled down at me.

"It wouldn't have been helpful." I glanced at the car as it pulled to a stop next to us. "Besides, Karma was doing enough jumping for both of us."

"True." Anarchy bent down and brushed a kiss across my lips. "I'm glad you're all safe."

"Me, too."

"I'll call you later."

"Just come over."

The look in his eyes could have melted a polar ice cap. It certainly melted me.

I climbed into the passenger seat and took a deep, much-needed breath. "We need to stop by The Alameda."

"We're not going home?" Grace asked.

"I thought we'd pick up your car."

"Right." She nodded.

"Chauncey looked so surprised." Karma pulled into traffic. A smile flirted across her lips.

"True." I had words for Karma. Many words. What had she been thinking going after a killer by herself? Did she have no regard for her own safety? How had she got past the ticket agent? I kept those words bottled up inside. "He looked almost relieved."

"Relieved? The man is going to jail for the rest of his life." A smile played across Karma's lips. "Maybe he was in shock."

I hadn't seen shock. I'd seen relief. As if he'd been arrested for something he didn't do. Then again, I supposed we all saw what we wanted to see.

I closed my eyes, rested my head against the back of the seat, and thought. If Chauncey hadn't killed Winthrop, Marcy, and Frank, who had?

We all saw what we wanted to see. Especially me. I opened my eyes. "Turn the car around."

"What? Why?" Karma demanded.

"They've made a mistake. I need to talk to Anarchy. Right away."

Karma cut across three lanes of traffic and took an exit going well above the stated speed limit.

Grace squealed.

I held on to the door handle for dear life. "Getting us there alive would be a plus."

"I don't drive in San Francisco."

I wished I'd known that before we got on the highway.

Ten minutes later we were in front of Terminal A. What if I was wrong? I gulped. What if I was right?

I jumped out of the car and ran inside the terminal.

I spotted countless uniformed officers. I spotted Detective Peters. I didn't spot Anarchy or the Nelsons.

Detective Peters spotted me and sauntered over to where I stood. "What do you want?"

"I'm looking for Anarchy—Detective Jones."

"Gone. Took the perp back to the station."

"What happened to his wife?"

"She followed in a cab. Why are you so interested?" He regarded me with beady eyes.

"Chauncey Nelson isn't the killer."

"I suppose you know who is?" He stopped just short of sneering. Barely.

"I think so."

His beady eyes narrowed to slits. "You're the one who dragged us all up here."

Chauncey was guilty of insider trading not murder. I was sure of it. Sort of. "I'm sorry about that."

Now Detective Peters let his sneer sneak past his mustache. "Do you have any idea how much paperwork that will cause us?"

"Sorry about that, too."

Peters cheeks reddened and I decided leaving was an excellent idea.

I hurried back to the car where Karma still sat behind the wheel.

"Move over. I'm driving."

"What? Why?"

"I think we've all had enough excitement for one day."

With an eyeroll worthy of Grace, Karma exited the driver's seat and circled the car to the passenger's side.

We drove back to the city at a sedate, calming pace.

"Why did we go back to the airport?" asked Grace from the backseat.

"I don't think Chauncey did it."

That was met with a moment's silence.

Karma flashed me a look. "You mean I raced to the airport to confront a man who's not even guilty?"

"About that."

"Yes?"

"What the hell were you thinking?"

She took a deep breath and clasped her hands in her lap. "I was thinking I'd let far too many men walk all over me. I was thinking I wanted to be there when Chauncey got what was coming to him." She tilted her head and looked at the roof of the car. "If Chauncey didn't kill those people, who did?"

"I need to confirm one thing before I'm sure."

"With whom?"

"Hester Nelson."

Grace finally spoke. "You know who did it?"

"I think so."

"So why are we driving so slowly?"

"We're not driving slowly. We're driving the speed limit. Chauncey has been arrested for the murders. The real killer isn't going anywhere."

We drove to the police station. I put the car in park but left the keys in the ignition. "You two should head to The Alameda and pick up Grace's car."

"And leave you here? No way, Mom."

"We're not going anywhere."

"Fine." I wasn't in the mood to argue. "I'll be back as soon as I can."

"We're not waiting in the car." Grace opened the car door and got out.

Karma did the same.

"Fine." I too stepped out of the car. "But I need to speak with Hester alone."

"Duh." Grace rolled her eyes.

"You'll tell us what she says?" asked Karma.

"If you want."

We stepped into the police station where the scents of cigarette smoke and desperation assaulted our noses.

I marched up to the front desk. "I need to speak with Detective Jones—Detective Anarchy Jones—please."

"He's busy."

"My name is Ellison Russell and I have information about his case. It's important."

The man on the other side of the desk looked as if he'd heard every story ever told. "Sure it is."

"Please. Just tell him Ellison Russell is here."

"I'll let him know." He rose from behind his desk. "Have a seat."

As if I'd ever sit in one of those chairs. They looked like a prime place to catch an unmentionable disease.

A few moments later, a uniformed officer appeared. "I'll take you to Detective Jones, Mrs. Russell."

"Thank you." I turned to Grace and Karma. "You can go home. I'll call a cab."

"We're not going anywhere." Grace wore her most stubborn expression. "Not without you."

My heart warmed. "I won't be long."

I followed the officer into the bowels of the station.

He led me to a desk." Wait here, please."

A few endless seconds later, Anarchy joined me. "What's going on?"

"I don't think he did it."

Anarchy's mouth moved but no words came out.

"I need to talk to Hester."

"Ellison, he had means and motive." Anarchy rubbed his jaw. "He assaulted a police officer."

"He's definitely guilty but not of murder."

"And you think talking to his wife will clear the whole thing up?"

"I do."

He led me to a private waiting room where Hester sat twisting her handkerchief into a rope.

"Hester." I took the seat next to hers. "Are you all right?"

"Ellison, what's happening?"

"Chauncey is in a lot of trouble."

She shook her head. "He didn't murder those people. He wouldn't."

"I believe you." Well, I believed the expression of shock and surprise I'd seen on Chauncey's face when Anarchy told him the charge. The man had looked relieved.

"You do?"

"I do. Thursday morning, did Chauncey meet with Frank Wallace?"

"Yes. Frank came to our suite." She glanced down at her hanky. "He was an hour late."

"Oh?"

"I think he'd been with a woman. He had that look." She wrinkled her nose. "And that smell."

Ick.

"What time did he arrive?"

"Just before ten."

"And they were together the rest of the morning?"

"As far as I know. I went shopping."

I patted her hand. "I don't think you need to worry."

"Really?"

"Chauncey's still in a great deal of trouble."

She regarded me with suddenly ancient eyes. "He hit a police officer."

"Yes."

"And he's been trading on inside information."

She knew?

"You look surprised," said Hester. "Don't be. My husband is a crook not a killer."

When I stepped out of the waiting room, Anarchy was waiting for me.

I looked up at his lean face. There were tiny lines around his eyes and a tautness to his lips that spoke of exhaustion.

I hated to add to his burdens. "You arrested the wrong man for murder."

"Then who?"

"Although Chauncey is guilty of insider trading on an epic scale."

"Who, Ellison?" Anarchy was a homicide cop.

"Ruth Marshall."

Later that night, Anarchy arrived at my house with take-out Chinese and a bottle of wine.

He stood in the foyer and kissed me. Slowly. Deeply. Till I was breathless.

Finally, I pulled away. "Grace and Karma are in the kitchen.

They're dying to know what happened."

"You were right. Ruth killed them."

"She confessed?"

He nodded. "She—"

"Wait. Not another word until Grace and Karma can hear. I don't want to make you tell the story twice."

We walked back to the kitchen with Max closely behind us. Max was a huge fan of Chinese food...and Italian food, and Mexican food, and Spanish food. In a pinch, he'd probably even go for my cooking.

"What did you bring?" asked Grace in way of welcome.

Anarchy held up the bag. "Moo Shoo pork, chicken fried rice, Gung Bao chicken, and pan-fried noodles."

"Yum." His choices met with her approval.

We grabbed plates, served ourselves, and ate at the kitchen island.

"She confessed?" asked Karma.

"She did."

"To all three murders?"

"Yep." Anarchy added plum sauce to the heap of Moo Shoo piled on a pancake. "Ruth was willing to put up with her husband's philandering. She never thought he'd get serious with one of the women."

"With Joanie." I lifted a forkful of fried rice to my lips.

"With Joanie," Anarchy agreed. "At first she thought she could regain her husband's interest by beginning her own affair. When that didn't work, she killed him."

"Why kill the woman at The Nelson?" Karma asked.

"Marcy was working late the night Ruth killed Winthrop. She knew Ruth had been in the office."

"And Frank?"

"Frank told Ruth about the insider trading. She saw a way to frame Chauncey Nelson for all the murders." Anarchy grinned at me. "It almost worked."

"How did you know?" Karma stared at me over the rim of her

wine glass.

"I didn't want to think the wife did it. I saw what I wanted to see." I'd been blind. "I wanted Ruth to be innocent so I chose not to believe Joanie. But what if she was right? What if Winthrop meant to divorce Ruth? Leave her for a younger woman?"

"Mrs. Marshall would be just another divorcée," supplied Grace.

"Ruth didn't want to be a divorcée. She liked the way she lived."

"What I don't get—" Grace wolfed down a bite of fried rice "—is why she confessed. Could you prove anything?"

Anarchy grinned. "There was a certain amount of bluffing involved."

"But why kill Mr. Wallace?" Grace spoke around a full mouth of rice.

I gave her a severe, Mother-worthy look and mouthed *manners*.

She rolled her eyes.

"She never cared about Wallace," said Anarchy. "Frank Wallace was a way to get even with her husband. After her husband was dead she was done with him. She used his death to make Nelson look guilty. "

"And it worked," I agreed. "I thought Chauncey Nelson was guilty." I lifted another bite of rice to my lips. When I put my fork down, everyone was staring at me.

"But you figured it out," said Grace.

"He'd still be in jail for murder if it wasn't for you." Anarchy grinned at me—that grin—the one that made my heart go pitter-pat.

I choked on my rice.

Karma whomped me on the back. "Hopefully he's still in jail for hitting you and for insider trading."

"Do you need water?" asked Anarchy.

I nodded.

Anarchy stood, fixed me a glass of water, and put it carefully into my hands.

I drank.

He replied to Karma, "The feds are very interested in talking to him. Apparently he had similar deals with small brokerages in St. Paul, Tulsa, and Birmingham—places the examiners don't look for insider trading."

"So, it's over?" asked Karma. "No more bodies?"

Anarchy donned a wry expression and draped an arm around my shoulders.

Grace grinned. "Over until Mom finds the next one."

JULIE MULHERN

Julie Mulhern is the *USA Today* bestselling author of The Country Club Murders. She is a Kansas City native who grew up on a steady diet of Agatha Christie. She spends her spare time whipping up gourmet meals for her family, working out at the gym and finding new ways to keep her house spotlessly clean—and she's got an active imagination. Truth is—she's an expert at calling for take-out, she grumbles about walking the dog and the dust bunnies under the bed have grown into dust lions.

The Country Club Murders
by Julie Mulhern

Novels

THE DEEP END (#1)
GUARANTEED TO BLEED (#2)
CLOUDS IN MY COFFEE (#3)
SEND IN THE CLOWNS (#4)
WATCHING THE DETECTIVES (#5)
COLD AS ICE (#6)
SHADOW DANCING (#7)
BACK STABBERS (#8)

Short Stories

DIAMOND GIRL
A Country Club Murder Short

Henery Press Mystery Books

And finally, before you go...
Here are a few other mysteries
you might enjoy:

MACDEATH

Cindy Brown

An Ivy Meadows Mystery (#1)

Like every actor, Ivy Meadows knows that *Macbeth* is cursed. But she's finally scored her big break, cast as an acrobatic witch in a circus-themed production of *Macbeth* in Phoenix, Arizona. And though it may not be Broadway, nothing can dampen her enthusiasm—not her flying cauldron, too-tight leotard, or carrot-wielding dictator of a director.

But when one of the cast dies on opening night, Ivy is sure the seeming accident is "murder most foul" and that she's the perfect person to solve the crime (after all, she does work part-time in her uncle's detective agency). Undeterred by a poisoned Big Gulp, the threat of being blackballed, and the suddenly too-real curse, Ivy pursues the truth at the risk of her hard-won career—and her life.

Available at booksellers nationwide and online

Visit www.henerypress.com for details

CROPPED TO DEATH

Christina Freeburn

A Faith Hunter Scrap This Mystery (#1)

Former US Army JAG specialist, Faith Hunter, returns to her West Virginia home to work in her grandmothers' scrapbooking store determined to lead an unassuming life after her adventure abroad turned disaster. But her quiet life unravels when her friend is charged with murder – and Faith inadvertently supplied the evidence. So Faith decides to cut through the scrap and piece together what really happened.

With a sexy prosecutor, a determined homicide detective, a handful of sticky suspects and a crop contest gone bad, Faith quickly realizes if she's not careful, she'll be the next one cropped.

Available at booksellers nationwide and online

Visit www.henerypress.com for details

NUN TOO SOON

Alice Loweecey

A Giulia Driscoll Mystery (#1)

Giulia Falcone-Driscoll has just taken on her first impossible client: The Silk Tie Killer. He's hired Driscoll Investigations to prove his innocence with only thirteen days to accomplish it. Everyone in town is sure Roger Fitch strangled his girlfriend with one of his silk neckties. On top of all that, her assistant's first baby is due any second, her scary smart admin still doesn't relate well to humans, and her police detective husband insists her client is guilty.

Giulia's ownership of Driscoll Investigations hasn't changed her passion for justice from her convent years. But the more dirt she digs up, the more she's worried her efforts will help a murderer escape. As the client accuses DI of dragging its heels on purpose, Giulia thinks The Silk Tie Killer might be choosing one of his ties for her own neck.

Available at booksellers nationwide and online

Visit www.henerypress.com for details

GHOSTWRITER ANONYMOUS
Noreen Wald

A Jake O'Hara Mystery (#1)

With her books sporting other people's names, ghostwriter Jake O'Hara works behind the scenes. But she never expected a séance at a New York apartment to be part of her job. Jake had signed on as a ghostwriter, secretly writing for a grande dame of mystery fiction whose talent died before she did. The author's East Side residence was impressive. But her entourage—from a Mrs. Danvers-like housekeeper to a lurking hypnotherapist—was creepy.

Still, it was all in a day's work, until a killer started going after ghostwriters, and Jake suspected she was chillingly close to the culprit. Attending a séance and asking the dead for spiritual help was one option. Some brilliant sleuthing was another-before Jake's next deadline turns out to be her own funeral.

Available at booksellers nationwide and online

Visit www.henerypress.com for details

CPSIA information can be obtained
at www.ICGtesting.com
Printed in the USA
LVHW051505170519
618251LV00012B/266/P